DERBY
HORSE

MARA DABRISHUS

Dabrishus, Mara, 1981 -
Derby Horse / Mara Dabrishus

Editor: Erin Smith
Cover: Shutterstock

ISBN: 0-9961872-7-8
ISBN-13: 978-0-9961872-7-5

www.maradabrishus.com

DERBY
HORSE

MARA DABRISHUS

For Carolyn Starkey,
who's been with me since the beginning.

Chapter One

PALM TREES SURROUND the gate at Palm Meadows like sentries, tall and imposing. I've grown used to them this winter, and I'll miss them when I'm gone. My eyes stick to them as Dad steers the rental car toward our allotted stalls. It's still dark—the sky streaked with purple in the east, evidence of a slowly approaching sun. It will be here before we know it, so it's best to hit the ground running.

As dark as it is, Palm Meadows is full to bursting with horses already winding around the barns, their heads down on long reins, breath misty in the temporary Southern chill. Exercise riders curl in the saddles, wearing clothes meant for the weather later—T-shirts and tank tops, crash vests strapped on over their torsos. Their jeans ride up along their mount's sides, exposing the tall boots underneath. Grooms bounce in and out of stalls, tack in hand, buckets kicked into the aisle. As one string leaves a barn, a groom with a pitchfork shows up soon after to clean up the night's mess.

It's a well-oiled, chaotic machine. When I open the rental car's door I take a deep breath of it.

Smells like home.

"We don't have much time this morning," Dad barks the second his feet hit the gravel. "Let's get these strings moving. Martina's pony girl on Maggie. Juls, you're on Feather. First set out in ten."

Martina and I share a look, but Dad's already on his way to the office to double-check the morning sets.

"Someone is eager to get back on a plane," I say.

Martina smiles slyly. "More like someone has an Eclipse Award, and is in danger of it going to their head."

I grin, the award ceremony still fresh in my mind from last night. Galaxy Collision may be a broodmare now, ensconced in a storied Kentucky farm, but last night her career earned Blackbridge Farm an Eclipse Award. Our mare was the best older female of the year, something Dad has been working toward since . . . forever?

I imagine the statue is sitting on Delaney's bedside table right now, waiting to fly home to New York for a lonely future as a mantle ornament. Now that Blackbridge is a one-horse operation, it's not likely to have a companion.

But by the way Dad struts down the shedrow, it's entirely possible to think there's more of those little statues in the future for Barn 27. After all this time getting our hands dirty, Galaxy Collision could be just the first *of many*.

Maybe. That's hopeful thinking for you. Every win feels like a step on a ladder to something greater, but there's still a barn that needs run and horses that need fed. In the background, it's never glorious. Dad knows that better than anyone.

"Dad has never cared about those things before," I say, opening the trunk of the rental and pulling my duffel out, hiking it onto my shoulder.

"There's always a first time," Martina says. "Of which all of this is." She motions to Palm Meadows—the giant white pavilion with its airy, cinderblock stalls.

We've been here over a month, escaping the bitter New York winter for enough sunshine to bronze skin. The horses we've brought are at the end of their winter vacations or are now training toward races at Gulfstream and Fair Grounds—Southern tracks without a hint of ice. Today we're either leaving them or taking them back with us to our snowy home. Dad just has to say the word and their fates are sealed: Sunny Florida or Bitter New York.

"I'm willing to admit it's been a nice change," I say, shutting the trunk with a slam as Martina slides a look at me—she knows better than anyone how much I didn't want to come here. "Lighter has definitely turned around."

A shrill whinny pierces the air. I glance into the barn, where Lighter's body moves through the shadows toward his stall guard. The metal gate clanks, holding in place. Just inside, I catch sight of Lighter's dark brown eye watching me steadily.

He blinks, and so do I.

"He has good timing," Martina says, walking ahead of me to the tack room. "If I didn't know better I'd think he was determined to avoid the trip back to Belmont."

I pause outside of Lighter's stall as Martina disappears into the tack room. The colt presses his nose against the grate and lets out a whooshing breath.

It will be strange, leaving him here, but that's what we'll do. If he impresses Dad during this morning's breeze, it's the Florida road for Lighter, racing under palm trees all the way to Kentucky for the Derby. It's Plan A. I have to stop myself before I think too far, along all the alternate paths, the scenarios rife with possibility, because *the Kentucky Derby.*

Twenty horses, two minutes, red roses and feathered hats and glasses packed with mint. It's an experience more than it is a race, and we're standing at the beginning of the long journey to the starting gate. Anything can happen on the way, so I opt to focus on what I know: Plan A.

"Taking a moment to appreciate the coming chaos?"

The voice pulls a smile out of me and I turn toward Beckett Delaney as he walks down the shadowy aisle. He's all lanky strides and sun-kissed skin; the blue Florida mornings have agreed with him, and his dark blond hair has lightened, glinting gold. When he gets close enough, he curls an arm around my waist and kisses the side of my head.

"Do you mean this morning or the next four months?" I ask, rising on my toes to kiss him on the lips. He makes an appreciative noise, despite the fact that I must taste like coffee and toothpaste, and squeezes my hip.

"Can't it be both?" he asks when I fall back to my heels, his characteristic smile tugging at one side of his mouth. A slither of warmth glides down my spine, and abruptly cuts off when Lighter rams a hoof against the grate. I shoot the colt a look.

"Knock it off," I command. Lighter stares at me with pricked ears, totally unconcerned as he continues to slam his hoof against the metal like an ingrate.

I sigh and look at Beck. "Belmont is going to be positively silent without Lighter around."

He shrugs a shoulder. "Assuming you're even around to appreciate the silence."

"Why wouldn't I be there to revel in the Lighter-less quiet?" I ask, smiling up at him. "Where am I going?"

"Jericho," he says slowly, to which I raise my eyebrows.

"And?" I prompt, looking up at him when he doesn't find anything else to say, preferring instead to look at me like I'm an unsolvable math problem. A laugh bursts out of me, spurring Beck to add a concerned frown to the mix. "Just because I'm going to college next week doesn't mean I'm suddenly lost for time," I say. "No class starts as early as the track does in the morning."

"You are way too bright-eyed and bushy-tailed," Beck tells me, shaking his head. "It's unnatural."

"It's a side effect of being overly caffeinated at an early age," I beam up at him, although he doesn't look convinced. "My whole life has been this," I say, waving a hand at the shedrow. "All I've ever done is weave my life around racehorses. Adding in college will be a piece of cake."

"Are you going to say 'hear me roar' next?" Beck asks slyly.

I laugh, a retort halfway up my throat when Dad's assistant trainer, Paul, calls down the aisle, "Daylight's burning, folks. First set should have been out five minutes ago."

"The sun isn't even up yet," I yell at him over my shoulder. He fixes me with a look I know well. It's the do-as-I-say stare, which does not pair well with his sleep-rumpled hair and stained jeans. Paul is the racetrack come to life. He's been known to sleep on the backside, bedded down on the ratty sofa and giving Martina heart attacks when she opens the office in the morning.

But that's another era now. Since Leo is still recovering from his literal brush with Lighter last month, we're leaving Paul behind here to keep things running instead. No more sleep-deprived assistant trainers camping out on Barn 27's office sofa and using the hose for basic hygiene after today.

It almost feels a little freeing.

"If you're looking for Feather, Izzie already has her waiting in the yard," he barks at me.

"Thanks, Paul," I call as Gus skirts around him, tack in hand.

"Get going, lady," Gus tells me, nudging my shoulder before he lets himself into Lighter's stall. "Boss man says."

I sigh and drop my duffel at my feet, rooting through it to pull out my safety vest and shrugging it on. Beck stands back as Gus leads Lighter into the shedrow, the colt all coppery energy under the dim lights as he goes floating into the yard, pale tail swishing in his wake to where Pilar stands in the darkness, waiting on him. Just beyond, I see Izzie and Feather, the lithe bay filly camouflaged by the early morning hour.

There's a line of horses outside, all of them waiting and ready to go.

"Morning, Izzie," I say when I get to the filly, scrubbing my gloved fingers underneath Feather's mane. The filly cocks her head, enjoying the scratching. Izzie smiles at me, her two-toned hair pulled into a hasty bun and her eye makeup ridiculously on point considering the hour.

"Morning, Juls," she says in her perky, never tired way.

"So do you want to stay or do you want to go?" I ask her, pulling down Feather's stirrups. "Now's the time to tell me so I can sway Dad's decision appropriately."

Izzie laughs and pretends to consider my question. As Feather's groom, there's no chance Izzie would leave her. Where the filly goes, Izzie goes.

"We both know Feather's staying in Florida," she says. "I know you'll miss me while I'm gone, but I'm sure you'll learn to cope."

"Pilar and Gus are staying, and now you?" I ask, glancing over at Lighter. Pilar is already in his saddle, gathering the reins. Gus stands at the colt's head. There's no way either of them will leave Lighter—Gus because he loves the colt and Pilar because she wants the challenge. If she can ride Lighter in the mornings, the better her position to eventually ride him in the afternoons.

I sigh. "It's going to be a lonely winter."

That does it. Izzie sniffles and pulls me into a hug, her voice muffled against my shoulder. "It's not going to be the same without you around."

Even though we knew this was coming, have been preparing for this split for days, it's still hard to say goodbye. To the horses, and to the people. I know I'll be plenty busy in New York, but everything's going to be different at home.

Which is equally weird. Shouldn't something feel the same?

"And what am I, nobody?" Beck breaks in, mock offended as Izzie pushes back and laughs, rubbing at her eyes.

"Are you planning on riding in the mornings?" I ask, to which he makes a face. I lift my foot, wiggling the toe of my boot at him in a wordless question. "I rest my case."

He chuckles and grasps my leg, lifting. I'm airborne for a split second until I meet Feather's saddle. The filly shifts under my weight, and I run my fingers through her mane, determined to make this ride on her a good one. It's going to be a while before I'm back here, perched in her saddle.

"Be good while I'm gone, you hear me?" I tell her, Feather's ears swishing back to listen.

Izzie pats the filly's forehead and looks up at me. "Are you ready?"

"Always," I say.

The filly bobs her head once, ears swishing back, and then we're off.

~~

We enter through the gap in the training track, sticking together as we turn to start jogging clockwise. The horses jump into the two-beat, and I rise out of the saddle, bridging the reins at Feather's neck, and settling her into the rhythm. *One-two, one-two.* She huffs and blows out a breath, the milky mist dissipating around her chest and sweeping through her legs.

We're quiet this morning. Jorge hums the latest song stuck in his head, eyes on the track between Kickabit's ears. Mom is a study in silence, her pink vest Day-Glo bright in the darkness. Underneath her, Zaatar's gray body reflects all the colors of the pastel sunrise on the horizon. Martina keeps a firm grip on Lighter's lead, full attention on the colt. Pilar is silent in his saddle. Our quiet is uncharacteristic for the track, which is peppered with laughter and shouts, people keeping in constant contact.

I suppose we're all feeling the imminent split.

"Okay, gang," Martina announces, her voice breaking the stillness. My fingers twitch on the reins, and Feather jerks her head up, as if to say I've ruined her chi. We come to a rolling walk along the outside rail by the finish line. Martina turns Maggie, letting her stand with her head pointed toward the infield.

This is standing time. Lighter tosses his head up and down, sidling back and forth.

"Heads up," Jorge says, ignoring Lighter's attention-seeking antics for the drama coming down the inside rail. Two horses spray dirt in a furious attempt to get to the finish first. The leader labors past the sixteenth pole, his ears pinned back and his rider urging him to step up the pace.

On the outside, a chestnut strikes. The colt's rider hovers over the colt's saddle as the chestnut plows by with his head down, mane ripping off his neck in the wind. His body is a collection of bunching muscles, his breath barely winded as he flashes past us and hits the finish with a lead change. Right to left. Then he gallops into the turn, head still down, his rider beginning a slow ascent to standing in the stirrups on the way into the backstretch.

"Damn," Pilar whispers as Jorge whistles through his teeth.

"Doesn't get much more classic than that," he says, running a hand down Kickabit's mane. All of us, I notice, stare across the infield at the chestnut as he's drawn down to a rollicking canter, then a ground-eating trot. A pony comes loping up from the sidelines to greet them, and from here I can see the flash of wide smiles.

"Danny Miller knows what he has there," Mom says clinically, as though she's describing the anatomy of the fetlock while I do a double take.

"Danny Miller?" I ask, twisting to look at her and then back at the chestnut. Danny Miller's giant string of horses cycles through Kentucky Derby preps like they're allowance races, racking up enough wins and points to put one, maybe two, Danny Miller horses in the gate at Churchill every year. But Danny is based in California, so he definitely doesn't have an allowance race in mind if he's in Florida.

"And Tahr," Mom elaborates, my mouth dropping open at the words she doesn't say—*Breeders' Cup Juvenile winner, Eclipse Award winner, champion*. Tahr is all of those things, and more precisely he was supposed to stay in California.

"They shipped him in last week," Martina says, as though bored by it all. "Danny supposedly wants to avoid running him against another colt of his at Santa Anita."

Mom gives me a look out of the corner of her eye. I realize she's looking past me, down to the viewing stand where Dad waits with his arms resting against the rail, binoculars and stopwatch in hand. Beck stands next to him, eyes on Tahr.

I afford a quick look down at Lighter's chaotic blond mane. It sticks up like he has bedhead around his ears, spiky and untamable. Then I catch sight of Tahr walking toward the gap with his pony, mane neat along his neck and coat hardly washed out with sweat. It looks like he barely moved a muscle, much less obliterated the competition.

"Well," I announce. "What are we waiting for?"

I put my heels to Feather's sides and she jumps into a trot, wheeling into the center of the track. I don't wait for anyone to keep up, rising in the stirrups and pressing the reins against the filly's withers.

On my inside, Mom appears on Zaatar, the filly shaking her head petulantly until Mom lets her stroll out into a hand gallop, increasing her speed until all I see is the filly's dappled hindquarters and whipping dark gray tail on their way into the turn.

"Gotta keep up, July!" Mom shouts at me over her shoulder, which makes me smile because my job is chase, overtake, keep Feather on the task of running to the wire and then gallop her out another furlong once we're done. Mom is playing rabbit, giving Feather a moving target. Once she's got five lengths on me, churning into the backstretch and fast approaching the marker where we'll start the breeze, I let Feather shift into a ground-eating gallop.

She huffs, flicks her ears forward and swishes them back as her hindquarters catapult us into not-quite-racing speed. I crouch low in the saddle, hovering over it and sighting over the filly's ears at the track zooming along underneath her hooves. Zaatar's dark gray tail flickers behind her as they gallop down the backstretch and hit the turn, changing leads in a flying shift of hooves.

Feather hits it milliseconds later, her mane licking back with stinging slaps at my cheeks. Glancing down at the digital numbers ticking along on my wristwatch, I let out a breath. The filly is hitting her marks just like we want her to, so now it's time to let her go.

Lowering myself in the saddle is all it takes. Don't have to chirp or shake my reins at her—Feather gets the message like I've put a bullhorn to her ear and shouted go. She launches into full flight, hindquarters bunching and shoving her through the air with such force it pulls at my bones. Her hooves hit the dirt hard, and I skate along on her back with my knees absorbing the revolving tumult of her body as she gains on Zaatar's gray tail.

I squeeze my fingers on the right rein and Feather bears out on the turn, steamrolling up on Zaatar's outside on our way into the homestretch. The quarter pole goes flicking by, lost in Feather's mane. All I hear is wind and the breath of horses stretching out, eyeing each other as we draw even down the rail.

I don't need to look at my watch to know how fast we're going. The wind drones in my ears, muddying the thunder coming from the two fillies striking the dirt. Zaatar tries to stick to the lead, but Feather pulls past her at the last second, leaving Zaatar behind as she hits the wire.

The end of a breeze is a gradual thing. At the end of a race, it's all neck-slapping and butts in the air, easing off the horse the second the wire slips overhead if not before. In a breeze, we let them keep running, slowly, slowly bringing them back down to earth in the turn. Feather is already in the backstretch when I decide it's time to put my butt back in the saddle. She breaks into a riotous trot, chewing on the bit and looking around like she can't believe what happened and wants to know who witnessed her speed.

"Everyone knows you're super," I tell her, watching her ears flick back as I run a hand down her mane, ending in a hearty pat to her neck. Mom tugs Zaatar down to a floating jig next to me, the filly's head in the air and eyes rolling, her nostrils red-rimmed.

"Getting full of herself," Mom says when Feather squeals, bouncing a full body length away from Zaatar and keeping me on my toes. I nudge the filly to the outside rail and bring her down to a walk, her shivering energy still roiling underneath her skin.

"Thinks she won one race and suddenly she's a diva about it," I say, wincing at the memory of Feather's slipped saddle in her last race. Luckily, Khalid Sahadi—the filly's owner and the reason we're in Florida—didn't see it as a total disaster, mainly due to my sparkling commentary about the filly's future.

Classic distance were the exact words that came out of my mouth on that sunny Florida afternoon. The last thing you want to do with horses is promise more than you can deliver, and here I went and said *classic*.

Where had my brain been when I promised Khalid Sahadi that Feather could handle the Classics? Oh, I know. I was trying to save my skin as Mom was trying not to hit the ground. At the time, it didn't seem like such a bad idea. Besides, everyone wants a horse headed to Churchill Downs in May—Oaks or Derby. It's every horse owner's fantasy.

Now? Feather hasn't yet won a race, but in fantasyland she's got all four hooves firmly planted on the road to Kentucky. Looking across the training track to where Dad is standing, I wonder how much of a fantasy it really is now that my words have wormed their way into Khalid's thoughts.

"I heard Feather is staying here the rest of winter," Mom says, her barely-there Spanish accent slipping through her words. "She'll have plenty of time to establish her divaness."

"I had a feeling," I say.

Mom eyes me, amused. "Khalid liked what you had to say at Gulfstream."

"I only said it because I panicked," I admit. "I shouldn't have promised him anything."

"Maybe not, but she was full of drive before her saddle slipped," Mom shrugs, and my face flames because the guilt is still there. *My fault.* Mom shakes her head at me. "Horses spit the bit out over less, July. Look at how far she's come in such a short time."

I cast a look down the filly's shoulder, feeling her solid footsteps ferrying me down the outside rail. She's not even breathing hard, and she schooled Zaatar in the stretch like they weren't even in the same class.

And maybe they aren't. Maybe Feather has blossomed into something better. She certainly feels like she has. The only way to really be sure, though, is to test it. Race her. Find out if the training has stuck.

"Then I guess Florida it is," I say, giving Feather a pat. She cocks an ear back at me, half listening. I lean over her neck and whisper, "Don't embarrass me out there, okay? I do a good enough job of that on my own."

As if on cue, Lighter goes flying by on our inside, his head somewhere in the vicinity of his knees and his hocks popping up every other stride. His blond tail bobs and flips with each kick, and Pilar sits through it like she was born to it. Her arms strain in efforts to get the colt's head up, somewhere near a semblance of control.

Luckily, Martina has her eye on them. Maggie swoops up just as the colt's gait breaks, my sister rising in the saddle and stretching to snag the colt's bridle. Lighter flings his head up, brown eyes rolling. I can see the whites from here.

"And then we have Lighter," I say, keeping Feather well away from the whirlwind that is the blond colt gallivanting toward the outside rail, Maggie pinning her ears and switching her two-toned tail like an aggravated housecat.

I look back over to Mom, who can't seem to hold back her grin as we trot toward the spot on the rail occupied by Dad and Beck.

"Please tell me Lighter's staying in Florida," I call out to Dad, envisioning bone-chilling mornings at Belmont Park, my hands rubbed red and Lighter casually crazying up workouts.

Mom's grin turns into a cackling laugh as we walk off the track in Lighter's wake, the colt scattering wood chips and swinging his butt off the path into the grass so he can better torment Maggie.

"It's my pleasure to inform you, July," Dad says dryly as Beck gives me a wild, obvious grin, "that Lighter is staying right here."

Relief floods me.

Sweet, *sweet* relief.

Chapter Two

"Up you go," I murmur to Kali through the scarf wrapped twice around my mouth, my voice muffled by the damp wool. The filly huffs at the ramp and taps one hoof at it experimentally, as though testing to make sure it doesn't give way before she pounces onto it and drags me into the trailer's dim interior.

I secure her and scratch her neck—one of the only places she's not covered with blanket because it is *cold* in New York. Bitter, freezing, wish-I'd-stayed-in-Florida cold. The horses hang out under heat lamps as inches of white fluff layer over the ground. Out beyond the barns, the all-weather training track is a ribbon of dark brown dirt, groomed and prepped like we're not in the midst of winter wonderland.

Kali snuffles my hips, expecting her treat for loading like the professional racehorse she used to be. Shivering, I hunker into my coat and pull the mint out of my jeans pocket, untwisting the cellophane with my teeth because I don't dare take off my gloves. The filly sucks the mint out of my hand and crunches, spiking the trailer with peppermint-tinted sugar I can barely smell through the scarf.

"All set?" Beck appears in the doorway, travel mug in hand. His knit hat is jammed over his hair and his ridiculous T-shirts have been relegated to undershirt duty for sweaters that are not nearly as interesting. It's hard to believe we were frolicking in the sun two days ago, but bundled-up Beck is just as appealing as summer-fun Beck, so I'm not going to complain.

"As set as we're gonna be," I say, rubbing Kali's nose and walking up to him. He tugs my scarf down just enough to kiss me, our cold noses brushing and coffee-stained breath misting in the air. Ah, New York in winter.

"Sure you want to dedicate your entire day to moving?" I ask him as he laughs, walking off the trailer ramp and helping me close it up tight. *Bang, clack, clang,* and Kali is ready to go.

"School doesn't start until tomorrow," he points out. "And I'm kind of a master procrastinator, in case you hadn't noticed. I'm fine using you as an excuse to not prepare for classes."

"So heartwarming," I sigh, putting a hand to my chest. "I'll be sure to tell Mom you're helping us unpack her new apartment only because you really didn't want to do those advance readings."

"Hey," Beck says, pointing at me as I grin at him. "I'm offering an essential service. Someone has to make sure that apartment doesn't implode from mother-daughter tension. Other people live in that building, July. I'm thinking of them."

"Then you can start by getting the truck's heater running," I say, digging into my pocket and tossing him the keys. "I'm going to tell Martina we're leaving."

"Godspeed," Beck says, climbing into the truck's cab and cranking the engine into a roar as I duck into the shedrow. Thoroughbreds blink at me from their stalls, resting on three hooves as they doze. The ones we brought back from Florida have their blankets on and look miserable, ears cocked back as they rip at their hay nets. I'm positive Lighter and Feather are gallivanting through Florida sunshine in their round pens right about now, living it up as I wait for the first crocus to tentatively peek out of the frozen ground. I can't even think about Gus, Pilar, and Izzie. I miss them too much to let myself dwell on their absence.

Slipping into the heated office, I find Martina curled around her cell phone. She cuts a look at me before she murmurs a soft, "Yeah, okay, tomorrow."

Then she tosses the phone onto the organized neatness of the desk.

"You know," I say, leaning against the door. "We all know you and Matt are a thing again. You don't have to whisper."

Martina gives me her no-nonsense stare.

"Are you leaving?" she asks, ignoring my comment.

"Yup," I confirm, letting it go. Martina and Matthew are like an experiment in a Petri dish. I'm going to have to let them grow a little before I start poking at them. "Are you coming to Mom's later?"

Martina sighs. "I suppose I should," she says. "I did agree to this crazy plan."

"I think since she's meeting us halfway and all . . ."

She waves her hand at me. "I know, I know," she says. "It will be better than last fall."

I stare at her for a beat, not comprehending my sister's breezy tone. Is this . . . optimism?

"Wait," I say, holding up a hand. "Who are you and what did you do with my sister?"

"Consider it a provisional period," she says with the tiniest of devilish smiles. "I'm giving her three months before there's a thorough review."

Whew. At least I'm not going crazy.

"I think you're letting your office manager powers go to your head," I tell her, and she laughs.

"And you're going to be late dropping off Kali," she tells me, pointing at the door. "I'll see you at Mom's in a couple of hours. *Go.*"

I slip back into the bitter chill, dashing out of the shedrow and hunkering into my coat when the breeze kicks up, smacking me in the face on my way to the gurgling truck. When I climb into the cab, the heater is just starting to emit a slither of heat, which isn't enough to defrost my numb cheeks.

Beck sips at his travel mug, one hand on the steering wheel.

"Ready to go?" he asks.

I nod, ready as I'll ever be, and the truck starts its rumble toward the gate. Toward Jericho.

～

City chaos recedes into suburban sprawl, where Jericho's equestrian complex sits ensconced in bare trees and brown pasture. White fences wink between tree trunks, a startlingly green roof peaking beyond scraggly branches. My heart speeds up when I see the fleet of trailers parked in the giant lot in front of the complex. Beck pumps the brakes, turns the wheel, and I cling to the passenger door handle like he's on a racetrack instead of slowly pulling a horse trailer carefully toward our destination.

Beck gives me a look out of the corner of his eye. A knowing look.

"You okay over there?"

"Fine," I reply tightly. "Just going over all of my life choices up to now."

He laughs, lifting his hand off the wheel to wave it at the windshield. "Look at this place, Juls. There was no way you'd wind up anywhere else."

Swallowing, I look past the giant barn complex to the rolling hills surrounding it. Paddocks line up in two tidy rows beyond the parking lot, a line of trees running between them. On the other side, the fields keep going. Jumps startle out of the manicured ground, and I remember the photos I browsed online of students schooling horses over a green cross country course. Somewhere on this property is a sandy dressage arena, where I assume I'll be spending plenty of time.

A surge of excitement spikes through my nerves.

"Okay," I admit, shifting eagerly in my seat and letting go of my death grip on the door. "This looks amazing."

"There it is," Beck says, pulling the trailer into line with all the others and cutting the engine. "Bright, shiny optimism."

I smack lightly at his knee, and he gives me his cheeky, 'I'm adorable' smile. The one that always makes me wonder how we happened in the first place, especially now. If someone had told me years ago that Beck Delaney would be driving me and my Thoroughbred to college I'd have died laughing.

"Let's get checked in," I say, pulling my hat back on over my static-charged hair and opening the cab door. A stiff winter breeze hits me hard in the face, knocking my breath out of my lungs.

God, I cannot wait for spring.

We weave through the trailers, through other girls unloading horses and equipment, hugging parents and rushing to meet friends. I keep my eyes open for Madeline, my old friend from Woodfield and the only person I'll know going into Jericho. She said she'd be moving in today, getting her mare, Cricket, set up in her new stall in the boarder barn before classes start tomorrow.

Another spike of excitement hits my blood, along with a twinge of undeniable nerves.

Inside the complex is an additional layer of chaos. The entry area is a churn of people, and I stumble to a halt in the center of it.

"There," Beck says, pointing to the registration tables, where fewer people are clustered. January is mainly for returning students, I remind myself. Not new ones. I'm one of probably only a handful of wet-behind-the-ears students stumbling in from the cold.

Weaving through people, I wash up against the tables and find a girl not much older than me beaming up from where she's hunkered in her green Jericho College parka. Her dark brown hair is pulled into sloppy pigtail braids, but her light blue nail polish is perfect, like she just arrived from a manicure.

"Name?" she asks, blinking big brown eyes at me.

"July Carter," I say, then remember the trailer out in the parking lot. "And Kaliningrad."

The girl flips through a stack of glossy green folders. Each one is emblazoned with a white horse jumping over the college's name, knees tucked neatly and body arched. She pulls one out with an "ah-ha!" and presents it to me with a flourish. Then she scoots down the table's length and starts sorting through a box, tugging out another, smaller envelope with Kali's name printed across the front.

"Your horse's information is right in here," she says, handing it to me. "Stall number, tack room info, etc. All of your information is in your welcome packet, including your class schedule. You'll need to go to main campus for your photo ID, but you can do that later. You have your horse with you?"

I manage a nod and she grins up at me, obviously sensing how overwhelmed I am.

"Cool!" She points behind her. "The boarder barn is that way. You'll find her stall in there, past the show barn. It's all connected. If you haven't seen it yet, you'll get the gist right away."

I keep nodding, even though the creeping realization that I *haven't* seen this place yet rises like a looming omen. I just applied. Sight unseen. And then I went to Florida for nearly two months, only coming back in time to arrive with my horse. Who does that?

Crazy people. That's who.

"Alrighty," Beck breaks in when I completely fail to say a word. He slowly reaches around me and massages Kali's envelope out of my death grip. "Think we have everything. Right, Juls?"

"Yeah," I croak, edging stiltedly away from the table as the girl's peppy smile becomes something a little more worried. I stumble over myself, reaching out for the solid, sure part of me. This was my decision, and I was accepted here. Me and my horse. *Stop acting like a meek mouse, July.*

"I'm good," I assure her as Beck steers me out of the waiting line. "I'll see you around, I'm sure."

Her smile reappears. "Count on it. I'm Ava, by the way. I'm always the one riding the big gray horse of doom."

"Sounds entertaining," I say, eyes widening.

"Oh," Ava laughs as the next girl leans into the table, waiting for me to move along. "You have no idea."

I give her a parting wave as she turns to the next girl, her

Welcome-to-Jericho smile beaming. Then I let out a breath. Beck gives me a knowing look, because he notices. Of course, he notices.

"See," he says, taking my hand as we slip through the crowd and back into the cold. "Already made a friend. You'll be a natural at this college thing."

A bark of laughter escapes me.

"I'm a basket case," I tell him. "No point in denying it."

"Welcome to college, Juls," he says, walking with me through the maze of trailers. "It's not like any of us go into these places knowing exactly what we're doing."

"Including you?" I challenge as we stop outside our rig.

"You didn't see me on my first day at Columbia," he says, shoving Kali's envelope in his back pocket and helping me lower the ramp. Kali peeks at us from her spot in the trailer, hay poking out of her mouth and ears swiveling forward. Beck lets the ramp tap against the blacktop with a clang and steps back, rubbing his hands on his jeans.

"What did you do?" I ask slowly, one foot on the ramp when I stop and turn around, catching his wince. Beck's first full day of adult responsibility in the city had to have resulted in at least one story. I'm busy conjuring riotous images in my head when my phone buzzes from my back pocket, distracting me as Beck scurries past and up the ramp, disappearing into the trailer.

Movers are here. When are you finished?

Mom's text hovers on the face of my phone. She's moving into an apartment near the track. To be honest, it's good to have some space between us.

"It's growing room," Mom had said when she pointed out the distance.

And she's right. Maybe it will be what we need—her here, but not too close. She can be our mother again, on Martina's and my terms. It's exactly what we need, I think. Baby steps.

Soon, I text and send it off with a little whoosh.

Behind me, I hear Kali's scrape and thud of hooves on the trailer floor and hop off the ramp when Beck brings her down to solid ground. My filly lifts her head at the new surroundings, the sea of trailers and blacktop, and gives a ragged snort that billows milky white in the cold.

"Where are we taking her?" Beck asks, tugging on the lead when Kali paws a hoof at the blacktop, inspecting the footing. I reach under his coat and pull the envelope out of his back pocket, yanking open the flap as Kali sticks her nose in the winter breeze and whinnies, full and throaty.

"Let's find out," I say, and slide Kali's future into my hands.

~⌁

Snow flitters through the air when Beck and I arrive at the apartment, which is really the first floor of a brick house sitting on a quiet, tree-lined street only a stone's throw from Belmont Park. All the streets are named after flowers—Mom's is Zinnia Street, near the corner of Geranium.

On our way up the walk to the house, I dodge a mover and his dolly and push the front door open tentatively, peering inside. Boxes clutter the hardwood floor leading to the kitchen, where I find Martina digging glasses out of a box on the counter, frowning at each one.

"None are broken," she reports to Mom, who whirls in with another box, her jet-black hair pulled into a bun at the top of her head.

"We'll need to wash them all, though," Martina continues,

handing the last glass off to Mom, who sticks it into the dishwasher. "To keep July happy."

I clear my throat, just as Beck covers his laugh with an obviously fake cough. Both my mom and sister turn around, surprised.

"Hey," I say, pulling off my coat and looking for somewhere to throw it, settling on the corner of the kitchen counter. "I'm not concerned with the state of your glassware unless I'm drinking out of it."

"Living with her is like having a personal maid," Martina says to Mom, ignoring me as I poke through the rest of the boxes towered on the floor. "I'd say you're missing out by living alone, but she also enjoys lectures on proper dishwasher loading technique and Goo-Gone. It's horrifying. This is really for the best."

Mom smothers a smile with her hand as I give my sister my best fake glare.

"Says the person who turned the last load of whites a dirty pink," I point out. "Maybe you should be taking notes during my lectures."

"Are they always this bad?" Mom asks Beck, who shrugs as he pulls off his hat and runs his fingers through his hair, making it stick into wild tufts.

"It's more that they're constantly together now," he says. "There's no alone time anymore."

"Please," I scoff. "I've been taking care of Martina for—"

I cut myself off at my sister's pursed lips, the subtle tightness raising her shoulders. She pauses while lifting another glass out of the box in front of her, giving me a look that says completely and without question *do you really want to go there now?*

Because yes, I've been taking care of Martina since Mom left. The little things—laundry, chores, dinners cooked and cleaned up after—to the big things, like offering her a shoulder she could shove

24

away when she could have cried on it. I did that, because who else would? We're sisters, and we were alone.

Now here we are, moving Mom back into our lives. Albeit a few towns over. This was something we all agreed to in order to close the wound, stitch it up, give it enough space to breathe and heal. Rubbing salt into it now is a mistake I snap off at the root.

"I can see I'm going to have to separate you two while we work," Mom says lightly, breaking the awkward silence. "For efficiency and everyone's sanity."

"There's a conspicuous number of boxes in what's probably the living room," Beck says, nudging me out of the kitchen. "Think we can tackle it?"

"By all means," Mom says, waving us down the hallway as another dolly of boxes arrives. I dodge around the mover again and stumble after Beck, arriving in a room cluttered with cardboard and plastic-wrapped furniture.

"Perfect," Beck says, clapping his hands together and rubbing them at the sight of the box towers. Most are the height of his chest. "This should take several hours."

"Anything to put off spring semester readings?" I ask, picking at the tape on the closest box. "Really?"

"You're not a college student yet, Juls," he says, pulling his keychain out of his pocket and finding a tiny Swiss Army knife, sliding the blade into a box seam to pull back the flap. "You'll understand in a couple of months when the excitement wears off."

"It's starting to occur to me you're a horrible influence," I say, and then give him my patented stink eye. "What *did* you do your first day at Columbia?"

He sucks in a big breath. "Juls, if I told you I may have put a fish in a friend's dorm vent that happened to get lost somewhere in the ductwork, rendering the whole building uninhabitable until it could be found . . . You would tell no one, right?"

I stare at him a beat too long, and he offers me a tentative shrug like *what can you do? Sometimes fish get lost in vents.* I shake my head and then look down into my box.

Books. So many books. I lift a few up and wave them in the air.

"Look," I grin. "It's like the universe is mocking you. As punishment for your fish story."

Beck grimaces and pulls a handful of books out of his own box. "Damn it."

I drop the books back into the box.

"Okay, you've got to go," I tell him as his head tips forward in defeat. "Get your readings done. You can't anger karma like this and get away with it."

"When did you start believing in karma?" he asks, pushing away from the boxes slowly. The way he looks at me makes my skin heat up, and I bite my lip until the truth spills out of me.

"Maybe somewhere between Florida and New York," I say, shrugging a shoulder. "Hard to say exactly when."

"Uh-huh," he says through a knowing nod, catching my hips in his hands and drawing me into a lingering kiss. Martina and Mom are just down the hallway, but I push into him and smile against his mouth, poking at his chest when he draws back enough for me to see his face clearly.

"Readings," I order him. "Go."

He sighs. "God, what is it about bossy girls?"

"You like them, that's what," I tell him, pushing him in the direction of the hallway as he sluggishly shuffles to his coat, shrugging into it grudgingly. We both dodge around the mover again at the door, and Beck stops at the threshold.

"I'll call you tomorrow," he says. "After your first-day-of-classes headache has subsided."

"It's a plan," I tell him, giving him a final kiss. "Now go be responsible."

He groans but goes, pushing his hands into his coat pockets and walking into the riot of falling snowflakes. I rest against the door-jamb, watching until his broad shoulders disappear into the storm. Behind the houses, I can see just a sliver of the Belmont training track's looping turn. It's a field of white. Silence descends, the snowstorm like a giant eraser, blotting out sound and any trace of movement. The air feels still.

"Excuse me," a deep voice startles me and I twist, the mover smiling at me with chapped lips, cheeks pink from the cold. I scuttle out of his way, watching him drag the empty dolly down the steps and over Beck's nearly gone footprints. Inside, Mom and Martina are laughing. Actually *laughing*.

Which reminds me—I have work to do.

Back with my boxes of books, I haul one over to the built-in bookcases and start sorting. Alphabetical by author, obviously, which would be easy if they were in any sort of order. These look organized by color, which is madness. I dig through them, fingertips brushing against a leather-bound book at the bottom of the box. Hauling it into the light, I find it's not a book at all.

It's a photo album. When I crack it open, the first page is a collection of faded snapshots of a chubby baby perched on the Western saddle of my dad's old track pony, Stuart. The appaloosa stands with his ears pricked, lead line in Dad's hands while Mom leans against the gelding's side, arms draped around the baby in support.

Everyone is all smiles. Except the baby, who is all coal-black hair and trepidation.

"That was Martina's first ride," Mom says over my shoulder, startling me. I jerk a look up at her, finding her standing in front of me with a mug of steaming liquid she holds out to me. "Cocoa," she says. "We found the kettle."

"Thanks," I say, putting the open album down and taking the warm mug, blowing the steam away.

"Where did Beck go?" she asks, picking up the album and looking at it tenderly, drawing her fingers over the images before flipping the page to another collection of baby images. Martina, in all her fat baby glory.

"I made him go read for class," I say. "Someone had to do it."

She smiles at me wryly. "Always taking care of people," she says. "You were always like that."

"Am," I say softly. "I'm still here."

Mom blinks at me and nods. "Of course," she says, and lets out a breath. "Sorry, I'm just so nervous. Both of you girls are in the house with me and I hardly know what to say. I feel like every second is an opportunity I'm failing to grab."

"You're here," I say. "That's all we really wanted, Mom."

She nods.

"And here I'm going back to Florida in a couple of weeks," she says, sighing. "I get here and then the next second I'm gone again."

I tense, then tell myself to stop it. There's nothing to worry about because I'm going to be there too. There's no missing seeing Feather and Lighter run. Racing is a family endeavor now, just like it used to be. Although it's hard to navigate this turn. We've been doing this without her for so long.

Mom raises an eyebrow at me, reading me like an open book.

"I'm not going anywhere, Juls," she says, putting the album down and looking at me, unwavering. "A few races over one weekend and I'll be back on a plane for New York. With you."

"I know," I say, waving her off and trying to ignore the way my throat is closing. It's ridiculous. I'm currently helping her move all of her belongings into a little house in snow-covered New York when she could be skipping through California sun.

She's *here*. And more importantly she's going to keep coming back here, no matter where the racing world takes her.

Mom puts a hand on my arm, stilling my nervous gestures.

"July," she says. "This is my home now. Agreed?"

I nod tightly, swallowing down an old, desperate feeling. The one I had so long ago, back when she told us she was going to California. *I'll be home before you know it,* she'd said. *Don't worry, July.*

"Agreed," I say, pushing through the hoarseness in my voice to go for light and airy, untroubled when the old problems are so close to the surface I can see them in detail.

"Tell you what," Mom says. "We'll do something while we're in Florida. The three of us. A mother-daughter night away from horses. How does that sound?"

I nod, because all of a sudden it sounds good. Great, even. If she's with us, she can't think about being elsewhere.

She draws me into a hug, smoothing a hand over my hair. "This will be good, July. You'll see."

And I want it to be. I do.

I only wish we could guarantee it.

Chapter Three

I keep obsessively looking at my course schedule. The slip of paper is wrinkled and folded, worn at the edges from my worrying fingers, but I can't stop myself. Flattening it against my car's steering wheel, I run down the list of classes again as if I haven't memorized them. Date, time, instructor name, and room number have been committed to memory much like Secretariat's winning time for the Belmont Stakes.

Two minutes, twenty-four seconds.

I've been sitting here longer than two minutes and twenty-four seconds. The parking lot of Jericho's equestrian center is scattered with cars. Girls hop out of them and trot across the ice-slicked pavement to the warmth of the building, looking like positively normal college students. And still I sit, staring at the schedule, eyes sticking on my first class of the day.

Horse Care Practicum. MTWRF 7:30am-9am.

With a glance at the car clock, I have ten minutes to get going. Folding the paper back into its worn creases, a knock on the car window startles me from picking up my book bag off the passenger seat.

When I look up, Madeline is grinning at me, waving.

"Are you ready?" she asks as I push the car door open and drag my bag after me.

"Are you *kidding?*" I ask, hiking my bag's strap to a more comfortable spot on my shoulder.

"Yes," Madeline replies, blue eyes sparkling. "You look like you're about to hyperventilate."

I take a big breath of cold air as we walk into the center, just to prove to myself that I'm *not* hyperventilating. I'm just a person walking into a new situation when all I've ever been used to is Barn 27 and racetrack backsides. Sure, I should count Woodfield and the handful of summer shows I did on Gideon back when there was time and motivation, but this is something different.

Thankfully Kali and Madeline are here. It occurs to me how staggeringly lucky I am that Madeline declared her major this semester, landing us in the same boat every weekday morning until May. We're both in Practicum, and I could use the friendly face while I get my feet wet. I need a little bit of the familiar right about now.

We walk down the aisle of the boarding barn, my feet carrying me to Kali's stall. The aisle is swept clean, stalls glowing of oiled wood and pristine black bars. My filly is a shavings-coated nightmare inside the bars, her chestnut coat speckled with bedding.

"Well, at least you've given me something to do between classes," I tell her as she comes to the bars, pressing her nose against them and whuffing at my fingers. Madeline chuckles as she checks in on a much more pristine Cricket, then nudges me down the aisle.

"Let's go," she says. "We're going to be late."

I give Kali another stroke down her nose and take off after Madeline, following her through the connecting show barn and down the middle aisle separating two huge indoor arenas leading to the adjoining school horse barns. The college has a horde of school horses for all the horseless girls taking Fundamentals of Riding and Principals of Whatever Random Discipline You Desire. If I didn't have Kali, I'd be riding a schoolmaster in a couple of hours for my dressage class.

Part of me wonders if that's such a good thing, Kali being so green yet in the midst of so many meticulously schooled horses. But if we both aren't learning, why did I bring her here at all?

Madeline takes a quick glance at her watch and pulls a grimace, jumping into a jog for the fire doors at the end of the hall. She hits them with a clang, looking over her shoulder at me.

"Come on, July!"

I shove all thoughts about being ready aside. I *am* ready. And so is Kali. Otherwise, we wouldn't be here, right?

Right.

I shrug my bag higher onto my shoulder and break into a run, chasing Madeline all the way up the stairs.

∽

"It's hard not to feel insulted," Madeline says after Practicum as she swipes Cricket's burnished bay coat with a dandy brush. The mare's coat hardly needs it, but grooming is part and parcel of riding. You just do it, regardless of if the horse looks dirty or clean. It's reflex, which is why going over all the safety features and dos and don'ts of the stable in the last hour and a half feels so basic. We've done this all before.

Hang the halters like this, keep the saddles facing just so, run your hand down the leg to get the horse to pick up its hoof. Like I said—basic.

"Baby steps," I say from Kali's stall, where the filly steadfastly ignores me in favor of her hay. Madeline nods and deposits her brush in her tack box, digging for a comb before returning to Cricket and working on her tail.

"I get it," she says, picking at a stubborn shaving caught between strands. "I just don't like treading water."

"Says the person about to walk into an intermediate dressage class," I point out to her. She wrinkles her nose.

"Point taken," she says. "I'll shut up. Besides, it will be good to work with the school horses, and I've always wondered what it was like to wake up this early. Must be what you did every morning."

"Try a little earlier and you'll be in my daily ballpark."

She turns large eyes onto me. "What? No. You're not still doing it, are you? Both?"

"Of course," I say, shrugging.

Madeline stares at me through the bars, arching one eyebrow. "And tomorrow?"

"Tomorrow, too," I say, as Kali swings her head around to nudge my leg. I put a hand on her massive shoulder and nudge her back. "Most of the horses are still in Florida anyway, so it's a quick morning."

"I don't know how you do both," Madeline says, shaking her head and picking up her burnished saddle from its post on the wall. She swings it onto Cricket's back and re-positions it, smoothing the saddle pad before going back for the girth.

"Neither do I," I admit.

"Even going to the big races is kind of off the table now, isn't it?" Madeline asks, buckling up the girth and finding the right holes.

"Those are on Saturdays, aren't they?"

I tilt my head at her. "What do you mean?"

"The syllabus for Practicum," she says, looking at me over her shoulder and then pausing when she seems to realize. "You should read the last page."

Ducking out of Kali's stall, I pick up my bag and pull the syllabus out, unfolding it and flipping to the last page where, in big bold type, I find the words "weekend assignments" written over a list of dates.

"Crap," I mutter, a wash of adrenaline slipping over me when I match the dates up to what I know—I *know*—are the prep races we're pointing Lighter to in Florida. February 4th—the Holy Bull. March 4th—the Fountain of Youth. The syllabus insists I'm learning the finer arts of feeding and trailering instead.

"This is not happening," I say to the paper, and then tear my eyes up to focus on Madeline, who bites her lower lip apprehensively.

"Maybe you can get your absences excused?" she asks hopefully.

"There are only four weekend dates listed," I say, resting against Kali's stall and glaring back down at the syllabus—a semester's worth of work I probably already know and don't need to go over. I'd drop the class if it weren't required. I know it in my gut. The Derby preps are too important. And what do I tell Mom and Dad? What the hell do I tell *Beck?* They're too—

"July," Madeline breaks through my rapid-fire thoughts, hand on my arm. "You're going to have a stroke if you keep thinking about all the people you're letting down."

God, was I saying all of that *out loud?* My face flames red.

"Come watch the intermediate dressage class," she insists. "It will be good for you. Sophie is an amazing instructor. You're going to love riding with her, and I could use the cheering section."

"Sure," I nod, folding the syllabus in my shaking hands. "Of course."

Madeline nods smartly and buckles her helmet, then turns to undo Cricket's cross ties, leading the mare down the aisle toward the indoor arenas. I turn to follow, pausing to tuck the Practicum syllabus into my bag. Out of sight, out of mind, right?

Then I scurry to the indoor.

～～

"Outside rein, Maddy!"

Sophie Moreau's voice carries from the middle of the indoor arena, where she stands with eight horses trotting circles around her. It's almost as if she serves as an anchor for the riders, the central point around which they all cycle. Her gravity is weighty, which seems funny because she's dwarfed by the horses. In fact, she's almost hidden by her winter coat, her tiny frame swallowed by green puff. All I can reliably see of her is the halo of short black curls adorning the crown of her head, her near-black skin glowing under the giant fluorescent lights beaming down onto the arena.

Madeline and Cricket churn up dirt as they pass by my perch in the bleachers, the mare's outside shoulder jutting out and her neck bowed in toward the arena.

"Pay special attention to her shoulders," Sophie continues, her hawk-like gaze on Cricket. "She's been popping that outside shoulder the last ten minutes."

Madeline nods, ponytail bobbing, and straightens Cricket out on the turn. The mare swishes her black tail and comes underneath herself, head lowering and white froth dolloping at her lips.

"There," Sophie croons. "Much better."

I catch the barest smile flash across Madeline's face before it's wiped away, total concentration returning to the mare underneath her. From experience, I know she's not paying attention to anything else. It's just her and Cricket and where they are in the arena so they don't cross paths with anyone else, like Ava, whose big gray gelding spooks at nothing and careens sideways off the beaten path in a flurry of hooves and snorts. Before Sophie can say a word, Ava has the gelding put back together, trotting animatedly back into line.

"Nice recovery, Ava," Sophie says, a wry smile slipping up her lips. "Remember to half-halt. Holy has a tendency to start running after a spook."

Ava doesn't say a word, too busy putting Holy back on the bit. Holy snorts, flicks his ears back, and molds himself into the image of a forward, uphill dressage horse on his way past me. Sophie calls for the riders to bring their horses in—a big gather-round.

Checking my watch, I realize with a jolt I've been sitting here the entire class period. My dressage class? It's next. Scrambling out of the bleachers, I dash down to the boarder barn, winding around cross-tied horses and more girls. Ponytails, headbands, paddock boots and half chaps blur on my way. There isn't time for excuse me's or sorry's. I arrive at Kali's stall and find her covered in shavings again, because of course.

"Really?" I ask her, and she gives me a white-ringed eye roll before shoving her nose back in the hay.

Letting myself into her stall, I wrestle her away from her precious hay stash and get her clipped to the line attached to her stall bars. Then it's a mad dash to the tack room, another blur of pony tails and paddock boots, and I'm arriving back at her stall just as horses are being unclipped from cross ties, shod hooves clopping away from me. *Damn it.*

"Why do I suck so much at this?" I ask Kali, who twists one ear around to listen to me as she sniffs aimlessly at the bars. I dig out a brush, swiping the shavings off her glowing red coat. I don't have time to tackle her tail, so she's just going to have to go into the arena with a little natural ornamentation.

Cricket's behemoth bay body goes cruising past me as I tighten Kali's girth, my fingers tripping on the clanking buckles.

"July," Madeline says from outside the stall.

"I know, I know." I lean out of Kali's stall, grabbing her bridle off the hook. "I am not making the best first impression."

"It's fine," Madeline says, although her eyes say something else. Something far different. Something between *you are getting docked several important points for the day* and *this is Sophie Moreau!* The dressage queen of Jericho isn't going to wait for me.

Kali mouths the bit curiously as I get the headstall over her ears, buckle up the rest of her with shaking fingers. When I turn to the stall door, I realize my helmet, gloves, dressage whip . . . all of it is still in my bag, where I left it sitting in the tack room.

"Oh my god," Madeline says, pulling her helmet and gloves off, shoving them into my hands, along with her long, ultra-pink dressage whip. "Take these and go. You don't have time."

"Thank you," I say, breathless. "I owe you."

"Of course you do," she says, pushing Cricket into the middle of the aisle as the big mare curls around her, trying to rub her head against Madeline's hip. Madeline waves me off. "Good luck!"

I'm too busy shoving her helmet on and adjusting the straps to say anything, my tongue tied with nerves and Kali following me hesitantly with her head up, ears swiveling, not entirely sure about the situation I'm rushing her into.

"I need you to be on your best behavior," I tell her, pulling Madeline's gloves on and putting the whip in my left hand as we come up to the arena just as the door's closing.

"Hold up!" I call, getting an eyeful by none other than Sophie Moreau herself. My urge to stammer starts immediately, which is interesting considering how little I have ever stammered.

"I'm sorry," I start, stumbling over words. "I was . . ."

"Not important," she says, waving a hand over my excuse. "I saw you in the bleachers. Try to be more mindful of the time. It literally counts around here."

The burn of adrenaline licks through my veins, rising in a flush along my skin. Great. That's just awesome. I'm a harried wreck and my off-track Thoroughbred is eyeing the arena like it might bite her. Couldn't have made a better first impression.

"Your mare likes to roll, by the looks of it," Sophie says behind me once I get Kali into the arena and the door slips closed behind her. "You'll get the 101 on grooming in Practicum," she assures me as my flush deepens, probably turning a crimson shade of mortification.

I open my mouth, and then shut it. What can I say? There's nothing *to* say. It's done. I'm done. The rest of the semester is just going to be me trying to live down this moment.

Wordlessly, I lead Kali to the mounting block by the door and tighten up her girth, my ears still burning and my fingers numb. Six other students are mounted and walking their horses in rangy circles in the arena. I catch the side-eye of one girl as she walks by on loose reins, silently studying Kali from the back of her warmblood. I force myself to focus, tugging on Kali's stirrup leathers and mounting up. Sophie is already motioning everyone toward her as she walks to the center of the arena.

Kali throws up her head and dances two steps to the side when I ask her to halt. I sink deeper into the saddle, my fingers tighter than they need to be on the reins. Kali grudgingly stops and huffs out a long sigh—long enough to wring a few smiles from the other girls.

I want to bow over Kali's neck and hide my face in her mane, but that would be rather obvious, especially when Sophie turns her attention to me.

"Let's go around," she says, tilting her head at me. "Get introduced."

"July Carter," I manage, heart pounding. "And this is Kali."

"Kali the Roller," Sophie nods.

"She's very good at rolling," I admit, my lungs still too constricted to let me draw a normal breath. Sophie eyes Kali up and down, but says nothing, moving on around our circle.

Jessica. Ashley. Olivia. Luna. Emma. Possibly there's an Avery in there. I blank out during show-and-tell and can't remember the names of the horses is my life depended on it, my attention on Kali as everyone else gets to know each other, know the horses we'll be riding all semester. Quietly, I tug a long shaving out of Kali's mane and let it drop to the dirt.

"So here's what we're going to do today," Sophie says after she introduces herself, leaving off her accomplishments. They don't need to be said. We all know her from the regional shows, and her shiny USDF gold medal.

"We're going to take stock," she says, "which is something I like to do every time I get up on my fifteen-year-old seen-it-all mare or my wet-behind-the-ears know-nothing gelding. I take stock, which means . . ."

I stare at her as she talks, going into a zone of what it means to listen to the horse underneath you, make sure they're listening right back.

"Sometimes it gels immediately," Sophie says. "We're on the same page from the word go. Other days . . ." she laughs, shaking her head. "Sometimes I spend a full hour walking in squares. Halting, walking, and turning. But we're taking stock and we're trying to listen, figure out what each one of us is trying to say. Some days are clearer than others, and today we're going to find out how on the same page you are with your horse. School horse or owned, this is your ride for the semester, so it's best to find the page now."

God, this sounds like something I need to do with Jericho as a whole. *Halt, walk, turn. Halt, walk, turn. Find the same page and listen.* It sounds so easy, but Kali shifts underneath me as Sophie starts going over the fundamentals, her off-track Thoroughbred impatience shivering to the surface.

This is going to be a challenge. I'm going to call it now.

"Let's start with Avery," Sophie says, pointing to a girl as I quietly pat myself on the back for remembering there is an Avery in the class. Avery nudges her horse out of our line, halts and nudges him back into a walk. Turns on a dime, halts, walks. They finish the square with Sophie's constant chatter, a stream of *there, do you feel that? He's listening to you.*

Avery beams, giving her bay gelding a hearty pat on the neck when the square is completed. The next girl goes and the next. Different stories for each, different squares for each. The horses know what's up, making us riders the learners. We're the ones striving to reach out, find the horse underneath us and build the connection from the ground up.

Kali stands underneath me, obviously bored as she sticks a leg out and fiercely rubs her face against it.

"July," Sophie says, and if it were possible to sit on the edge of a saddle, I'd be on it in an instant. My back goes straight, and Kali's head shoots up, her whole body lurching to the side. Sophie raises an eyebrow. "It's obvious someone is listening. Time to see if she'll listen on the square, too."

"I'm happy to try," I say, digging down for some old part of myself. The person who knows just what I'm capable of, who isn't ever late or caught unaware. I'm on top of this. I've been riding horses since I could walk. Since *before* I could walk. I know how to halt, walk, and turn.

I put my heels to Kali's sides and she strides out across the dirt happily, eager to move. Then the halt and her ears swing back, her reaction quick to the weight in the saddle and my closed fingers on the reins. I can't resist giving her a little more attention, encouraging her to tip her head down, be square. We've worked on this, after all. Florida was all about this when it wasn't about Lighter, and Feather, and Beck. Might as well show Sophie Moreau we know how to look pretty despite the shavings in Kali's tail.

I keep my legs on Kali's sides, thinking about those schooling sessions on the Palm Meadows track. I squeeze harder, feeling Kali's mouth, the reins a tense line up to my elbows as my filly thinks about lowering her head that extra centimeter further. *Almost there . . .*

I watch her ears swivel and her chin lower down, down, my thoughts flitting back to Florida. To the trips I won't be taking anymore because I have to master basics. Kali snorts like she knows exactly where my mind is—not on her—and flings her head up, balking just before I can get her to my goal. I give her space, rush to ease the reins, but her hindquarters dance to the side anyway, followed by the rest of her.

"Gather her up, July," Sophie says. "Try again."

Kali's body kinks underneath me, refusing to travel straight, refusing to turn, refusing any attempt to halt square. I have a crooked, confused horse, and I managed to accomplish all of this in less than five minutes. There's little I can do other than exactly as Sophie says: try again. Wipe the slate clean.

I straighten Kali and put my legs to her sides, asking for go. Kali, horrible racehorse though she was, understands *go.*

Kali goes, leaping into a springy trot. She's full of snorts, her head up too high and her body quivering with the undeniable urge any horse has when left leaderless: run. Kali is two seconds away from dumping my commands and listening to her instincts.

"Straighten her neck out," Sophie commands, jettisoning her earlier polite tone in favor of do-as-I-say-*now.* "Then half-halt, July. Do you know what . . .?"

"Yes," I interrupt through my unkinking of Kali. Of course I know what a half-halt is. The tips of my ears heat up from having to answer that question. Kali's neck goes from an awkward angle off her shoulders back to the comfy middle, right as I sit back in the saddle, asking her to come up underneath herself. Gather. *Come back to me, Kali. Please, for the love of god.*

Kali's stride stutters back into a walk, and I tap her off the wall. She turns with a swish of her tail—happily, like she wasn't just thinking about taking all of my decisions and trampling them.

With a squeeze of the reins and a shift of my weight, she halts.

Square. Then she bobs her head down and mouths the bit like I always wanted, but never asked for quite right.

Sophie raises her eyebrow. "Did you ask her for that?"

Can I say I asked for half of it? The rest was just a happy accident? Something tells me Sophie already knows, and before I can say a word, she motions me forward.

"Pick her back up, July," she says. "Once more, but this time it's going to be your idea."

I pick Kali up, my heart feeling battered, and we walk.

Chapter Four

"She fell apart," I say as I drive down the Northern State Parkway, still shivering from the extra adrenaline coursing in my system from my epic fail of a first day. "And I, in case you were wondering, was a total wreck of a human being."

Beck makes a disparaging noise through the car's speakers.

"Come on," he says. "It couldn't have been so bad you were at human wreck level."

"It was bad," I groan, telling him the whole story, from Kali's insistence on kicking shavings around her stall like she's constantly tossing confetti in the air to Sophie's certain look. The one that says *so you're going to be the problem student this semester.*

"I just have to do better," I say, standing by my filly. Kali may have fallen apart, but that's on me and my fuzzy signals. "Like, dressage-princess-with-OCD kind of better."

"I'm not sure I'm liking this," Beck says, the humor in his voice translating loud and clear through the scratchy cell connection. "Bossy race girl I can handle, but dressage princess? What is that, anyway? You're not going to start gluing rhinestones on your jeans, right?"

"Wrong discipline," I tell him, and then make a face. "Although thank you for reminding me—I can't go to the Holy Bull in February."

A distracted pause crackles through the speakers, city noise replacing Beck long enough for me to imagine him on the sidewalk somewhere on Columbia's campus, breath puffing from his lips in the cold as he trundles to his next class. Once, not too long ago, I thought that would be my life. I thought I'd be city-bound. Instead I'm working toward more horses and now, ironically, it's horses keeping me from, well, horses.

"What?" Beck asks, and I can picture his face screwing up into confusion. "What do you mean you can't go?"

"I have four weekend assignments in Practicum," I sigh. "And guess when they fall."

Another pause. Then: "Damn it."

I flinch, even though Beck doesn't sound angry. Disappointment laces his words, and I can't help but feel like I'm letting him down. I'm letting Lighter and Feather down.

"I'm sorry," I say, feeling an intense urge to babble, to find a way to make this better when I'm not sure how.

How do you explain not being able to follow through with plans made because you have to learn how to trailer a horse? I've known how to do that for years. It's engrained in my soul, like a cosmic tattoo I'll never be able to remove.

I take a deep breath, remembering. Baby steps.

This isn't about me.

I start to explain, but Beck beats me to it.

"No, I get it," he says. "It sucks, but I get it."

"I'm sure you'll have a great time in Florida," I offer. "Sunshine and fruity drinks, right? Maybe Lighter will even win."

He laughs. "Yeah, probably I would. And maybe Lighter will. But I'm not going to see it in person because I'm not going."

"Wait," I stumble, almost veering onto the shoulder. The car's tires hit the warning strip meant to jar dozing drivers back to bright-eyed alertness and my teeth rattle. I yank the car back into its lane, fully awake. "You can't just do that."

"Why not?" Beck asks, in his most blasé way that infuriates me to no end. "Lighter will run with or without me around. Not to wreck my own highly important self-image or anything, but I'm not tremendously important to the cause, Juls."

"You're the *owner*. The Holy Bull isn't just a race. It's a stepping stone to the Kentucky-*freaking*-Derby. It's not something you fail to attend without a good reason."

"Juls," he says over my rising tirade. "Hey," he laughs. "Rein it in and take a breath. I know I need to go, but I don't want to. There's a vast difference. I'm not going."

"Why?" I ask, still mortified.

"Because you're not going to be there?"

I can see the invisible question mark zooming into the air from the streets around Columbia, slipping in through my car speakers and hitting me square in the face.

Because I'm not going to be there.

My heart melts, which is such a strange, alien feeling.

"Oh," I say, dumbly. My voice is about as loud as a squeaking mouse, and I'm surprised Beck hears me. But he does, if his chuckle is any indication.

"Yeah," he says. "*Oh.* Look, Juls, Lighter stopped being a fun project a long time ago. I'm not a horse owner for the sheer desire to be a horse owner, you know? I'm in it for entirely selfish reasons at this point, most of them tied up with you. You've got to know that by now, but if not then I need to make myself clear."

My foot slips off the accelerator, my brain somewhere else entirely. I'm not in this car, not driving it on a busy interstate, maintaining the proper distance between vehicles. I'm in la-la land, swept up in pretty words.

Which is why when a honk startles me back to my present situation I slam my foot on the pedal and nearly give myself whiplash.

Right. Okay. I can function like a normal person—I can.

"You okay?" Beck asks, sounding worried.

"Fine," I chirp. "Just, you know, nearly driving off the road over here."

"Yeah, maybe I should have waited to tell you that when you weren't driving sixty miles an hour."

"No, I accidentally forced your hand," I say. "And it's not unappreciated, you know? I want to know those things. I guess I just didn't realize you felt that way about Lighter. About the whole racing thing. A—"

I'm babbling. I snap my mouth shut, trying to think of the right words to say.

"About you?" Beck asks, guessing.

"Well," I say, the old shyness rising in me. "Maybe not about me."

There's a pause, like he's digesting this.

"Good," he says, finally. "Then it's decided. I have a television. What more do we really need? You'll just come over to my place for the Holy Bull."

A little part of me shivers. I'm quickly rewriting my winter Florida fantasy, replacing it with Beck's cramped brownstone dorm room he shares with two other probably equally slovenly college boys. It's not what I imagined twenty-four hours ago, but this is better.

This is what I wanted—living the college girl life with my horse, getting the best of all possible outcomes. And here Beck is, finally inviting me in.

I smile. No—I *grin.*

"It's a date."

~~

Walking into the house, the first thing I do is trip over Smoky. My cat winds around my legs, plaintively crying, probably because she hasn't yet been fed. Normally this is a task that falls to me, but with all the newness to this day I let it slide.

Dropping my bag at the base of the stairs, I follow her excited trot down the hallway into the kitchen, which gives me a perfect view of Leo balancing precariously on an exercise ball and twisting from side to side, a medicine ball clutched in both hands. He's been exercising nonstop since the hospital discharged him last month and Dad exiled him back here to recuperate. Needless to say, Leo's chances at heading our newfangled Florida barn took a header the second Lighter ran him down. Dad has promised him the job of foreman at Barn 27 now that Paul is in Florida, but Leo has to be of sound body and mind before he's allowed back on the track.

I watch his back as I dish out Smoky's food into her bowl, my cat digging her claws into my leg right above my half chaps, because she knows my weak spots.

"Okay, okay," I mumble at her, unsticking her sharp little nails from my breeches. "You don't have to tear me to shreds; I'm sorry."

"She's been whining for hours," Leo chimes in from the living room, moving the medicine ball from right to left and wincing as he goes.

"Thank you for helping," I shoot back at him, putting Smoky's bowl on the floor and leaving her to chow down. I cross over to the living room, falling onto the sofa, exhaustion suddenly peppering every inch of me. It's a different sort of tired than what I'm used to from the track.

It feels weird to be home in the early afternoon, pale winter sun still shining through the windows. It's hard to remember when I last saw my house during daylight hours. I won't be able to get away with this all the time—this casual sitting here after my classes are done. I can feel the track whispering to me even now.

"How was the first day?" Leo asks, putting the medicine ball down by his feet.

"Equal parts enlightening and terrifying," I say, getting a sideways glance from Leo as he starts his crunches.

"College tends to be like that," he says between reps, sweat glistening at his temples. His hair is starting to grow back in thick, black fuzz all over his head. The scar on his scalp is only just visible beneath it all, making me wince when I remember the sound of Lighter plowing him down, his head bouncing off the gravel.

I would like to never experience that again. Of course, here I am in the horse world. I'm going to see such things again. Only a matter of time. Maybe it will even happen to me.

"You're pushing it again," I tell him softly, and he laughs, finishing up his crunches and bending over, resting his elbows on his bare knees.

"You would, too," he points out. "If you were stuck rehabbing instead of doing what you wanted to do."

"Going to the track, you mean," I say. "Dad told you . . ."

"I need a clean bill of health." Leo rolls his eyes. "I feel like a lame horse about to get a vet check."

"You're almost done with physical therapy," I point out. "Another couple of weeks and you'll be back at Belmont."

"But not Palm Meadows," Leo says, sighing and looking up at the television, where TVG shows brilliant images of Gulfstream Park, all verdant turf course and startling blue sky. It's not hard to see what Leo's missing.

"No," I say, watching his shoulders sink and grappling with something to say. It's unnerving watching Leo like this, like he's a shade of his former confident self. "But look at it this way," I continue. "Being Dad's right hand man at Belmont is valuable. You will be the foreman of Barn 27, Leo. Saddling horses in the afternoon and everything."

He barks out a laugh, nodding. "Point taken."

"You're welcome," I say, hoping my little pep talk has done the trick. If only I were so good at talking myself up. I'd be unstoppable.

The image on the television shifts to two men in suits and gaudy ties, papers covering the desk in front of them as they chatter about past races. That's handicapping—forever discussing the past in an attempt to predict the future.

Then the image shifts and my breath stops in my throat as Feather's last race spills across the television screen. I'd like to squeeze my eyes closed and not witness the ridiculously avoidable tragedy that was the slipped girth, but no such luck.

There it is, squeezed back on her ribcage, just as Feather's trying her hardest to fight to the front. Mom shifts her weight, and that's it. They're done.

"Now, this filly obviously has class," one of the talking heads says, smiling at the camera. "My understanding is she was saddled by Rob Carter's daughter, and this was the first horse she's sent forward. Despite the *wardrobe malfunction,* I have to say this filly showed serious effort."

"Positive commentary," Leo says over the anchors' giggles, giving me a look out of the corner of his eye as the anchors move on to workouts, their words meant for the handicappers glued to the screen.

"For Feather," I grouse, still stuck on that slipped saddle like I'm hanging on a rein, insisting on a result I know I'm not going to get. I want to stop thinking about Feather's slipped saddle like I want to stop thinking about Kali falling apart in the arena, shavings in her tail and my fingers clammy in Madeline's gloves.

"Juls, equipment fails all the time," Leo says, standing up. "Try to cut yourself some slack."

"I should have double checked," I say, frowning at the television. "I was nervous and you know how Feather is—she was hyper to go. I just didn't think to make sure."

"And look where we are now," Leo says, falling onto the sofa next to me, smelling like sweat and boy. I wrinkle my nose as his shoulder brushes mine. "Feather is in a Kentucky Oaks prep race, where she wouldn't have been had she not done well in that maiden. We all know she would have won."

"If . . ." I start again, and he rolls his eyes.

"Stop it," he chides me. "Enough wallowing. If anyone should be wallowing, it should be me. You're stealing my thunder, Juls."

I look over at his halo of growing hair.

"Yeah, sorry," I say, admitting it. "You're right. Things turned out okay. And without me around next weekend she might just win."

"What do you mean without you?" Dad asks behind me, and I startle, twisting around. Dad looks at me expectantly, and Leo startles to standing, bounding to his feet in an extra show of how ready he is to return to the track.

Dad raises an eyebrow at me. "I'm assuming you've got somewhere better to be?"

"School," I sigh, letting my head fall back on the sofa cushions as I explain myself. Dad looks at me like I'm trying to explain Latin to him. Frustration builds its way back up my throat. "I know how to do all of this," I say. "I shouldn't have to stay home to go over things I already know."

"I understand the reasoning," he interrupts me, shaking his head. "You know how we've always done things at the track, but they'll have their own set of rules, July. You're learning how they expect these tasks to be done. You plan to be there long enough that it will matter whether or not you know their rules."

I groan, because he makes sense.

"Fine," I sigh. "Then you'll have to know Beck isn't going to Florida for Lighter's races either."

He shrugs. "Owner's choice. Beck doesn't concern me, Juls. You do."

A flush hits my cheeks, and I look back at the television, even though they're so past Feather I have no reason to stare at it. Leo slinks out of the room as though given a wordless order as Dad sinks down onto the sofa next to me, vacantly staring at the screen for long enough that I think he might have forgotten I'm still sitting next to him.

"How did the first day go?"

I glance over at him, surprised to find him looking at me.

"Terrible," I admit. "I was late to nearly everything, and Kali proved beyond a doubt she's nowhere near the same page as me, which makes me wonder if I'm just pushing her into something she has no business being involved in. Meanwhile, Saturday classes. Who has classes on Saturdays?"

"College students," Dad says without missing a beat, making my flush deepen.

"Touché," I nod.

"Look, Juls, you'd be missed at the barn," he says, "but . . ."

"No," I interrupt, emphatic. "Nope. Gus, Pilar, *and* Izzie are gone. You need me."

"Not as badly as you seem to think," Dad counters. "School comes first. I've always said that, and it isn't going to change because you're in college."

"But it's *college*," I stress. "It's flexible. I can do both. Besides, you can't run me off. I'm an adult; I can decide where I want to be."

Dad looks at me like I've surprised him, and maybe I have. But I've always been the adult in the room, starting when I was barely thirteen. I've always kept the ship running, and I'm not about to stop now.

"You're right," Dad says, blinking at me and giving a stilted sort of nod, as though he's trying to come to terms with my adultness. "You can decide where you want to be." Then he looks at me hard. "But don't lie to me, Juls. If it gets too hard to do both, you're going to tell me. Understand?"

"Understood," I sigh. "Although, let's face it, you'd rue the day I left. It would be chaos in a heartbeat."

"Damn straight," he says, clapping a hand on my knee and standing up, leaving me to the television just as my phone beeps and I turn it over to read the incoming text sent from my best friend, Bri Wagner.

How did the first day go?

Bri is basically a bloodhound. It's like she can sniff out exactly when she's needed—even if she's miles away in the city—because if I need help with college girl things I'm certainly not going to Leo.

I tap the face of the phone.

So much to say. But more importantly, I'm going to Beck's for the Holy Bull. Want to come?

The little thought bubble sits there quietly, waiting for Bri's answer, which comes crashing in with a little swooshing noise that makes me smile.

!!!

And then, so big and insistent I laugh out loud, *OF COURSE.*

Chapter Five

Walking out of the subway takes the breath out of my lungs when I hit cold city air. Bri hunches into her coat next to me, burrowing her nose in her scarf and hiding even more in the wool she's wrapped around herself. Her long dark hair billows out underneath her knit hat, which she has pulled over her forehead as far as she can make it go. She squeezes her eyes shut and groans.

"I swear my eyelashes are freezing together," she says, scrunching up her nose, which I can only barely see above her scarf.

Despite the snow coming down all around me, I'm feeling pretty good from Feather's head bob loss earlier in the day in the Forward Gal. She rushed up at the end, bounding underneath Mom like she had something to prove, but came up short. Hopefully this means she wants more distance, not less. The real wild card is whether she can hold her own against better fillies, because they always get better from here on out.

"I'm thinking Florida thoughts," I say to Bri, voice muffled in my own scarf as we cross the slush-slicked street.

"Does it help?" she asks, hunching her shoulders as a stiff early February breeze blows into us, knocking me back a step when I try to navigate climbing over a snow pile on the sidewalk.

"Not particularly," I admit, taking the gloved hand she offers me so I can clamber over the mound of snow and get my feet underneath me. "Right now my embarrassing memories of the last time I was here are keeping me warm."

She snorts, eyebrow rising against her beanie.

"And left me to fend for myself," she reminds me, the flush on my neck actually starting to make me a little more comfortable in the cold. "I can imagine that would be a memory to keep you warm out of shame."

"We don't need to speak of it ever again," I tell her, and she laughs, continuing on down the sidewalk.

"I'm not the one bringing it up," she says. "I'm over it, Juls."

"That's big of you," I tell her. "I'm just wondering what everyone else up there is going to think."

"Everyone else should mind their business," Bri says smartly. "They didn't know what the situation was, and I don't think Beck's the type to bare his soul. You'll be fine. And if you aren't . . ." She motions to herself. "I am here to rescue you."

"How did I get you as my best friend again?" I ask, tilting my head to consider her, because I'm honestly not sure how this happened.

"Luck," she says, nudging my shoulder with hers as we walk. "You don't deserve me."

I can't help but think back to Bri and Beck showing up in Florida in December, Jericho's acceptance letter in hand and reason on their lips. There's no way to know what would have happened had they both stayed in New York, letting me stew alone in Palm Meadows, but I can safely say if they hadn't shown up I wouldn't be here—walking to Beck's brownstone dorm on the day of Lighter's first Kentucky Derby prep race.

"I really don't deserve you," I agree. "You're integral to my life, Bri."

"So happy you finally admit the obvious," Bri says, trotting up the salted brownstone steps. The salt pops and crackles under my snow boots. When we crowd into the vestibule, Bri motions at the intercom. "You can do the honors this time."

I stick my tongue out at her as I press Beck's button, the door giving off a fuzzy hum before the lock unlatches. Bri shoulders into it, and I push through behind her, eager to start unwinding the scarf from my face. Bri peels off her hat as we walk up the stairs, shaking away the melting snow as I stamp my boots on the carpet. Slush falls off of me in chunks to join the salt stains.

"This is disgusting," I proclaim, dangling my scarf's damp form in front of me as we hike our way to the top floor.

"Welcome to winter in the city," Bri says, pushing through the door to Beck's floor. "Snow drifts and walk-ups. You're always hot and cold and more than a little damp at the same time."

"Sounds like the track," I say, just as Beck opens his door, getting an eyeful of both of us. We must look like chilled, drowned rats, because he laughs.

"Honestly, I wasn't expecting vagrants to be all that interested in the Holy Bull," he says, leaning a shoulder against the doorjamb so he can take his time enjoying this. "Did you guys get hit with a snow plow?"

"I am not dignifying that with a response," Bri replies, flicking her wet fingers at him, which does nothing to dampen his glee as he stands aside, letting us into the packed apartment.

People cluster from the door to the kitchen, and in the middle of the melee I catch glimpses of familiar faces—the boys who witnessed the night last fall when everything went wrong pepper through the crowd. Sunglasses Girl sits on the sofa with a tumbler full of something amber, her blond hair braided and sleek. Her outfit is old school Jackie O equestrian, right down to the knee-high leather boots that suspiciously don't have a line of salt stains crusting the heels.

It occurs to me I still don't know her name. I assume she has one. That would be normal, after all.

Then it hits me, again, that I need to talk to these people. There are too many to reliably be called upon to remember, and the last thing I want to do is indulge small talk that will undoubtedly involve Beck and that night last fall when our brand new relationship cracked and fell apart. For a minute, I'm glad for my damp wool coat, because the flush on my face deepens. At least I have a cover.

Thank you, snow.

"Devon's room is collecting an impressive pile of coats," Beck says, breaking me out of my internal conflict over my lack of social skills. "I'm not sure how thrilled he was about that, but it was either have the party here or do the catered thing at my parents' place. This seemed more . . . homey."

I've been to precisely one *catered thing* at Beck's parents' house. I was afraid I would break something the Smithsonian would be grieved to find destroyed by a clumsy teenager, so let's just say I'm glad for small favors. There's absolutely nothing in Beck's apartment that can't be broken, besides my pride.

Beck is all smiles, and the television is blaring the day's undercard through the din of the crowd. People are putting bets in through their phones and tipping back bottles of beer. It's a party, I remind myself, not an inquisition.

"I, for one, could use a beer," Bri says, shrugging out of her coat and putting it on top of the pile on Devon's floor. "How long until the Holy Bull?"

"One more race," Beck and I both say, as Bri looks between us like she might have been expecting something more like a time.

"Which means I have time to get a beer?" Bri asks hopefully.

"You have time to think about it for at least thirty minutes," Beck says. "It won't take that long because there are basically two choices, but you're free to mull that decision over until it gets weird."

"Then I should start the selection process now," Bri says, bouncing out of the room and disappearing into the crush of people, leaving me with Beck, who watches me with glittering, mischievous eyes.

Of course, he looks incredibly tempting in his Henley, because he seems to understand by some intuition how to be appealing without looking like he's too aware. Part of me wants to pull the Henley up by the hem, see what bizarre T-shirt he has on underneath in this room that is smelling increasingly of wet wool.

"Want to get out there?" Beck asks, hooking a finger through one of my belt loops. "Meet the folks?"

I take a visible deep breath.

"They aren't that bad," Beck says. "They're just your average trust fund kid, the brilliant full-ride-scholar . . ."

"All of whom know a little something about me, I imagine?" I ask, watching his mouth shift to the side.

"Not *that* much," he insists. "I wasn't being very clear with you last fall, and I wasn't being really clear with them either. Elyse nearly had my head about it."

"Sunglasses Girl?" I assume. He nods.

"She told me to get my head out of my ass," Beck tells me, to which I raise a questioning eyebrow. "We both kind of owe her some gratitude, I think."

"Sounds like a fun conversation I'm about to have." I peer into the packed room, catching Bri weaving through the masses with two bottles clutched in her upraised hands.

"Victory!" she announces as soon as she gets to us, depositing one sweating bottle in my hands and tipping hers back to drink. "We'll be warm in no time."

I look down at the bottle, its label already askew from the condensation. I'm not normally a big drinker, not with the track always looming in the early morning hours of my life. There's no way I can nurse a hangover and pilot a thundering Thoroughbred at the same time. I value my life.

But this is college, I remind myself. I did say I was capable of doing both, didn't I? What's one beer?

So I bring the bottle to my lips and drink.

~~

When the camera first catches sight of Lighter, the whole aparment erupts into rapturous cheers. The colt walks the paddock at Gulfstream, yanking on Gus's arm and coiling into a coppery strand of muscle. His pale tail is held just high enough to show his excitement, and his arrogance. Not nervously high, not apathetically low. Just right.

"You know he won me, like, a hundred bucks at Saratoga," Devon announces from the sofa.

"That was me," Elyse corrects, leaning forward to give him the evil eye. "You had no idea how to handicap, remember? Who showed you which horses to pick for your trifecta?"

Devon rubs a hand over his mouth as the rest of Beck's inner circle nudge each other, grinning at the brewing conflict. Jasper, the Rhodes Scholar in sweats; Lucas, the squash player wearing a legitimate bow tie and flat cap; and Sebastian, the playboy who won't stop winking at me.

"I might have needed some coaching," Devon allows.

"Coaching?" Elyse asks, lifting her eyes to me. "You should have seen him, Juls. He didn't know what a bullet work was, not to mention morning line odds. I practically had to explain fractions. *Fractions.*"

"Hey, I know what fractions are," Devon says defensively.

"He does now," Lucas breaks in, a whole cascade of laughter rolling in his wake as Devon grunts and leans back into the sofa, waving us off.

"Fine," he says. "Elyse picked the horses. I ride her glorious coattails."

"Of course you do," Elyse nods, taking a sip of what I now know to be bourbon. "And had Beck introduced us to Juls last summer imagine how much more glorious I'd be at picking winners? Two track brats? We'd have been unstoppable."

Elyse, I have come to find out, is from Kentucky. Her accent is thick and her taste in beverages is questionable. She's been in Manhattan since high school, when her father moved Bluegrass Thoroughbred Partners' base of operations to New York, managing horses for giant groups of owners, everyone chipping in to pay for the horse's upkeep and training, then sharing in the glory—if there is any. With Bluegrass, there's been plenty of glory. My very eloquent response to Elyse saying its name like it was nothing was *what?*

And then she asked me if I wanted a bourbon.

"Wait," Beck breaks in, "I've seen July bet on horses, and it's safe to say she's horrible at it."

"Because I don't do it," I point out, and Beck motions at me like I'm proving his argument.

"I rest my case," he says. "Not even my horse could sway her."

"Doesn't matter," Elyse dismisses this. "Insider information is better than none."

She turns back to the television as the camera leaves Lighter and moves on to Tahr, all blood red in the Florida sun. He looks even more magnificent on camera than he did that morning at Palm Meadows. Clearly Florida is treating him well.

Elyse watches the paddock preparations with detached commitment. I know the feeling. There's no knowing how all of those weeks and weeks of training will end. You have to give yourself over to the not knowing, detaching yourself just enough to get through the next few minutes. Get the horse saddled. Get the jockey on the horse. Make sure all the ducks are in their rows, the horse is ready, the jockey is ready, and then see them to the track, where everything is up to mostly luck.

Sometimes not even the best, most talented, most prepared horse wins. So you detach. Only when the horses are in the final stretch does it all reconnect and adrenaline takes over, pushing you to start screaming at the top of your lungs, jump, wave your arms around like a fury.

Sometimes, especially with trainers like my dad, not even then.

They've seen too much.

They know better.

I haven't reached that point yet, and I have a feeling Elyse hasn't either.

When the jockeys leap onto their mounts, I catch sight of Mom with her boot in Dad's hand, both of them working in tandem to get her airborne. She leaps and lands in the saddle like she weighs nothing, settling herself and collecting the reins. Lighter doesn't even flick his ears at the weight, walking with an animated jig next to Gus all the way to the sun-splashed track as the announcers chatter about his comeback after so many months away.

Then the camera moves to Tahr. The big red chestnut with the splashy blaze looks just as good, walking easily under one of racing's best jockeys—Samuel Ramirez. All the other horses are treated to slap-dash coverage, all of them at long odds thanks to Lighter and Tahr. The Holy Bull is a two-horse race as far as the racing industry is concerned, with the other eight contenders whittled down to potential upsets. They're the ones for handicappers to box in with their picks, the ones to choose if you're feeling bold and want to make money looking for a longshot winner.

I ignore them, focusing on the track, on the way Lighter warms up. His coppery coat is clean of sweat, pale mane fanning off his neck as he canters around the bend of the track and slows, turns around with his pony and presses his muzzle into the patient gelding's neck.

"He looks good," I say, as though to reassure myself. Elyse nods in silent agreement.

The starting gate looms in front of them, horses clustering behind it as the gate crew gets busy. When one of the assistants takes Lighter forward to the five hole, my heart starts its treacherous pounding. In front of me, on the sofa, Elyse leans forward. At my side, Beck is a silent wall, eyes glued to the screen. Bri bounces on her toes on the other side of me, her beer sloshing in its bottle.

Quiet presses down on the entire room in the split second it takes for the last horse to load. Then the bell shrieks out of the television before the rough gunshot of the gate doors banging open.

All the horses leap and plunge, hooves hitting the dirt and digging in. Their hindquarters bunch, necks bobbing, riders already working to get to the sweet spot first. Mom hustles Lighter through horses—the very opposite of what happened in his last race, which was so long ago now I hardly remember what happened.

Rain, some bit of me reminds myself. *Mud up to your ankles.*

We'd had to make up ground then. Today is shiny and clear and Mom is taking Lighter to the front. Our ditzy blond colt leads the way into the first turn, a bay named Arco Iris quick on his heels. To the outside, Tahr stalks a half-length back in third as they go into the turn.

So there it is. The first turn on our road to the Derby complete. Of course, Lighter has the gall to prick his ears.

The horses move down the backstretch, Mom keeping Lighter steady down the straightaway. Acro Iris runs in his kickback, falters just enough to let Tahr move into second, but gets himself together to retake second before they hit the last turn. Who knows what the other horses are doing—the camera doesn't care about them. The announcer gives them a cursory once over, but by the time Lighter switches leads it's obvious who needs screen time.

Lighter kicks away from the crowd, Mom still keeping him under wraps. Behind him, Acro Iris tries his little heart out under the crack of the whip, but he falls behind Tahr, who moves up under urging.

My hands find the back of the sofa and squeeze as everyone in the room falls into disarray. Screams spike through the air, curse-riddled excitement rolling through us as Tahr stretches out and gains just as Mom shakes the reins and becomes a flurry and an afterthought all at once. All eyes are on the horses. Tahr gaining, and Lighter speeding up. Both are moving faster.

Faster.

The wire approaches somewhere off screen, making it hard to tell when this will be over. Elyse leaps to her feet, screaming at the television for Lighter to freaking run.

Mom looks under her arm, sees Tahr gaining like a fiery locomotive, and flips the whip down on Lighter's hind end. The colt leaps, stride lengthening and ears slipping back flat against his head.

And still, Tahr *gains.*

"Shit," I hear Beck whisper under his breath. A litany of it, over and over until the red chestnut is even on Lighter's outside and the colts stretch as one to the wire that suddenly appears like an oasis in the desert.

Saved.

But as the horses flash underneath it, and my throat opens enough for me to speak, it occurs to me I have no idea who won.

Elyse falls onto the sofa, exhausted. Confusion wheels through the crowd, questions popping around us asking *what do they do now?*

Beck runs shaky fingers through his hair as the camera follows the colts into the bend, both jockeys standing in the stirrups before flashing back to the grandstand, showing Tahr's trainer, Danny Miller, standing anxiously. Worry lines crease around his signature mirrored aviators before the camera cuts to Dad standing silently, watching. Waiting.

"Either way this turns out," I hear myself saying, "it's a good comeback."

"And points to the Derby," Beck says absently, keeping his eyes on the television as the rest of the runners are stripped of their tack and taken back to the stables. Only Tahr and Lighter remain, walking circles in the dirt as people discuss and a replay starts on screen.

The entire crowd starts hollering when Lighter and Tahr, in a slow motion grind, hit the finish line. Lighter's nose is just centimeters ahead.

A flash in the real world, and gone.

I bite my lip as Bri does a little dance. "See!" she exclaims, high-fiving Devon and Jasper before she turns to me with an excited flush on her face. "We can all stop worrying now."

I nod, because it looks so tempting. So real.

But where's the real finish line? Even Beck doesn't move until the official numbers are posted, flashing on the giant board situated in Gulfstream's infield as large as life. The five over the three. The *hold all tickets* sign stops flashing, replaced with the definitive word: *official.*

Lighter has won.

Then the entire room falls apart.

∿

In Saratoga, we always went to Rustic after a win. Or, really, if we had even the slightest of reasons, like we really tried hard that day and we're bone tired. Or it's a dark day and there has to be at least one good reason to get off the farm. Time away is important, no matter how you spend it, even if it was always at Rustic.

For Columbia kids, it's The Library. Not to be mistaken for *the* library, because there are no books on the premises. What they do have is a variety of board games and a lax attitude toward fake IDs, of which I have none.

"It's like you missed out on some fundamental college 101 experiences," Elyse says over the crowd noise, which is deafening.

"Since she just entered college I'd say that's an affirmative," Beck says dryly next to me.

"Oooh, where?" Elyse asks, leaning forward over the table.

"Jericho," I say, pointing . . . in a direction I am not sure is east, actually. I lower my hand quickly. "Equine studies program."

"Really?" Elyse's eyes light up. "I'm jealous. But, honestly, the horse thing is all my dad. I rode them, but I'm not brilliant. Not make-it-a-career kind of brilliant, anyway. You must be really good."

"Or crazy," Bri pipes up, smiling at me when I shoot her one of our understood looks. "It's not like I was the one at the barn this morning learning how to feed horses when I know how to feed horses, which I don't, of course."

Elyse frowns. "I get it, though. Not everyone knows, and you're a freshman. Freshman get the worst assignments."

"Hear, hear," Bri says loudly, lifting her drink.

"I think it's about time to cut this one off," Beck says as Bri giggles her way into another sip.

"At least I'll be warm on the ride home," she comments, and Beck just shakes his head at her.

"Think again," he says. "I'm not putting you in an Uber, a cab, or letting you roam the subway by yourself at this rate."

Bri pouts. "But July will be with me."

Beck opens his mouth, then shuts it. We all look at him curiously. Me. Bri. Elyse.

An awkward silence descends.

"I," he starts slowly, then pauses to drain the last of his beer. "Am going to get another one of these."

Then he's gone. Elyse smirks at his back.

"He's so bad at this," she says wisely and then clarifies for me when I look at her questioningly over my soda. "The whole boyfriend thing."

I raise an eyebrow, and Elyse groans, letting her head fall forward in a luxurious wave of blond hair. Absurdly, I almost want to reach out and prevent it from touching the dirty table.

"As one of his few female friends," she tells me, straightening and flicking her hair back into place, which it does with a maddening ease, "Beck kind of runs things by me."

My face? It instantly heats up.

"Oh, god."

Elyse startles. "Not about you, so much," she rushes to reassure me. "Mostly about how he's an idiot. I hear a lot of Beck-is-an-idiot stories. It's actually what made me consider him friendship material instead of boyfriend material, because he's either not talking or, when he does, it's to tell me he's being an idiot."

"July knows how to pick them," Bri comments from her section of table.

"I'm still basically on *oh my god,*" I say. "What has he told you?"

"Oh," Elyse shrugs. "I know a lot about you, of course. Enough to put together he's crazy about you, and when Beck's crazy about anything he's inevitably an idiot about it. This? Right now?" She points between me and Beck, who's waiting on his beer at the bar. "That was him hoping you'd stay at the apartment tonight."

I stare at her, my brain short circuiting.

Stay. At the apartment. In Manhattan. With Beck.

I'm sure the level of red on my cheeks has approached a magma level of hot.

"I'm embarrassing you." Elyse makes a face. "Forget I said anything. It's not my business anyway."

"Really isn't," Bri says, having completely lost her filter. I feel like hiding behind my hands, or ducking under the table, anything to escape my current reality, which is a little shell-shocked. But who am I kidding? Of course this would come up. I'm eighteen, not a nun.

Granted, I didn't anticipate this conversation happening with Sunglasses Girl—Elyse, I tell myself, *Elyse*—but that's life for you.

"You're right," Elyse tells Bri, who smiles winningly. Then she looks across the table to me. "I'm sorry, July."

"Nothing to be sorry for," I mumble, too busy looking across The Library to where Beck is standing, ensconced in friends still patting him on the back for the big win. Beck smiles, ducks his head under the onslaught, and we haven't even been hit yet by the reaction of the racing world.

I haven't looked at the online reaction, the commentary on the stories that have surely already been written on *The Blood-Horse* and shuffled to the back pages of major news sports sections across the country. The Holy Bull isn't a big race, but its fallout can be. It reshuffles the future Derby field, changes odds, and gets handicappers talking. In the morning, Lighter will be on top ten lists and everyone will be asking Danny Miller what he's going to do with Tahr now that he's been beaten. When reporters ask where we'll find Lighter next, they'll do it knowing my dad's quiet answer: the Fountain of Youth.

Then the pressure will *really* be on. I look at the way Beck hunches against the bar and feel another pang of guilt that he's here with me instead of there, celebrating, like he should be. The next race could be wildly different, and the race after that might not happen at all.

But he's *here,* I remind myself. With me.

Elyse is wrong. Beck, as it turns out, is being the perfect boyfriend.

"Hey," I slip up next to him just as he gets his beer and his credit card back. "Tabbing out early?"

"It's almost one," he points out, signing the slip of paper and tossing the pen down. "And I have this feeling you're going to want more than an hour of sleep before you get to Belmont tomorrow."

Right. Time. It hasn't really occurred to me. Nor has Belmont.

"Chances are they won't be training tomorrow morning," I say, pointing to the snow coming down in thick, white puffballs. "If the city can't keep up with it, Belmont's maintenance crew has no hope."

"You're overestimating New York's snow cleaning capabilities," Beck says, sending me a sideways smile as I stare at him impatiently, because he's really going to make me say this, isn't he? He pauses, because Elyse is also wrong about something else: Beck isn't actually an idiot. Sure, he can act in ways no one else would, and he's made me want to scream on numerous occasions for all sorts of reasons from purple hair pranks to abandonment in far off states, but he's not an idiot.

He takes one look at me and puts his beer down.

"Look, Juls," he says, turning toward me. "I didn't mean for that . . ." He waves in the direction of Elyse.

"No, I know that," I say, tilting my head at him as he shifts on his feet. "It was awkward, and then Elyse explained it to me, which made me feel both stupid and *more* awkward."

He sighs. "It's okay," he says, recovering. "I'll have to kill her later, but it's okay."

I smack his shoulder and a fleeting smile flickers across his lips.

"Don't kill Elyse," I tell him. "Despite the mortifying embarrassment, two good things happened."

"What good could have come from any of this?" Beck asks, rotating his beer on the bar in what I'm coming to understand is a nervous tic.

"For one thing, Bri is too far gone to remember any of our conversation," I say. "So there were no witnesses besides Elyse, and despite having just met her I actually really like Elyse."

"Figured," he says. "Horse girls somehow manage to gravitate to each other in a crowded room. It's amazing to stand back and watch."

"Second thing," I continue, poking him to get his attention, "is she did you a favor."

He stops rotating the beer. "Explain to me how that's possible?"

"You said something cryptic and then ran off," I point out. "How am I supposed to know what you really meant if not for your apparent translator to decipher for me?"

"Elyse is definitely not my—"

"In any case," I talk over him, "she did you a favor, because now that I know what it is you've been planning all this while, you can now ask me appropriately without needlessly worrying I'm going to do whatever negative thing you think I'm going to do."

"I don't know, Juls," he says, shrugging a shoulder. "We don't have the best track record. You might forgive me a little bit for the delivery."

"No," I stand firm, smiling up at him. "Try again."

"I just figured you'd want to head home, what with the track and . . ."

"You are really bad at this," I groan, letting my head fall back.

"Maybe I'm a little gun shy," he starts, and I shake my head, crowding closer to him.

"Stop talking," I insist, kissing him firmly. Right there at the bar. Because sometimes things really do need to be shown instead of said, and haven't I been the perfect poster child for pushing actions instead of words? Sure, I've been Miss Chatty lately, talking about all the things I haven't been able to say, but this time it seems words aren't good enough. This time, they need a little help.

He kisses me back, one hand on my waist and fingers digging into my sweater. Fuzzy eagerness blooms softly in my stomach, followed by a rush of warm want. His fingers find bare skin, and I gasp against his mouth just as he pulls away.

Suddenly I'm in a bar again, but it doesn't matter because no one notices this seismic shift I'm standing on. No one cares. It's just me and Beck, his eyes shining in the dim light and my thready breaths coming in quick sips as I make up my mind.

Right here.

"So what do you want to do, July?" he asks me, fingers burning paths across my skin. I lean into him. Look up.

And I say it.

"I want to get out of here."

Chapter Six

It's always startling when you're not sure where you are in the hazy moment between sleeping and waking. Somehow, no matter how coherent you were when you decided this is where you will sleep, the waking is always jarring. Like this morning, when I expect my dark bedroom in Garden City and am met instead with Manhattan streetlights shining cold and silvery through the giant window in Beck's room.

Beck's room.

I've never been in any of his rooms before. Not the one in the family brownstone in the city, not the one in the now-sold estate in Saratoga, and certainly not this one. This temporary set up that smells of boy and dorm and old house. I don't know how I ever managed that, knowing him as long as I have, but then Beck was mostly such a mystery. Such a summer project, flitting in and out of my life like a firefly. Being invited to rooms would have been absurd.

Besides, he's never been to mine.

But this boxy little room is not entirely what I expected of him. For one thing, it's mostly bare. The walls are clean of stuff aside from dust, markings of previous posters hung by former tenants. The only pieces of furniture consist of the bed, a dresser, and a desk doubling as a night stand. There's a laptop sitting closed on the desk, a lamp, various pens scattered across the surface. The dresser is a mess of paper on top—unruly stacks of textbooks and notepads. A hamper overflows from an open closet onto the scuffed wood floor.

So this is what boy rooms are like. It's basically the opposite of me and my overstuffed sanctuary at home, where every bit of wall is a canvas for something and every inch of space is to be used. The hamper, however, I identify with. Somehow, my room is where I let everything go. I let it rest there, undisturbed, so I can sit and not have to think about anything else.

Maybe this is the same thing for Beck. Clear out a space of everything and sit in it, so you don't have to think about the reminders of life outside the room.

"You're thinking about something." His voice rumbles sleepily behind me, and I tense, caught. Then I melt a little as the sheets rustle and he drops an arm around my waist, presses his naked warmth against my bare back and a kiss against the nape of my neck.

"How do you know?" I ask, burrowing under the covers next to him and feeling his smile against my skin. It may be warm in the room, but the window is frosty with new snow. I can imagine the chill.

"You're awake, for one thing," he says, and I roll over, grabbing my pillow and smacking him with it. He snags it out of my hands, and shoves it under his head.

"Rookie mistake, Juls," he says, settling back down on his now luxurious amount of pillows. "Now what are you going to do? Not so powerful without a pillow are you?"

74

I flop down next to him, using his shoulder to prop up my head, all of my tangled hair cascading down his arm.

"Easy," I sniff. "I wouldn't test my ability to improvise. I really wouldn't."

"I'll keep it in mind," Beck says, chest rumbling by my ear. "Although this is fine by me, if you were wondering."

I peer up at him, grinning. "I wasn't."

"Sure," he says, and turns over, kissing me.

Which is when I remember we're not wearing clothes and the bed suddenly feels very warm. My skin flushes as I'm drawn back to last night, to the laughing and fumbling under the covers, to the not knowing what I'm doing and the certainty that now I kind of do. And with Beck, whose fingers slide to the back of my neck, drawing me down toward—

"The track," I announce suddenly, pushing away. Beck looks at me quizzically, hair askew. My fingers might have pushed it into its current state of chaos.

Then he groans, flopping onto his back.

"What time is it?" I ask, twisting to look for my phone.

"Probably past time," he says as I find my phone on the floor by the bed, next to my jeans and my sweater, which puddle forgotten on the hardwood. I swipe at it and the time glows up at me.

5:13am.

And there, underneath the time, is my sister's enraged text: *WHERE. ARE. YOU.*

"Well, that's not great," I groan, grabbing my clothes off the floor and blushing at the torn condom wrapper that falls to the ground.

"What isn't great?" Beck asks, sounding concerned as I pull on my shirt and then yank the sweater over my head, get it backward, and tear it off again.

"Work," I say, standing up and pulling on my jeans. Beck looks at me from the bed like I'm a crazy person speaking words he doesn't understand. "I'm late."

"Work?" he echoes.

"Work," I confirm. "You know, it's this thing we do in the mornings?"

"It's snowing," he says. "Didn't we confirm it's snowing?"

I stop mid-attempt to put my sweater back on, looking at him lying there tantalizingly on the chaotic bedsheets. No. Must focus.

"And yet the world still somehow found a way to make us all get up and exercise Thoroughbreds," I sigh.

"I think the world owes us one," Beck says, dragging himself out of bed and fishing his discarded jeans off the floor. I quickly look away, because I'm still somehow able to be embarrassed, so easily flustered by something I shouldn't be. I *know* Beck now, but it still feels absurd. Like a fantasy I'm living instead of real life. It's sinking in, slowly. Little by little, like easing into a hot tub one inch at a time until the temperature feels right on your skin.

That's Beck and me. We're easing our way in.

I get my sweater on right this time, pausing as I pull my hair out of the collar when a flurry of knocks peppers the door.

"July?" Bri's baleful voice floats through the wood. "I think I'm going to be sick."

"Oh, no," I leap off the bed, ripping open the door to find Bri standing there with a halo of bedhead hair. It didn't take much convincing to get her to spend the night on Beck's sofa, tucked under a blanket Devon fished out of his closet and a garbage can positioned strategically by her head. I figured she would sleep well into morning, but of course Bri would surprise me. She's a hardwired overachiever, after all.

"My phone is dead," she announces, blinking blearily and holding up the little black device, then looking down at it like it's personally disappointed her. Before I can say anything she sighs and shoves the phone into her pocket, shaking her hair out of her face and losing her balance, stumbling into the doorjamb.

"How is it even possible she's awake?" Beck asks, mostly to himself as I shake my head.

"No idea," I say as she falls into me. I stumble under her weight and glance back at him. "And there's literally no time to take her home. I need to be at the track in the vicinity of immediately."

"Okay," Beck says, pulling a sweater on over a T-shirt that says *Go Hedgehogs!* in blocky type before he takes my place under Bri's arm. "What do you think, Bri? Want to go to the track?"

"The where?" she asks, looking up at him like he's speaking gibberish.

"More importantly," he says, steering her out of his room. "Can you not throw up in my car while we drive there?"

"Does your window roll down?" she asks plaintively, and he throws a look at me.

"You drive a hard bargain, Bri," he says, patting her head as I mouth *thank you* at him on our way out the door.

~

The track is clear of snow. Of course it is. Horses pepper the long, dark stretch of dirt even as the snow starts coming down again, their bodies sliding through the flurry. I watch for Dad's saddlecloths as we drive by, Bri groaning from the Mustang's backseat and the heater blasting warm air in my face. Beck taps the steering wheel like none of this is concerning—not my blatant lateness, not Bri demanding I never let her drink that much again, and certainly not the fact that he's the one driving us all the way out here from Manhattan.

I'm sure weirder things have happened, but all it takes is Martina giving me her glare from the shedrow as Beck parks the car next to his brother's Bentley to know my absence has been missed.

"Is there coffee?" Bri asks hopefully, still unmoving from her prone position in the backseat.

"There'd better be," I sigh as Beck opens his door, letting in a blast of frigid air.

"Up and at 'em, girls," he announces, eliciting a sharp intake of breath from Bri as she sits up abruptly and blinks at her surroundings. Beck helps her out of the car, then holds onto her arm as she doubles over to dry heave. Martina's glare turns into the evil eye from her position inside the barn.

"This is embarrassing," she informs me as I slip out of the snow and into the covered shedrow, where it might be a few degrees warmer.

She looks at her watch, and I wince. I know the time. The time is not good. "Are you going to tell Dad?"

"The question is who *isn't* going to tell your Dad," a voice I'm not expecting chimes in. Leo stands in the doorway to the office, waving at me. My mouth falls open.

"Whoa, wait," I say, jumping after Martina as she turns and heads into the office, Leo stepping aside for her. "What is he doing here?"

"You didn't show up this morning," she says, "so I called him."

"He's not supposed to be on the track," I remind her, and Martina shrugs.

"That's not my problem," she says. "You weren't here and I need all hands on deck when half my workforce is literally in another state. We're short-staffed, July. You know that."

"And I'm here now," I say as Beck leads Bri to the coffee machine, readying her coffee as though he's had her preferences memorized for years and putting the steaming mug in her hands. Martina looks at them like she's watching a play in a foreign language she doesn't understand.

"And you've brought the visibly hung over and the eternally talkative," Martina says over Bri's meek protest and Beck's cavalier shrug. "Are you trying to make my life harder?"

"Yes," I sigh. "That's exactly it, Martina. I live to make your life harder."

"Maybe we could just get to work instead of arguing?" Leo asks, which feels wrong because he is not supposed to be the logical voice in the room. I should be pulling my spare duffel out of its dusty corner in the office and getting ready with the next set, because Martina is right: we are short-staffed. And gaining extra hands in the middle of winter? Not the easiest thing to do.

"I agree," Matt Delaney says from the doorway, appearing in totally out of character jeans and a horse slobber-streaked down coat. I'm not sure I've ever seen Matt outside of tailored suits, and if I didn't know better I'd think he's been doing actual work. In the barn. I stare at him in utter confusion, questions warring up in me as he nods toward the shedrow. "Because Star's van is here."

The whole world slows down. Then it stops entirely.

Star is supposed to be upstate in a comfy stall, cooling his heels and decompressing from track life after his less-than-stellar Breeders' Cup performance. He most certainly is not supposed to be on a track-bound van, because that would mean he's set to go back into training . . . a whole month early.

"Say that again?" I manage, looking between Martina and Matt. My sister lets out a frustrated breath and Matt tilts his head at me, considering me in bewildered silence. I swing a glance at Beck, who is utterly stone-faced, and it occurs to me that outside of Bri, I might be the only one who doesn't know what's going on here.

"Star," Matt repeats himself for my benefit, and then focuses on Martina expectantly. "His stall is ready, right?"

"Finished it myself," Martina says with a pointed look at me on her way back into the shedrow. Matt turns to follow her as I jump to keep up.

"What is happening?" I ask, rushing to defend myself on our way down the shedrow. "I didn't even know Star was showing up."

"Neither did I until this morning," Martina says, batting away my excuse. Because that's what it is—an excuse. And not even a good one. I should have been here, but I can't seem to choke out the apology to smooth everything over. Martina knows that college is going to take up time, but I can just see her face now if that's what I say. College didn't keep me in Manhattan until well into workouts. That was Beck, his warm bed luring me into some semblance of a normal life.

As I watch my sister turn her back on me to sign the paperwork the driver hands her, I'm left with the van and Matt, who stands by my side with his hands shoved in his pockets and his ears pink from the cold.

"Whose idea was this?" I ask him, not ready yet to concede defeat. He peers at me over the puffy collar of his coat.

"Would you believe it was my idiot brother's?" he asks, and then chuckles at my shocked silence. I'm tongue-tied as I try to figure out the why, not even hearing the clank of the ramp when it hits the slushy gravel and the scrap and clomp of Star's hooves. Matt shrugs, his eyes full of Star as Martina leads him down the ramp. "Beck convinced Rob to put Star back in training up at the farm. Kid's full of surprises."

"And bad timing," Martina says, brushing at the fat snowflakes that break apart on her cheeks. They cling to Star's dark mane, his near-black body peppered with white on his way toward the shedrow, where Beck stands with a shoulder resting against the open doorway, bare hands cupped around his steaming coffee mug. I glower at him, and he smiles, giving me a little wave.

"You have got to be kidding," I growl, pulling him into the empty feed room off the middle of the shedrow. He holds his mug up, coffee lapping over the edge and trickling across his fingers.

"Hey," he protests as I slam the door behind us, "this is coffee. I'm surprised you'd disrespect the beverage like this, Juls."

"What are you doing?" I ask, ignoring the coffee while also painfully aware that I haven't had any yet. I'm not in any condition to ride a horse, much less discuss why Beck has put Star into training on the farm we sent him to last year to rest and recuperate.

"Dad might be nursing a small going-out-in-glory fantasy," Beck says, flicking the coffee off his fingers and putting the mug on a nearby shelf. "I happened to mention the Dubai World Cup after the Breeders' Cup . . ."

I swear a ringing starts in my ears.

"The what?"

"... and he's been talking about it ever since," Beck finishes, raising his hands. "So I called your Dad while you were in Florida. Asked him how likely it was to send Star to Dubai."

"Do you even have money to send him there?" I ask, feeling like I'm going mad.

Beck grins. "That's the thing. All expenses paid. Dubai picks up the check."

"And to keep a horse in training since, when? December? Who's paying for that?"

Beck's grin flickers, begins to turn into a wince.

"Don't say it," I start, just as he admits, "Lighter's earnings."

"Damn it, Beck," I groan, because in no way is it okay to keep the one remainder of Blackbridge afloat with Lighter's earnings. As much as I liked the idea of keeping Star around Barn 27 a while longer, it was selfish—another horse I've gotten used to keeping close. He should have been auctioned off with Galaxy, and Blackbridge should have died a dignified death at the Breeders' Cup.

"It's a loan," Beck insists.

"I don't care!" I insist right back. "What is he hoping to accomplish? Star can't win that race, Beck. We both know it."

"Maybe," Beck agrees, because at least he hasn't gone off the deep end, too. "But after we get a published work or two into him here and start him in a decent prep, your Dad thinks it's not out of reason to think he could do second or third. That would be two million dollars, a million?"

"So it's a money grab," I confirm, and he raises his hands in frustration.

"Maybe it is," he admits, "but isn't that racing?"

"Not in simple, blunt terms," I say, holding fast to my position.

Saying people are only in racing for the cash when so many lose their hearts and their sanity to it is disrespectful to the people who live in it every day. Like me.

Like Beck, even.

"Lighter is more than a cash grab," I point out as he rocks onto his heels. "And so is Star."

Silence descends on the room, doubt nipping at me. Star is the last Blackbridge horse. More importantly, he's not mine; I don't get to call the shots. But here I am, arguing over him anyway when Delaney can send him wherever he wants and Beck can bankroll it for as long as he can.

"What am I going to do, Juls?" Beck asks me softly, breaking the stalemate. "Tell my dad no when there's no good reason not to run?"

And this is where I'm going to lose, because how could I have possibly won this fight? This is my problem—always picking the wrong battles. I nod shakily.

"You're right," I admit, my tongue sticky in my mouth. "I know you're right. Star is your dad's horse, and Lighter is yours. You can do what you want with them and your money, but I'm working with the horses. I'm not doing my job if I'm not standing up for them."

Beck runs his hands through his hair, obviously flustered with where this is going. Especially since I just inadvertently suggested no one else is thinking of the horse. But then, they aren't, are they? It's just that they're depending on us to do that for them. Beck and his father, both.

Like always.

Finally, Beck shakes his head.

"It might just be a pipe dream, Juls," he says. "If Star's prep race is a disaster, no one is pointing him to Dubai. You know that as well as I do."

I nod, biting my lip as he eases up to me. I don't move when he slips a hand into my messy hair, cupping the back of my head and drawing me up against him.

"And Lighter really is not a cash grab," he says as I burrow into him, thankful that he's not pushing me and my opinions away. "I enjoy the mayhem he rains down on you guys far too much to sell him, even if he weren't on the Derby trail."

I snort a laugh against his chest.

"You two are a perfect match," I say, lifting my chin. "Have I ever told you that?"

"Not in as many words," Beck says, "but I could have guessed you thought as much."

I let out a breath, the tension in the room unwinding right along with it. Beck's fingers tangle in my hair as I look up at him, surprised to find seriousness still cluttering his face and crinkling around his bright green eyes.

"I know you're just looking out for Star," he says, surprising me again with the seriousness in his voice. "But give everyone else some credit. Even if my dad were mad with power, he listens to Rob. And I'm holding a weird number of purse strings, so if I don't think Star is ready to fly across the world and defend the family honor, he's not going. You're not the only one with sense, Juls. Trust us a little bit, okay?"

Trust us. God, I want to trust them. It would be so much easier if I could just let go a little, admit I have no control over what happens. I can stamp my feet and argue until my throat is raw, but where does it get me in the long run? This has always been the uncomfortable reality. He's the owner's son and I'm the trainer's daughter. That's what it always goes back to, doesn't it?

But then, I realize what Beck is saying. It's not trust *us*.

It's trust *me*.

"Okay," I say stiltedly, because the illusion of control is all I've ever had, and giving some of it up? It's not for beginners, and I feel unsteady with it. Still, I manage a shaky smile. "I can give you that."

He kisses me, rests his forehead against mine after he pulls away.

"Maybe Star will surprise you," he says. "And then who will have been the right one again in this scenario?"

"Oh, not this again," I say, breaking away from him. "The one time you were right was Lighter. There was no other time."

"There were other times," he defends as I make my way to the door.

"Name one," I challenge, hand on the doorknob when he catches up to me.

"That you love me," he reminds me, voice husky in my ear as he wraps his arms around my waist. "I called that one, remember?"

My heart does a little stutter, right before it starts to pump harder in my chest.

"Fine," I say, twisting in his hold just as he presses me into the door, my back meeting the wood. "You may have been right twice. I'll allow that."

"See, generosity is one of those things I like about you, July," he says, just before he kisses me, settling his arms against the door on either side of my head as he takes his time, moving from my mouth to my neck. My breath hitches when he gathers me up from the door, just as it opens and bangs into my shoulder blades, shoving me unceremoniously into Beck. We stumble, stepping on each other's feet, as Martina stands in the doorway with her fingers rubbing circles against her forehead.

"You know what?" she asks, raising her hand to stop my attempt to explain. "I don't want to know what you two are doing in here." She points at me. "You have a horse to ride, and you . . ." she transfers her glare to Beck, momentarily lost for words. "Are you capable of being helpful or are you just planning on popping up in the least expected of places?"

Beck smiles at her, wide and bright. "You know, Martina, I feel like you've never appreciated my—"

She rolls her eyes and points to the shedrow. "Get out of my feed room."

"Going," Beck says promptly, slipping past her. "Hey, maybe I can even . . . what did you call it again?"

"Check with your brother," Martina orders as Beck salutes her, disappearing around the corner as though he actually plans to do work, which I honestly seriously doubt. I stare after him, wondering what work and Beck must look like together, until my glowering sister pokes my arm.

"July," she says, making me jump.

"I'm on it," I say, and she shakes her head tiredly.

"Obviously not," she says, her welling exhaustion lapping at me. For the first time since I got to the track this morning, I really look at my sister. The messy ponytail is uncharacteristic of her, dark strands of hair falling haphazardly against her cheeks. I'm one hundred percent sure she hasn't taken a shower yet, which would be normal for most people on the track, but not Martina. She's not even wearing eyeliner.

What is going on here?

"Hey," I say, faltering underneath her steady gaze. "I'm sorry I wasn't here this morning. It's obvious you need the help. I was just—"

Martina groans. "Living your life," she finishes for me, waving me out of the feed room. "You're busy. I get it. Just call me the next time you can't make it, okay? Then I won't have to harbor increasingly elaborate revenge fantasies."

"I really meant to come," I start, knowing this isn't the end of the conversation, even if Martina looks too busy to have it. She rummages through the med shelf, making a face when she can't find what she needs. "Martina," I say to get her attention. "I was just late, okay? It won't happen—"

"I don't want your apologies, July," she interrupts. "I want you on a horse."

"I can do that," I say, nodding eagerly. "Who's the lucky ride?"

Martina snorts. "Ask our foreman," she says. "Leo's been grinning at the whiteboard all morning."

"You didn't," I groan. Giving Leo the power to control my mornings isn't an elaborate revenge fantasy. It's straight up mean. Martina knows that better than anyone, but then what did I expect? I didn't show this morning, so I didn't get to call the shots. Now I have to own it.

Then Martina smiles, finally satisfied. "Oh, I did."

Chapter Seven

"**K**eep those shoulders back, July!"

Sophie's voice rings up to the arena's rafters. I do as she commands, drawing my shoulder blades closer together and feeling my chest open. *Everything is connected,* I think. Move the heel an inch, the spine shifts with it. Move the shoulders, and suddenly Kali feels loftier underneath me, more willing to drive forward as we trot down the long wall.

If only I rode like this every day—mindful of all the little things.

I'm lost in thought as we circle around in the arena at Jericho on Friday morning, the weak February light streaming through the windows and casting pale rays on the dirt. It's been an entire week of riding—whatever Leo puts me on at the track, Dad's classic nonchalant nod approving whatever the whiteboard proclaims. My back aches, and my thighs scream, but I can also feel myself getting stronger. Wire-tight and ready for anything. Soon I could ride half the Jericho barn after morning workouts and feel ready for more.

Maybe this crazy schedule is actually working.

"Halt her," Sophie calls. "Keep your leg on. I want her focused on you, not the end of work."

I nod, bringing Kali down the second long wall, her stride lengthening until I call for the halt. Sinking weight, closed fists, calves on her sides . . . just enough pressure to round her into my hand and stop with all four hooves square.

It's a miracle.

Sophie nods just once and then turns to Emma. I let out a breath and give Kali long reins and pats, leaning over her neck to whisper *good girl* into her mane. My filly flicks her ears back and ambles forward, following my lead until I'm back with the group and she can huddle with her new friends.

Although their riders aren't quite friends of mine yet. Luna and Ashley chat about upcoming spring break plans. Jessica and Avery smile shrewdly at each other when Emma needs yet another reminder about diagonals. Olivia rolls her eyes and shoots me a look like *can you believe we're here right now?*

I smile at her and shrug. As much as I don't want to be in any introductory classes, I'm coming around to the need of them. As much as my ego bruises with each reminder that I've got bad habits to fix, Kali does better with each lesson as I roll my shoulders back and remember to breathe.

After the class, I lead Kali toward her stall, catching sight of Madeline and Cricket through the bars separating the mares.

"So are you going to sign up?" she calls over to me as she swipes at Cricket's burnished coat. I pull Kali's saddle off her back and pause, the heavy leather pressing into my breastbone.

"Sign up for what?"

"You don't know?" she asks, turning to look at me between the bars. She shakes her head, chuckling. "I swear you have tunnel vision *and* selective hearing."

"Hey," I say, threading Kali's bridle over my shoulder and stumbling over my feet when my filly shoves her head into my thigh, rubbing at her eye with the closest available surface—my brand new breeches. "In my world we call that focus-driven."

Madeline snorts and shakes her head, slipping out of Cricket's stall and grabbing my hand before I can make it to the tack room, dragging me to the bulletin board posted on the wall nearby and pointing at a giant flyer of a horse doing a half-pass—something I am dead sure would cause Kali to fall on her face if I tried. Above the rider's jaunty top hat are the words *Jericho Horse Show: April 9th*.

Wood Memorial Day, I think automatically, and then shake the thought away. We won't have a horse running in the Wood this year since—besides the fact that we almost never have a horse running in the Wood—Lighter will be aiming toward the Florida Derby instead.

"You're entering," Madeline says, her voice coming back to me through the haze of racing and horse show noise.

"Wait, what?" I stammer, looking at her like she's grown a horn on her forehead. What sort of madness is she suffering? I can't put Kali in a horse show now, not after she's only been off-track since September.

"I know what you're going to say," Madeline says, rifling through the envelope that's tacked to the board, pulling out two registration forms. "Kali isn't ready. She's an off-track Thoroughbred who barely knows about bend. I've heard all of your stories of woe, July. If you think they're swaying me, you are absolutely wrong."

"Clearly," I say, taking the form she shoves toward me.

"They have those Thoroughbred Makeovers now," Madeline says. "People turn around racehorses all the time, and quickly. Kali is improving—I've seen it, both at Woodfield and here. Whether or not you choose to believe it is your issue."

"She's right." I startle, because Sophie stands directly behind us, hands tucked in her coat and tall boots gleaming in the barn lights. Her posture is impeccable, as though she's always prepared to sit a horse, even when one isn't immediately available. Sophie looks from the poster to us, considering us with quiet appraisal—the way one would look at a horse during a vet check.

"I don't know," I start, preparing myself for all the reasons I can't enter Kali. Because she doesn't know how to transition from a trot to a canter without bucking, because her grasp of self-head carriage is more or less keeping her ears somewhere near my face, because even though she knows the basics she knows little else.

All fine reasons not to do this.

"There are plenty of open classes at introductory level," Sophie says, narrowing her eyes at me. "As easy as it would be to tell you to do a walk-trot test and get your feet wet, I'd like to see some canter work thrown in. Kali can handle it."

Can she?

Those are the first words that want to pop out of my mouth, but Sophie isn't the kind of person I feel comfortable pushing. This isn't the racetrack. Jericho operates under a different set of rules.

"Well," I say slowly, looking between Sophie and Madeline, who wear twin expectant expressions, only Madeline is bouncing on her toes.

"Please, July," Madeline pleads. "Please, please, please."

I haven't been in a horse show since riding Gideon for Wood-field, when he was younger and happier about getting trailered to show grounds. Even then, I knew what I had under me: a star schoolmaster who'd done it all before. Gideon knew the tests better than I did. Kali . . . not so much.

Standing there with the application in my hands, I can't help but think of the impending potential disaster. I also can't help but think this is exactly what I need—for Kali and for myself. Focusing on something that doesn't feel like a brush up might make Jericho feel *real*.

"Oh, for god's sake, Juls," Ava says as she leads Holy down the aisle, the gelding's gray coat so spot-free it must have taken her hours to clean given how she'd whispered his full name to me last week after he'd dumped her in the dirt: Holy *Terror*. "Enter and be done with it," she continues as she passes us. "We all do the Jericho show, so peer pressure."

"Peer pressure!" Madeline says excitedly, waving her form in front of her. "You have to do it now."

Sophie's lips quirk, and I let out a breath. I guess there's plenty of time to practice. Spring break is on the horizon, after all. And I'm nothing if not a riding machine these days.

"Well, who am I to be the weird one who won't participate?" I ask, which sets Madeline dancing in a small circle. Sophie nods her head, as stoic as ever.

"Glad to hear it, July," she says, and turns on her heel, following Ava and Holy down to the indoor as Madeline grabs my hand.

"Now," she says, pushing the tack room door open. "Let's find you a pen."

Chapter Eight

The shedrow in the morning is a line of yellow lights in the darkness. The softly falling snow looks like flakes of gold glinting in the air. I stand just inside the shedrow opening, Maggie's reins in one hand and my coffee mug in the other, greedily swallowing down the last lukewarm sip.

There is never enough coffee these days.

"There's a fresh pot in the office," Mom announces, sidling up to me. She looks ready to go on an expedition to the North Pole; a down coat engulfs her tiny frame and the rest of her is covered or wrapped in wool and fleece. No doubt there's thermal underwear underneath the many layers. If she's anything like me, she's wearing tights, too. It's never enough to feel warm. I wonder what she thought when she got home to our frosty hellscape after piloting Feather and Lighter in their races at Gulfstream last week. Maybe *what was I thinking?*

My breath mists in the air as I put the empty coffee mug down by the door opening.

"Thanks, I'll get a warm up when I get back," I say, catching sight of Star and Jorge making their way toward me from the far end of the row. Star looks inky in the light, and is swallowed up by the early morning darkness as he slips out of the shedrow. I gather up Maggie's reins and follow, my far splashier mare easy to see in the dark.

Mom follows me into the snow, sipping at her coffee. Everything is quiet, even when she starts, "I was thinking . . ."

I glance over at her, halfway to mounting up, and pause. My heels settle back in the snow.

"Since you weren't able to go to Florida," she says, a look of careful reflection on her face, "how about dinner at my place tonight?"

Mother-daughter night. Right. How had I forgotten? That was supposed to be our big icebreaker event in Florida, while we reveled over Feather and Lighter. Instead we've been encased in ice, it seems. Literally. I've been riding horses for a week straight, worrying over Spanish homework and Western Civ readings the rest of the time, so locked in my schedule that there's been no time.

Mom's face is open and earnest, waiting for me to make a decision. After all, we did agree that she would be in the passenger seat on this crazy family-togetherness ride. The least I can do is carve out some precious time. I do have to eat, after all.

"I can do dinner," I say, putting my foot back in the stirrup and swinging into Maggie's Western saddle. Mom smiles, her lips relaxing in relief that I've said yes. "Did you ask Martina?"

Then the worry mark appears between her eyes. "I did," she says. I raise an eyebrow.

"She says she'll try for seven o'clock," Mom says with a shrug. I smile. So like Martina to push control of the situation into her court.

"Then seven it is," I say, nudging Maggie over to Star, who stands totally still in the freshly trodden snow. The colt pricks his ears at the training track, chewing on the bit eagerly. I'm just as eager to get him to work, delve into something that isn't thinking about dinner with Mom and Martina. I don't want to start contemplating how to defuse landmines that haven't even been set yet, not with a fresh colt to ferry to the track.

"Nice to be back?" I ask Jorge, who grins at me ear to ear. His dark skin is darker still from Florida and Louisiana—all the warm places with their balmy winter racing meets. I envy his tan.

"You know it," he says, rubbing his hand through the colt's mane as I attach a line to Star's bridle. "Didn't know if I'd ever have another chance on this guy."

"And here you are," I muse, giving Maggie the go ahead. She sets off with Star ambling at her side. "For the Dubai World Cup no less."

He turns big, brown eyes toward me. "You're telling me," he says, sitting back in the saddle and letting out a big breath at the sky. "Almost overwhelming. Between you and me, Juls, I never thought I'd make it over there. Definitely not on this guy."

I don't say anything, because I think it's what everyone is thinking when it comes to Star. Not after a fourth-place finish in the Classic, and not when he was training so poorly we skipped the Jockey Club Gold Cup. Star is a good, solid racehorse. I don't want to make him out as worthless, because he isn't. He can hold his own.

He just maybe might not be one of the best.

"What's the plan?" I ask as we approach the gap in the training track.

"Five furlongs," Jorge says. "Gotta be razor sharp for the Razorback, girlie."

I nod. Star's prep for Dubai is coming up fast: the Razorback Handicap, Dad decided, in Arkansas. If he does well today, we'll breeze him again before we ship him south, to Oaklawn. If he does well there, it's off to sunny Florida to acclimate to warmer weather before Dubai. So much depends on this one breeze. It still feels like I've stepped into a fantasyland, with Star standing next to me in a frozen waste with a future of sand dunes and palm trees right around the corner. Everything is happening quickly, and Star stands next to me under his exercise rug without shivering a muscle, unbothered by time speeding around him.

I envy that a little.

After standing for a moment, Star watching the workouts pick up as more and more horses enter the gap, I tighten my hold on the lead line.

"Ready?" I ask Jorge, who nods.

"*Vamonos,*" he says under his breath, pushing his balaclava into place over his mouth and yanking his goggles over his eyes. It's too cold to go without them at a breeze—not if you don't want your eyes to tear up in about two seconds of looking straight into a headwind. It's not like you can just close your eyes when you're galloping a horse on a busy track.

Or *ever.*

I push Maggie into a trot, rising and falling to her rhythm as Jorge stands in his stirrups next to me. Star is comically larger than Maggie, so Jorge towers above me, looking like a giant even though he's so much smaller on the ground.

Galloping toward the turn, I let go, the lead line slipping free and Star kicking away from Maggie as we peel off toward the outside rail and they go shooting toward the inside, picking up speed until they hit their mark and it's go time.

Jorge is a blur in a dark morning. Star slips through the air faster and faster as Jorge becomes an afterthought to the colt's movement.

Maggie snorts underneath me, ambling down the outside rail to the backstretch, where we'll catch them once they're through. I keep an eye on them, trying not to lose them in the dark.

The training track isn't very big, but it's big enough to lose them anyway. I have them one second, and they're gone the next—lost in a flurry of horses and inky darkness. It's only when they flash by the finish line that they come plunging back into reality, Jorge slowly rising in the stirrups and Star listening as they curl into the turn, easing back bit by bit until they're in the backstretch and Maggie leaps to catch them. I reach out for Star's bridle, snagging it on the second try. Star arches his neck, gives us a wild white-ringed stare, and allows himself to be pulled down to a jigging jog, and then, finally, a rambunctious walk. My mare blows out a breath happily, her job here done.

"How was it?" I ask, even though I already know.

"*Chingon!*" Jorge laughs, slapping the colt's dry neck. "Freaking *chingon!* I don't know what they were feeding him up at the farm, but this is going to be Star's year, Juls. I can feel it."

Star snorts, a huge plume of breath billowing between him and Maggie, who walks him off the track with a casual lick of her lips, totally not as impressed as Jorge.

But me? A little warmth slithers around my heart, constricting at Jorge's infectious smile, and maybe—*maybe*—this Dubai thing isn't the craziest idea we've come up with yet.

~~~

At seven o'clock on the dot, I stand at Mom's front door, doing a little dance to keep warm as Martina rings the doorbell. Our breath mists in the air, and we're both uncharacteristically silent. Could be it's cold and we're focused on shivering. Could be neither of us know what to do.

No matter what? This is definitely a scenario neither one of us ever thought would happen six months ago. I think our thoughts are in the same place, somewhere between *how did this happen* and *what do we do now?*

The door swings inward, and Mom stands there in all her pint-sized glory.

"You don't need to ring the bell!" she admonishes us, laughing. "It's too cold outside to stand around waiting for me. Come in, girls."

I follow Martina inside the warmth of the house, shedding my coat and pulling off my snow boots at the door as Mom closes it with a whoosh of winter air. She rushes back into the kitchen, where smells of her cooking take me back to less complicated times. Onions and homemade mole waft over me as I move deeper into the house, padding over the hardwood in my socks.

The house is mostly put together. A few straggler boxes sit in the corner of the family room, but the kitchen is in working order. Although, it's the framed photos on the table in the hallway that grab my attention. Images of me and Martina, Mom and the horses, Mom and Dad, as if they had never broken up in the first place, litter the surface in organized chaos. I pick up one I recognize from the photo albums—Mom and Dad flanking Stuart, the barn's pony, Martina dwarfed by his saddle. She must have framed it recently, which makes me wonder about the rest. Did she always have photos of us in her house in California?

Or did they just show up, like she needs convincing that she belongs?

I put the photo down, telling myself to stop questioning her motives. Mom can do what she wants with her photos. She can do what she *wants*. We're all adults here.

Or so I like to tell myself.

"Juls?" Mom calls from the kitchen. "Want to set the table?"

At least one thing hasn't changed. I remember unsteadily learning place settings, Mom pointing out where the utensils went on each side of the plate, flipping the knives when I got it wrong. It was such a little, stupid thing, but all of a sudden it's all I can think about; her following me around the table, straightening as I went.

"Sure," I say, experimentally opening a drawer and finding kitchen knickknacks as Martina opens a bottle of wine and pours herself a healthy glass. Mom points to the drawer I need and takes a glass of wine wordlessly handed to her by Martina. I'm busy sorting out silverware when a glass appears in front of me as well.

I raise an eyebrow at my sister, who raises her glass at me in silent acknowledgement that this might be what we all need to make sure mother-daughter night goes smoothly.

"How's school, Juls?" Mom asks, pulling the casserole dish out of the oven. Another, stronger, wave of mole hits me and my mouth starts to water. "I see you both so often now, but . . ." She looks up at me and smiles bashfully. I get it, because horses always take up all the time you thought you had, and Mom is not exactly the best at usage of time. "I'm out of the loop, I guess."

Clutching a handful of silverware, I slip around her to the cabinets, hunting for the plates and trying not to laugh at the thought of Mom being here and still out of the loop. Always on different wavelengths—that's Mom and me.

"Good," I say, finding drinking glasses that look suspiciously like the ones we used to have before she left and setting three of them on the counter before moving on in my hunt. "I mean, it's basic right now. The horse stuff, anyway. Although my dressage instructor might actually succeed in teaching Kali how to bend without falling off the circle entirely, which will be helpful because I've entered her in the Jericho Horse Show in April and I can't have her not know how to turn a circle correctly in front of an audience."

Mom and Martina both look at me like I'm speaking gibberish, because things like bend never enter the lexicon of horse racing. When Martina rode, she was always pointing and shooting at something, not fastidiously thinking about angles and pounds of pressure put on the reins. When Mom rides, it's all about *go*.

"Tell me about the show," Mom says, pointing at the right cabinet. I open it up and find colorful plates, just the sort of thing that would appeal to my mother, which feels like another little kick to my heart. They're just plates—orange and red-glazed, chipped in a couple of places—but they're reminders, too. The life we used to live is in this kitchen, in this house, standing right here with me and Martina like she never left at all.

"Sophie, my instructor, wanted me to try it out," I say, sweeping the plates to the table and focusing on putting everything just so. "Everyone does it, apparently. So I can't be the only person not showing. It's the big end of the semester bash."

"In April," Martina says flatly. "Which is not the end of the semester, I feel the need to point out."

"Before finals," I amend. "Happy?"

She takes a sip of her wine. "Extremely."

"Well, I'd like to go," Mom says, bringing the casserole over to the table and dishing mole-covered shredded chicken and corn tortillas onto plates. "What day is it?"

I wince.

"Wood Memorial day," I say, watching her nod silently and push her thick, dark hair behind her ear. I remember most of my shows never quite working with her schedule. With racing's biggest purses to be found on the weekends, and most of the shows I ever participated in being on those same weekends, it boiled down to going it alone most of the time. Until she left. And after that I hadn't really felt like showing.

Oh, the irony.

"I'll try to make it work," she says, which is at least the honest thing to say. "There's no telling what will happen between now and the Wood, much less what will happen that Saturday."

"You might not even be in New York by then," Martina says unhelpfully. We both stare at her, and Martina takes a deep breath, like she just realized how that sounded. "I mean, there are other races. There's a lot going on that weekend."

"There is," Mom says quietly, sitting down at the table. She takes a stab at the chicken and looks at it in the silence that's descended before she puts her fork down and says, "I want to get something out in the open now; I'm not going to leave New York. So long as you're both here, I'm here. My schedule might not mesh with yours, but I *will* be here. It's what I think we agreed to in Florida, if I remember correctly."

"You do," Martina says, speaking up as her face flushes pink. "I didn't mean . . ."

Mom shakes her head. "It's important to me that you both know how serious this is. I'll still be jet-setting around the country, but I'm not taking my life with me anymore. I want you both to feel at home here. *I* want to feel at home here."

I stare at her, questions bubbling to the surface.

"Do you?" I ask, looking around the house, where she lives. Alone. Without us. We live in Garden City, where she's explicitly told us she won't invade. Because those were our terms.

"It's still new, July," Mom answers. "It will start feeling like home soon, but what makes it feel right to me is having both of you here. I hope you know that."

I nod quietly, and Martina plays with the stem of her wine glass, twisting it between her fingers, lost in thought. It takes a moment before she looks up at us, pushing her dark hair over her shoulder and giving one stiff nod.

Mom takes a sip of her wine, swallowing it down and licking her lips.

"On that note," she continues, "if all goes well with Star your father will be in Dubai for the better part of two weeks to oversee his training. We've debated when to tell you this, but I'm going to go ahead and say it: he wants me to move in with you girls while he's gone."

"What?" Martina asks, laughing in disbelief and maybe, I think, a little defensiveness. "We don't need to be babysat."

Mom sighs, putting her hands in her lap. "I was hoping you'd see it more as an opportunity to be together. Like . . ."

". . . we used to be," Martina finishes for her.

I don't say anything. The food on my plate is tempting, everything luring me back to a life I remember from years ago. It's soft and warm in those memories, maybe because I didn't know any better, or maybe because that's how old memories of your mother are supposed to be. I have two competing sets of vastly different memories: before and after. I don't know how to reconcile the two.

But I do know that I can't let myself be paralyzed by the opportunity to try.

"I'd like that," I say, almost to myself. Martina and Mom both look at me suddenly, like they'd both forgotten I was here in their quiet standoff.

"You can't be serious," Martina says, hands on the edges of the table, like she's prepared to shove away from us, leave in a huff. I'm almost expecting it.

"I am," I say, feeling surer of myself as I keep thinking about it. "She's right. Dad is right. If we're going to try to be a family, even one living in different houses, we should try to start acting like it. We have to meet each other halfway."

"This," Martina says, waving a hand at the house, "was supposed to be meeting halfway."

"It's two weeks, Martina," I say, trying for cajoling and coming off strained. I know how this sounds.

"I agreed to *this,*" Martina says, voice rising as she pushes back from the table, shredding all the delicate peacemaking that brought us here. I want to tell her to sit back down, plead with her to just see how this could work out, but she's already standing. "I didn't agree to more forced together time. I thought that was the condition upon which all of these decisions were made, and here we are, back where we started." She looks at Mom. "I'm not going to roll over and forget where you've been for the last four years. July shouldn't either, but she's more eager to forgive than I am."

She picks up her wine glass and takes a healthy swallow, then slams it down on the table, making me jump. Mom sits through it like a statue, watching as Martina stomps back to the front of the house, shrugs into her coat, and bangs through the front door.

Within a few minutes, her car starts up and slushes away through the snow. Well, there goes my ride.

Mom lets go of the breath she's holding.

"She's wrong," I say.

Mom shakes her head and says, "She's right."

I stop, swallowing down the sudden need to get up, pace around, work out this intense need to mend things I can't fix. Because that's exactly the problem: I can't make a whole family out of our broken pieces.

Mom sighs. "I shouldn't have said anything. I should have told your father it wouldn't work, but you know how your father is."

"Bright and shiny optimism," I nod. "I know it well."

"I'll tell him it's a no-go," Mom says. "You're old enough to look after yourselves, and Martina's right. I have no business living in that house, not after everything."

I sit, swallowing down my mother's admission of guilt. I'm drowning in it, and I have no idea what to say to make it better. The urge to play peacemaker is itchy on my skin, but this time there's no one to make peace with. Martina is gone, and there's nothing to say.

Mom pushes away from the table and offers me a sad smile.

"Come on, Juls," she says. "I'll give you a ride home."

When I get home, the house is dark except for Dad's office light spilling into the hallway. Mom doesn't come inside with me on the off-chance Martina has come home, which of course she hasn't. I imagine she went straight to the city and crawled into Matthew's arms, trying to pretend we don't exist for a while so she can cool off and show up at Belmont tomorrow morning with a level head.

I peek into Dad's office, finding him kicked back in his ergonomic chair and basking in the glow of a giant computer monitor. A horse walks across the screen, palm trees exploding in the background.

Fasig-Tipton's Gulfstream Sale is just around the corner; young horses are making their under tack debut to the racing world after being picked up at yearling sales across the country. This is when the pinhookers try to make their money back, like flipping houses only with baby Thoroughbreds. The horses breeze for their audience and then a few days later they're sold at auction. Every May we go to the Midlantic Sale in Maryland, looking for promising two-year-olds. But now we have the Palm Meadows barn, so looks like the Gulfstream sale is on the radar.

"See anything interesting?" I ask into the room, making Dad look up from his studying.

"Potential," he says, rubbing his eyes and then scrubbing a hand into his sandy blond hair before really looking at me. "Although there's potential in all of them. We'll have to see this filly breeze before I make up my mind." Then he squints at me, remembering. "I thought you were at your mother's."

"I was," I say, leaning my shoulder into the doorjamb. "Guess what news cut that visit short?"

He leans back in his chair, sighing as he clicks off the video. "I guess it was too much to hope for," he says.

"As much as it pains me to say it, Martina's right," I say. "The most unpredictable person in this house is Leo. Martina and I are fine on our own for a couple of weeks."

"You know it's not about responsibility," Dad says. "I trust you both not to burn down the house when I'm gone. I just thought you'd like time with your Mom, without me around to make it awkward."

"It's not you making it awkward," I say, trying to find the best path to say this. "Mom just got back. She's living in Elmont for the sole reason that it's not here. We agreed it was for the best that way because when she was here she was driving Martina crazy."

Dad nods, then looks up at me. "But not you, it seems."

I shrug.

"I'll talk to Martina," he says, which is what he should have done to begin with, although I don't say that because I seriously know better. "See if I can find a middle ground."

The middle ground was Mom's apartment, but I don't say that either. I only shrug and say, "You really think Star is going to Dubai?"

Because this is a lot of family turmoil for nothing if he flops in the Razorback. Dad only smiles, which I could take to mean anything if I didn't know him well enough to read every one of his silent tells.

This one screams *do you have to ask?*

So I nod, and slip out of the doorway. I have dinner to scrounge up.

Chapter Nine

"Remember to use all your aids," Sophie calls from the middle of the indoor. "Most riders work plenty with their reins, but the seat and the legs become neglected. This makes bend difficult to accomplish, because you can't do it by pulling on the horse's face alone. Bend has to happen throughout the horse's entire body or it doesn't happen at all."

Fitting. In a lesson dedicated to bend, of course we're going to hear a lot about the outside of things—reins, legs, shoulders, even weight.

Sophie pauses, studying one of the other riders before lifting her voice. "Outside leg, Olivia!"

Olivia turns pink and her mount instantly shifts underneath her, body more aligned on the circle. Everyone in the class walks on a circle, holding onto our reins by the buckle.

"When we take our hands out of the equation, you can feel how much your body can do," Sophie says. "Little shifts, a nudge, a turn of the shoulders speak volumes to a horse. Now, let's all turn in and halt. We have to talk posture."

Obediently, horses break off the circle, turning toward her. Kali meanders toward Sophie, eyeing the other horses and bobbing her head. It occurs to me that I haven't ridden her on a loose rein since the track, when she was a racehorse and I felt at home in her saddle, perfectly at ease with letting her have her head on the way back to the shedrow. Lately, all I do is ride her in connection, like I'm afraid of what she'll do if given half the chance to put her head down and bolt. All of that working on getting her to connect at Palm Meadows, and this is what I've turned into—someone who feels weird when I'm doing the opposite.

"Stretch the outside back and *down,*" Sophie says, doing an awkward hop as she demonstrates from the ground. "The movement should come from the hip, not the knee. If you bend the knee you're drawing the heel up, which pushes your outside hip up and forward, which allows—maybe causes—a horse to fall onto the outside shoulder. What happens when the horse falls onto its outside shoulder?"

"It becomes unbalanced," Luna says quietly as the rest of us stretch our legs. "You can fall off the circle."

Sophie nods. "Remember everything is connected. You move your leg wrong, you upset your weight distribution. Your horse feels that and reacts because horses are trained to listen. Every movement of your body is an aid, and every movement of your horse is a reaction to that aid."

I stretch my leg down and back, while Kali chews on the bit thoughtfully and ignores me.

"Today," Sophie continues, "we're going to start with loops off the long wall. I'll explain . . ."

I zone out, remembering loops off the long wall like I remember I have five fingers on each hand. In my head, I keep thinking about bend. What had Lisa always preached all those years at Woodfield? *Inside leg to the outside rein.* Outside rein moves the horse's outside shoulder into a turn. Inside leg asks the horse to step under itself with the inside hind leg.

Therefore, inside leg to the outside rein. Always.

"July?"

I startle, breaking out of my thoughts. "Yes," I say, clipped, like I was always listening as Sophie raises an eyebrow at me. There is no way I can cover for falling into myself, not listening whatsoever through her instructions. Sophie looks at me like she knows.

"You'll start," she says, motioning for me to lead the way. Okay, then. Might as well do all the things I already know to do. How many times have I bent a horse?

Every day.

How many times has Kali successfully turned a circle without popping her shoulder out? Well, that's a little harder to say. I give Kali the go ahead. There's no stutter in her step as she springs into a graceful trot, lifting her hooves like she was born to airily carry herself around a dressage arena. She even gives me some semblance of connection, lowering her head just enough to make it look good.

We turn onto the long wall, and I nudge her off of it.

Outside rein, outside rein, I think. Then: *inside leg, inside leg.*

The filly curls around my boot on the way toward Sophie, who watches me with her arms crossed, mouth uncharacteristically shut.

Silence from a trainer can be good . . . and it can be bad. I can't help but jump to what Lisa said precisely once in the many years I rode with her: *"You notice I'm not talking, right? It's because this is good work, Juls."*

I'm going to hope this is good work.

When I hit X I shift my aids. Inside becomes outside, outside becomes inside. Kali snorts at the change, tips her chin into her chest like a warhorse in a military mural might, and thrashes her tail as she bends toward the wall. Out of curiosity, I soften my inside rein and the filly stays in bend, still trotting toward the wall like nothing has happened.

Yes.

"Good girl," I croon to her as we hit our mark at K and collect, turning onto the short wall.

"Walk her, July," Sophie says as I smile. I feel like I'm splitting open from happiness, because Kali trotted in bend and didn't fall on her face when I tested whether or not we were truly doing it right. We were.

We were doing it *right.*

"As pretty as that was," Sophie says as I rock gently to Kali's big walk back to the group, "I asked for this exercise at the walk on the buckle before we tried it at the trot. Since you've proven yourself quite adept you can sit out the next few exercises."

The words sound like accolades, but the delivery really isn't. My face flames, evidence enough I've been caught not paying attention, my mind elsewhere when it should have been here. No matter what I think I know, it's not good enough when I have to pay attention to things so simple as walk *then* trot.

Sophie motions to Olivia, who slips her hand to the buckle and gives her mount a good nudge into the exercise. Once all of the girls have ridden through at a walk, successfully checking where their legs are, directing their horses with only their seats, Sophie nods and says, "Trot."

Then she looks right at me and shakes her head.

~~

They go through the exercise at the trot on the buckle and then once more, this time with the reins. Kali stands through it like a champ, watching with her ears pricked, while I sit in her saddle and tremble.

The rest of the lesson is a disaster. The loop off the long wall into a twenty-meter circle sees Kali popping her shoulder out. The loop into ten-meter circles at C, B, and A has her falling off the path entirely. I can't think about circles, much less bend, and Kali lets it be known what she thinks of my complete inability to get it together.

"I think that's enough for today," Sophie says, waving us off. I've already got my feet out of my stirrups, prepared to fling myself off of Kali and bury myself in work so I don't have to feel this hideous failure anymore when Sophie puts a hand on Kali's bridle, stilling me.

"Stay right where you are, Juls," she says as the other students' heels are hitting the ground, stirrup leathers running up and horses blowing happy sighs at another lesson over. Sophie points at my feet. "Put those toes back in your stirrups. You're not finished yet."

"But class . . ." I start, drifting off when she gives me a look.

"You have somewhere pressing to be?"

I close my mouth, and she nods.

"Do that exercise again," she says. "This time I want you to stop thinking about me and think about what you were doing during the first loop off the long wall. Keep your attention on Kali and where you're putting your body."

I nod shakily, gathering the reins and giving Kali the signal to move forward at a trot. The filly lifts off, her head up and her body stiff, obviously finished with my inability to talk to her. Immediately a rush of uncertainty hits my blood. I feel just as stiff as Kali, like we're both suddenly new at this.

And Kali *is* actually new at this, which doesn't help get me back on track.

"You know this horse, July," Sophie says from the ground. "Work with her. Get her attention back."

Outside rein, I think a little desperately, feeling the leather through my gloves. I squeeze it, pressing down on it to keep it firmly connected between my thumb and index finger. Kali cocks an ear back at me.

"There she is," Sophie says. "Now make the rest of it come through."

The inside rein. I twitch my fingers just a little, feel Kali's jaw loosen around the question I'm asking her. *Are you there? It's me. It's just me.*

Kali sighs and drops her head.

"Okay," Sophie says. "Now start the exercise at C. Forget everything else exists. It's just you and Kali."

I let out the breath I'm holding, my shoulders sliding back. Kali lifts into an airy trot, bending underneath me through the ten-meter turn, looping off the long wall and crossing the arena, changing bend and circling at B, looping across the arena and changing bend to turn and circle at A.

We hit the short wall again and I hardly know what happened. Kali churns excitedly down the next long wall and Sophie claps as I sit back, bringing Kali down and letting her drop her head into an exuberant, bobbing walk.

"That is what I was looking for from you," Sophie says, pointing at C. "Right there. If you rode like that all the time I'd just kick back and watch you do it, so what's the deal?"

I shake my head, no good excuse presenting itself for my total lack of coherence. I could blame Kali for being green, I could blame the class for being something I've done before, but really the truth is I have to blame myself.

"I wasn't listening," I sigh, the admission taking a little of the weight off my chest. I can breathe easier with it gone. "And then I fell apart."

"Look, July," Sophie says, crossing her arms and peering up at me. "Most of the girls in this class have experience; you're not the only one here who's been riding since you were probably walking. But some of these girls haven't, so I'm teaching to them just like I'm teaching to you."

I nod, throat closing because she's right. This isn't a class just for me. I'm so used to the opposite I can't see what's happening around me.

"That said," Sophie continues, "I'm hoping you can either brush up on your fundamentals here or at least realize you can use these fundamentals to better your horse. Six months off the track, you said?"

I croak out a small "yes."

"She's doing a lot for a recently off-track Thoroughbred," Sophie says. "You should be proud of her; I think you have a good one on your hands. But she needs foundation work, and this class can get her there if you stop getting in her way."

I keep nodding, like I'm bobble-headed, because there's nothing to do other than to agree. She's right; I *am* getting in Kali's way. We both fell apart because I can't expect her to be at my level, especially when I'm quietly panicking in her saddle.

Because horses can feel that, too. Panic might as well be an aid screaming *it's every man for himself!*

It's a wonder she didn't bolt on me.

Sophie steps back from Kali's head, looking her over. "She's cool. You can go ahead and put her away. Next time we're going to build off of this lesson, so I'd advise you work on these figures as I intended beforehand. We want Kali to have a foundation before she's expected to do it perfectly. Okay?"

This time, I manage to keep myself from nodding. "Okay."

∾

The rest of the week becomes dedicated to figures. Figures on the buckle, walk and trot, before figures finally—*finally*—in connection. If I'm not in other classes, not driving from the track to school, not sleeping, it's figures.

I'm going to start dreaming about figures soon, which is what Madeline says to me on our way out of the barn on Saturday afternoon after Practicum. "Just think, Juls," she laughs. "There'll be no escaping it soon."

"I don't think there's any escaping it *now*," I say, taking a deep breath of late February air. It's frigid, burning my lungs. "But Kali's improving," I add. "Sophie's right. The foundation I'm laying is helping. She's already moving underneath herself better, and it's easier to get her to bend on the circles when I have her in connection."

"There's something I'm going to tell you that you may not want to hear," Madeline says seriously as we walk up to our cars, "but Sophie is *always* right."

"I had a feeling," I say, grimacing because I still feel like such an idiot. I'm hoping I've schooled enough to walk into class next week and not embarrass myself again. I should be at Barn 27 right now, helping with the afternoon chores before the Razorback Handicap watch party. I begged off for a few more hours to give Kali one more ride, because the figures aren't going to ride themselves.

Madeline's right. Dreaming about them is the next logical step because they've taken over my life in only three days.

Madeline waves at me as she gets into her car, heading off. I climb into mine and sit in the chilly interior, waiting for the heater to kick on before I take off my gloves and hold my numb fingers to the vents. I don't know why I bother—I'm only going back to Belmont. Might as well stay popsicle-cold.

I stifle a yawn, wishing Jericho's equestrian center had a coffee maker. When I get to Belmont it's the first thing I make a bee line toward, passing Martina wordlessly and pulling the carafe off the hot plate to pour her freshly ground artisanal coffee into my travel mug.

"Figures?" Martina asks me, eyeing my breeches tucked into half chaps—not exactly racetrack attire. Around here it's all tall boots under jeans, or, considering the weather, ski pants.

"Figures," I confirm, taking a healthy, warm sip of needed coffee.

"How is Kali these days?" Martina asks, scrolling through our barn management system and not looking at me. I inch toward the desk, thinking maybe I've been forgiven for being a little too quick to jump at Mom's proposal last week. Although I'm cautious. Too many times burned, and all of that.

"She's starting to get the concept of bend," I say, taking another sip. "And I'm starting to learn how to teach her a little better. Being more patient is something I should have been to begin with."

"No kidding," Martina grouses, tearing her eyes from the screen to give me a knowing look.

"I don't know how training horses applies to letting Mom live with us for a couple of weeks," I say, digging in my heels. Stubbornness might not be a virtue, but this is an old game.

"I think it's exactly the same thing," Martina says. "We agreed we wouldn't let her push us, Juls."

I stare at her over my travel mug, because yes, I do remember this being the agreement. I'm just tired of treading water, waiting for things to happen instead of making them happen.

Which is exactly what keeps biting me in the butt.

"Did Dad talk to you?" I ask.

"In a manner of speaking," she snorts, viciously clicking the mouse and opening up another horse's profile, inputting what we did with it this morning in terms of feed and work with a few loud, deliberate keystrokes. I've never seen someone type angrily before, and now I can safely say it looks ridiculous. "He said you were still open to it."

"I am," I confirm.

"Which brings me right back to—"

"I'm not saying you aren't right," I interrupt her, watching her hands still over the keyboard as she looks up at me. "You're right!" I exclaim. "But it's not like she's moving in for the duration. It's just a few days of togetherness, which is what we wanted, isn't it? Ever since she left, we've just wanted her back. Now she is. She's doing everything we asked, and we're still going to hold her at arm's length? Punish her for trying? I don't want to drive her away."

"The fact that *we* might drive her away by having boundaries is my exact problem with this idea," Martina points out, which feels like a punch to the gut. "It means we're afraid to say no. That *you* are afraid to say no, because we assume anything else would mean she'd run away again. That's not fair, July. It's not part of the deal. I refuse to be afraid because I have standards people need to meet."

I open my mouth and shut it. She arches an eyebrow, knowing she's won because I have nothing to say. Sourness fills my stomach, and the coffee suddenly feels like such a bad idea.

Before I can say anything, Leo pops his head into the open doorway.

"Guys," he says, breaking the stalemate, "are we watching the Razorback or are we not watching the Razorback? It's going off in thirty and I think I can safely say I'm really looking forward to the warmth of the Belmont Café."

"Right!" Martina says, pushing back from the desk. "The Razorback. The watch party. We can go."

Martina puts the computer to sleep while I watch her back, trying to think of something to say.

"If you're going to just stand there . . ." she starts, as my thoughts form coherent sentences in my head and start rushing out of my mouth.

"She won't stay with us," I concede, and Martina stills. I shift on my feet, clenching my fingers around my cup and unclenching them, feeling awkward admitting what I've known and not wanted to voice. But here I am, letting it all fall out. "I don't want to be afraid either."

Martina is silent for a good too long, as though she's weighing what this means.

Then, finally, she nods to the door.

"So are we going to go watch Star or let Leo and the rest of them enjoy the heat alone?"

I scoff. "Oh, we're going."

And Martina smiles.

∾

The Belmont Café is the simulcasting room on the ground floor of the track's clubhouse. It's where the locals started coming after the off-track betting facility closed, sitting at their tables with their battered programs and chewed pens. Most people look like they've been here for years; some look like they never leave, with stains on their clothes to show off how little they care about the outside world.

Simulcasting is for the hardcore track-goer. The ones who see numbers instead of the horses flashing across the screens. Every so often you see newbies in the mix—adventurous dates and bachelor parties. But usually it's just the track people, eyes bleary from squinting at the television screens and the tiny print in the programs.

Over a hundred televisions cover the walls, some of them showing the card at Oaklawn leading up to the Razorback Handicap. Our crowd clusters in front of these televisions, watching silently as the horses warm up for the race.

"Hey," Beck whispers in my ear, making me jump and whirl around, finding him grinning at me mischievously. Behind him, Elyse stands aloofly in a wool dress and riding boots, her shiny blond hair easily the most stunning thing in the room. Sunglasses perch at the top of her head. She waves at me over Beck's shoulder, and I wave back.

"Who are you betting?" Beck asks.

"There's no time for that," I say, just as I notice the ticket in his hand. One hundred dollars to win right on Star's nose.

"That is optimistic," I raise an eyebrow. "We're . . ." I glance back at the screens.

". . . fourth choice," Elyse helpfully finishes, "in a handful of Kentucky Derby also-rans and local horses, it looks like." She looks down at the race program in her hands. "Star's the best looking horse in the field."

"See, Elyse understands. It's a good bet," Beck defends, putting his hands on my hips just as I want to point out that studying the past performances is not the same thing as training a horse day in and day out. Beck grins at me, as though knowing exactly what I want to say, and turns me around as the last horse loads, the back gates shutting closed behind its tail. "Besides," he says against my hair, "Star is family."

The gates open, every horse jumping and leaping onto the track. The announcer's voice is tinny as he goes through the motions of describing the action, almost drowned out by the whooping and hollering coming from the other end of the simulcast hall—people invested in another race, somewhere that is definitely not Oaklawn.

"Quark Star settles into third, two lengths back to Joyous Act, then Founder on the outside . . ."

When Star is midway through the far turn, Jorge twitches at the reins. It's hardly a movement—more of an adjustment than anything—and the colt lengthens his stride, shoving off with his hindquarters and beginning his run.

"That's it, Jorge," Elyse approves, as though she knows him well enough to shoot the breeze with him during morning workouts. It occurs to me that maybe she does. Her father's horses train here and she stands in the midst of pari-mutuel betting like she was born to it. Television light gleams off her eyes as she rises on her toes, excitement shivering on her when the horses scoot past the quarter pole.

Jorge shakes the reins, puts his head down, and *pushes*. Star switches leads and rolls in response, gobbling up the flagging leaders with late closers flying up behind him. Jorge glances under his inside arm and pumps harder, whip bouncing along the colt's outstretched neck.

"Yes!" Elyse screams. "Get up there, baby! Get up!"

Beck laughs, the reverberation vibrating across my back. Martina bellows at the screens, arms in the air as Star keeps pouring on speed down the stretch, holding off the late charges. Eyes slide over to us, a few knowing smirks peering from dirty tables, and a few screams of encouragement even joining us—because Star glides past the wire first, four lengths in front, like he wasn't even trying hard. Jorge stands in the irons and slaps the colt's neck.

Elyse flicks her golden hair out of her shining eyes and looks over her shoulder at me, for just a second, before her eyes lock on Beck behind me.

"Better start packing your bags," she tells him. "You can't miss out on the Dubai World Cup like you have Florida."

Like Florida, I think, brain suddenly derailing as Elyse continues to smile past me.

Is that what she thinks? Beck's missing out?

Or is it just what I'm always thinking?

A little pang of guilt chimes deep and resonates in my chest, but I push it away. Beck makes his own decisions, and he decided to stay in New York. With me. He isn't missing out on anything.

But even I know that's not at all true. He is missing out, even if it is his choice.

I clear my throat, and Elyse looks away quickly.

"Dubai, then?" I ask, not particularly aiming it at anyone as the camera pans to Star walking into the winner's circle, Jorge flicking flecks of dirt off his crop as he grins.

Beck pulls me into a hug, our feet slipping on the ticket-scattered ground. He kisses the side of my head and says, "Dubai."

Chapter Ten

"March is supposed to be warmer," Madeline grumbles as we trundle into the indoor arena, bundled against the cold that seeps through the walls. Kali and Cricket snort and flick their ears at the busy schoolers, students getting in extra riding time on the weekend.

"It's never warmer," I tell her. "This is New York, remember? March is designed to torture you with thoughts of spring but leave you with the harsh reality that it's still winter."

Madeline groans, stopping Cricket by the side of the arena and pulling down her stirrups. I tighten Kali's girth an extra hole—which she bobs her head at in silent disapproval—and buckle my helmet. Instinctively, I check my watch before I mount up, even though I have plenty of time before I need to be in the city, back on Beck's sofa for Lighter's Fountain of Youth watch party in the late afternoon.

Help Beck forget he's not in Florida! Elyse's group text chimed on my phone this morning during workouts. *Doors open at Gulfstream Park North (aka, Beck's place) at 3pm. Post positions provided!*

I can picture Elyse happily printing off Gulfstream post positions and handing them out to Beck's friends at the door. A little curl of something warm and uncomfortable tightens in my chest, because shouldn't I be the one doing that? I'm his girlfriend, after all.

I'm not doing any of the prep work for Lighter's watch party. In fact, it hadn't even occurred to me. Should it have? I think about Elyse's text and now I'm not sure. I have two precious hours to myself, and I have to use them on Kali. What time can I sink into party-planning—a skill I certainly *don't* have—when there's a week's worth of Sophie's lessons to put into practice?

Beck understands that. *I think.*

I shove away the uncertainty. Beck *does* understand. If Elyse wants to throw herself at the feet of the party gods, so be it. But this unfamiliar wedge of something I can't name pricks at me, reminding me that Beck isn't in Florida for a reason. The least I could do is get to the party a little early, laugh with his friends, put forth some actual effort when really I just want it to be us. Only Beck and me watching Lighter run hundreds of miles away.

But I can't have that, so I better get to work at forgetting about it and playing along.

I stick my foot into the stirrup and lift onto Kali's back, looking across the arena at the four other riders in various stages of flatwork. Ava and Holy, her big gray gelding, walk past us. Holy's on the bit, ears tipping back and his whole body coiled in wait for a transition she gives him with a near-imperceptible shift of her legs.

He goes bounding off at a canter, Ava's dark brown braid bouncing behind them. Kali watches like she's envious—but maybe that's me.

"We'll get there," I tell her, but not today. Not for a while.

The test we're aiming for at the Jericho Horse Show next month includes canter work, but no transitions to it from a walk. What we need to work on is bend at walk, trot, *and* canter. It's about balance and roundness, which means I have to get her straight and then I have to get her to bend. Then we'll work on her head not snapping up every time I transition her into a faster gait, because I can't wait to see the judge's commentary when Kali's ears brush my face somewhere between C and M.

I let Kali walk on the buckle while I get my thoughts organized. Cricket and Madeline walk somewhere behind me, both of us on the outside of the arena while the other horses loop around to our inside. Faster to the inside, slower to the outside—so like the track this way. I smile a little, thinking about how this is one thing Kali gets. I pat her on the shoulder and she licks her lips, bobbing her head and walking with pep in her stride without any urging from me.

There's no sluggish walking with Kali –another racehorse thing I appreciate. She'll have the walk portion of her introductory test totally mastered. The comments will say *brilliant, clear walk rhythm. Exemplary ground cover.* Maybe there will be exclamation points.

I pick up the reins as Ava and Holy canter past, Kali huffing in their wake.

"No need to get excited," I tell her, even though I keep an eye on Holy. There's no telling when he'll decide something previously inert and unthreatening will try to kill him, and Kali tends to react when other horses behave badly.

Holy seems to be in control of his emotions today, and when he's past us and three-beating a beautiful canter down the long wall, I ask Kali to trot. She leaps out, head flying up. I work at her until her head comes down, her jaw loosening around the bit just enough to feel her relax underneath me so I can start the dreaded figures. Looping off the long wall, Kali tries jutting out her shoulder as she goes. *Outside rein, inside leg, keep her neck straight, loosen at the poll . . .*

My thoughts run like a mantra, my body trying to be every aid Kali needs to hear and feel before she needs to hear and feel it. It's anticipation at its finest, which takes me straight back to exercise riding in the morning. Isn't this what I always do on the track? Anticipate every shudder of muscle and preparation to buck?

It's no different now. It wasn't even any different with Woodfield's schoolmasters. Gideon always needed constant supervision, because that's riding for you in a nutshell. Always anticipate, always be there to guide, because if you drop the ball the horse will pick it up for you. Gideon would slow down to a crawl, hardly wanting to gather himself back together again. With Kali, it's different, but it's not at the same time. She still needs me to ride every step.

Loop off the long wall, twenty-meter circle at C, outside rein, outside rein, outside rein.

I keep talking to her, whispering *good girl* and twitching my fingers on the reins. Kali flicks her ears back at me and rounds into my hand, arcing off the wall and crossing the arena in the circle of a freaking lifetime. Her ribcage bends around my inside boot, and it feels so heavenly in my hands I lose myself to the feeling of actual dressage. Kali and I put it together and got on the same page without Sophie or Lisa or anyone else to tell us how to do it.

A smile stretches across my mouth, giddiness climbing up my chest, when Holy goes flashing in front of us. All I see is a streak of gray, empty stirrups banging at his sides.

Kali veers off the path to avoid him, head up and eyes white-ringed. I sit through her sudden reversal of course, but then she decides to throw in a mad leap in the opposite direction, only to come up short when she runs straight into Cricket.

The thud snaps my head back. Then I'm airborne, flying over her head, somersaulting through the air, landing on my back in the cushy arena dirt that does not feel nearly as soft when you're actively pummeling it with your spine.

I hear the thunder of hooves, the ring of voices. My breath startles back into my lungs, which scream insistently at me to *stay put.*

When I open my eyes, Sophie fills my vision. Her face is full of worry lines.

"Where's Kali?" I ask, because my scattered, pain-numbed thoughts go straight to my horse. "Is she okay? Cricket?"

"Madeline has them," Sophie says, putting a hand on my shoulder. "They're both walking fine. Can you sit up?"

I think about the effort it might take to sit up, and immediately start to cry.

~~

Okay, so it was more like dry heaving rather than crying.

Extremely painful, ultimately embarrassing, dry heaving. I text Mom and Dad the most ridiculous, needlessly worrying phrase known to man: *I'm in the ER,* which brings on a waterfall of questions I stave off as best I can with Sophie sitting next to me, reading a magazine with cupcakes on the cover that couldn't look more out of place in her hands. I tell Beck I'm going to be late and his response is immediate.

I'm coming to you. Screw the race.

Nothing I can say will dissuade him, so for all I know he's actually on his way to Long Island when the nurse calls me in and Sophie quietly flaps her cupcake magazine closed, following me into triage.

The first thing anyone asks you in the ER when you're sitting in front of them smelling like horse and wearing breeches is, "Did the horse roll over you?"

I think of all the things that could have happened, and want to laugh.

"No," I say, thinking about Ava somewhere in the same triage unit, doing other tests. Sophie has slipped back and forth between us, called parents, been the adult in the room when all I want to do is curl into a small ball . . . if my spine would allow it.

I'm presented with a hospital gown instead. Sophie helps me peel off my riding clothes, because every movement hurts. Every bend at the waist feels like white-hot electricity zipping down my limbs, exploding in my fingertips. I shrug into the gown, red-faced and ashamed.

"Stop it," Sophie tells me, smoothing a hand over my dirty hair. "It's not beneath you to need help."

"I was more thinking about how I'm only wearing my under-wear now," I say, easing slowly onto the bed and wincing as I go.

Sophie smiles.

"I've been there," she says. "Second year of school, I got slammed into the wall by my horse during a class and she came right down on top of me. Broke my leg, was out of the saddle for months, and I had to undress in front of my trying-to-be-helpful instructor in the ER. We're just lucky, Juls."

I find myself wanting to laugh again. I wind up grimacing instead.

Sophie sits down in the arm chair next to me when the doctor whisks in through the curtain, my chart in hand and the predictable question on her lips: *did the horse roll over you?*

"No," Sophie and I both say in unison.

The doctor flips the chart closed.

"In that case," she says, "it's time for an x-ray."

∿

Laying on the sofa hurts. Sitting up hurts. Walking is slow and deliberate, like an elderly woman using a walker at the mall. I popped two painkillers at the hospital, after they told me I had nothing more than bruised ribs, but I can't avoid breathing, and breathing? It *really* hurts. Like fire wrapping around my lungs with each rush of air in and out.

I'm lucky; Ava got out of the hospital with a cast on her arm. I didn't ask her how bad it was. Seeing the turquoise peeking over her hand was enough.

"How are you doing down there?" Beck asks from his position on our sofa. I'm using his thigh as a prop for my pillow, my hair spread out across his jeans. I've wrapped the rest of myself burrito-like in a blanket, as if constraining my own movements will make breathing less painful.

Even though, the doctor's words coming back to me from the ER, I'll need to breathe deeply anyway, otherwise I have the fun of pneumonia staring me in the face.

This sucks.

"This is good," I say instead, and Beck raises an eyebrow at me. He knows a lie when he hears one, and I'm so bad at it I might as well be saying *all's dandy. Let's get back to the party.*

Only it's just us here in Garden City, the family TV broadcasting sunshine-full images of Gulfstream Park. This is actually what I wanted. Just us; no one else. What a weird twist of fate.

"Elyse must have been disappointed," I murmur, almost to myself. Beck looks down at me, tilting his head.

"She has plenty of people to keep her company," he reassures me. "I'm pretty sure my place is going to be a wreck when I get back."

I only nod, watching the television from my horizontal angle. Feather is walking quietly toward the gate, Mom in the saddle. The filly looks quiet—more so than usual—as if she's finally coming into her own when it comes to this racing thing. She's not sweating, even through the Florida warmth, and she stands calmly as the other fillies start entering the gate. No fidgeting, no fighting, no tossing her head around.

She just stands there, resolute.

"I'm impressed," Beck says. "She could hardly walk to the training track alone when we left, and now look at her."

"Guess time does fix everything," I mutter, and Beck laughs, pulling the blanket over my shoulder.

The gates crash open and Feather leaps, rushing down the stretch of dirt with Mom hustling her from the saddle. The fillies are all churning bunches of muscle, finding racing room as they charge past the stands and settle into positions going into the turn. Feather runs fourth on the outside, off the rail nearly five wide.

I want to groan, but something tells me that might be a bad idea.

The horses loop into the backstretch, drifting further apart as the leader keeps a half-length lead on a local filly. Mom sits passively on Feather—the filly running with her head down like she's not in a race at all but is instead breezing in her own private world. The filly to her inside doesn't seem to interest her, not until Mom starts to scrub at her in the far turn.

Feather, as it turns out, is ready to fly. She switches leads and catapults off her hind end, launching herself around the front-runners and passing them as they wink past the quarter pole. I blink, surprised.

Then my heart starts to race in earnest, and I shove myself up on my elbow despite my screaming ribs. Feather keeps digging into the dirt, the screaming announcer trying to keep up.

"It's all Feather today!"

Our filly flashes by the eighth pole, flicks her ears up at the looming finish line and swishes them back when Mom shows her the crop. *Mind on business,* Feather, I think. *Keep the momentum.*

But against what? I tear my gaze from her floating form and find no one behind her. The camera has sped ahead of them all to keep up with our filly, who leaps across the wire first.

It's a solid few beats before the next filly crosses it, and after that I'm too shocked to say a word.

"Holy crap," is all Beck says.

Mom pumps her fist in the air and slaps Feather's neck as they cruise down to a canter in the turn. Feather pricks her ears, clearly pleased with herself, as Mom draws her down to a bouncing trot and an outrider appears at her side to tow them home.

Beck looks down at me as I continue to stare at the television with my mouth hanging open.

"I take it you didn't know how well she was training?" he asks.

I look up at him and shake my head.

"Guess Feather is the stakes horse you promised Khalid," he muses, watching her enter the winner's circle with Mom beaming on her back. "Are you psychic? Care to tell me how Lighter's race is going to go?"

I laugh and ease myself back down to rest against my pillow. "I think it's plenty obvious I'm not psychic, especially where Lighter is concerned."

He grins down at me. "I still think fondly on last summer for the pure knowing of how right I was."

"Of course you were right," I huff. "Lighter is your horse. Everyone wants the next Derby winner in their barn, and for the amount you picked him up for as a yearling it's broadcast montage-level inspiring."

"I can't wait to film one of those for the Derby," Beck says, sounding at once dreamy and sarcastic, like he knows it's not going to happen. It's best to be realistic about this, after all. Lighter is a racehorse—one of thirty thousand three-year-olds in North America. Only twenty make the gate for the Kentucky Derby. Only one wins it.

"Knock on wood," I say, pointing at the coffee table. Beck leans forward and raps his knuckles against it.

"Superstitious all of a sudden?" he asks, settling back on the sofa. I get more comfortable against his side, watching the horses enter the paddock for the next race as the announcers break things down about Feather's race, everyone all smiles as they talk about her potential future as a rising star.

"Maybe I should be," I say. "A little luck might keep me glued to Kali's saddle."

Beck makes a face. "You couldn't have stopped the other horse from bolting more than you could prevent Kali from being where she was or how she reacted to it. Didn't you tell me falling is part of riding?"

"It is," I say, resolute. "And a few bruised ribs aren't keeping me grounded while Kali needs work. *I* need work."

"You've got time, Juls," Beck reminds me, because—it occurs to me with a rush of annoyance at myself—I haven't told him about the show yet.

"Not really," I sigh, the Jericho Horse Show spilling out of me. Beck tilts his head to look at me thoughtfully.

"Wood Memorial day, huh?" he asks, and I bark out a laugh that makes me gasp. Beck shakes his head. "No laughing, Juls."

"I keep trying to remember that," I say, "but then you're around."

"I am pretty amazing," he sighs, like it's such a burden. "But it sounds like you can do the show. What's a little horse dancing from letter to letter with some circles thrown in?"

"It has just become incredibly apparent to me that you don't know what I do when I'm not at the track," I say, and he nods.

"That is correct," he says. "But from what I can tell it's not a show you're aiming to conquer. It's a show you want to use for the sake of setting a goal for yourself, right?"

"More or less," I say. "It's definitely providing motivation."

"Then let it," he says, stroking a hand over my hair like he can soothe my worried brain. "And give yourself a break."

"I will try to remind myself to do that occasionally," I say as Lighter enters the paddock for the next race.

We're silent through the lead up to the Fountain of Youth. The announcers chatter about odds and past performances, preferring either Lighter or Tahr. Both camps insist one or the other performance by both colts in the Holy Bull was a fluke.

So it's a draw.

In the paddock, Lighter walks with Gus. He's perfectly turned out, blond mane and tail accenting his bronze chestnut coat. All of him burnishes in the sun, his little white mark on his forehead glowing. Mom stands with Dad and the Delaneys, talking and glancing at the colt every so often.

It must be odd for Beck to watch his family represent Lighter in the paddock, but I don't say anything about that, feeling already like he's made the wrong choice being here. He needs to be *there*, watching his colt skip from prep race to prep race. This isn't something you miss because your girlfriend had a couple of classes on inconvenient Saturdays.

I look up at Beck, his eyes on the screen, and don't see any sort of regret warring on his face. Maybe he's hiding it. He's good at that, isn't he?

Tahr walks by, his golden chestnut body a living flame in the paddock. Danny Miller stands in the background, his eyes hidden by his mirrored aviators as he talks to jockey Samuel Ramirez, fresh from California. Tahr's owner, Rickie Curbow, flits around them, his fedora shading his face and the little soul patch under his lower lip. They're here with one mission: destroy the Fountain of Youth field, complete with trampling Lighter.

Rickie Curbow isn't subtle. Leo sent me the link to the morning show *Works at Dawn*, which interviewed Rickie this morning in all his blustery glory, giant Dunkin' Donuts cup fisted in one hand as he laughed manically at the prospect of bouncing back this afternoon. Then he said the word *destroy.*

We'll destroy Lamplighter. Mark my words.

No one asked Dad how he felt about that, probably because they couldn't lure him in front of a camera. Beck makes a face when Rickie fills the television screen for a live interview, his larger-than-everything confidence booming into the living room.

"Rickie has the tact of a drunk bull," Beck sighs. "I kind of wish I'd talked to that reporter this morning."

I shoot a look up at him. "A reporter called you?"

"Guess Rob was busy," he says, putting his socked feet on the coffee table and stretching out like all of this means nothing to him as Mom gets a leg up onto Lighter. It's a ruse I recognize these days. "I was barely awake. Didn't seem like a good time to pick up phone calls from reporters."

"The difference between you and Rickie Curbow," I point out, watching the horses trail through the paddock, jockeys settling in saddles and getting last minute instructions. "He'd pick up."

"Yeah," Beck sighs, "I'm just going for the mysterious horse owner vibe these days. Rickie wouldn't be able to handle my game."

I snort, curling up against him. He drapes an arm over my body and we settle into pre-race quiet as the horses jig through the post parade. I haven't kept up with any of the horses, and certainly haven't been at Palm Meadows to watch the workouts, so I glaze over the parade of horses like most people—blind to the possibilities. I only see Lighter and Tahr, the two warring favorites.

The horses roll off into warm-ups, ponies alongside. Lighter dashes off by himself, pale mane sweeping off his neck and Mom a speck of black and white silks on his back. The white star stretched across her spine blazes in the Florida sun.

I drown out the commentary, all the *showing signs of sweat, looks fabulous in his warm-up, blah, blah, blah.* It doesn't matter. Once the horses reach the gate, I seek out Lighter again, finding him standing with his ears flicking back and forth like he's not sure what he signed up for. The horses move into line one after the next, and when the assistant starters come for Lighter he dances to the side, approaching the gate like a crab.

Mom straightens him out, and he goes into the last stall. It's only a heartbeat until the gates crash open.

All the horses surge, their bodies rocking onto their hind legs before they dig in with the tips of their front hooves, shoving into racing speed from a standstill. Lighter breaks wide, and Mom hauls his head toward the inside, pointing him toward the rail as the horses gallop past the grandstand.

Tahr blazes to the front, but Arco Iris beats him to the punch. Lighter is so lost on the outside he has to settle for fifth into the turn, his body a stream of platinum and copper in the middle of the track.

Along my side, I feel Beck tense. His hand on my hip curls into a fist as he worries his thumb against his index finger. I don't dare look up at him, because I'm too busy watching the race play out as the horses spill down the backstretch, entering the far turn and starting their final drives to get to the front—or stay there.

Tahr inches past Arco Iris, who is ready for him—speeding up and shoving his nose in front as they whip into the homestretch, switching leads and blazing. Samuel Ramirez transforms into a wild, flailing thing, pushing Tahr back into the lead.

Still on the outside, all Lighter needs to do is pour on speed. I know he has it. Mom knows he has it. All the betting public knows he has it, but no matter what Mom asks of him he remains bottled up, galloping down the dirt like he has nowhere to go and all the time in the world to get there.

"Come on," I growl at the screen, pushing myself up as my ribs constrict and scream. I can't help myself because this is so aggravating. "Get up there, Lighter!"

Beck doesn't say a word next to me, as if he's already accepted what I know deep down. Lighter isn't going to win this race.

In fact, he's going to lose quite grandly.

Tahr hits the wire first, Acro Iris slipping back into the pack to finish third. As lackadaisical as Lighter is running, he still manages fourth in front of a cascade of coming colts vying for the remaining Kentucky Derby points afforded the top four finishers. Lighter has just managed to nab five points by finishing just out of the money. Add on the Holy Bull and the Champagne Stakes, and Lighter has twenty-five total.

Tahr just earned fifty.

"Shit," Beck says under his breath as the horses gallop out in the turn, the camera on Tahr's chestnut body rippling with dark sweat.

"He can bounce back from this," I say quickly, drawing my legs underneath me and sitting up. I'm still shaky from the adrenaline rush, and now sick with the loss. "First place in the Florida Derby is a hundred points; if he wins that he'd go from the bottom of the list to the top ten."

Beck watches the screen, hunting for any image of Lighter. But the camera refuses us, focused on Tahr and Rickie Curbow leaping down the stairs to the grandstand, slapping the backs of strangers as he goes. He grins at the camera and points a finger at it like a gun, taking aim and firing.

My heart does a little squeeze, the pain in my ribs forgotten.

"If he does well in the Florida Derby . . ." I start again, telling myself what I want to hear when Beck shakes his head. He's already thinking what I'm refusing to let myself acknowledge. What I don't want to look in the face.

"If," he says, and turns off the television.

Chapter Eleven

The commentary on the racing websites is, shall we say, *uncharitable* about Lighter's loss in the Fountain of Youth. Even after the weekend is over and the dust should have settled, the discussion still rages. Naturally, I can't stop reading it.

Flash in the pan. Spit the bit. Looked sore. Obviously unprepared. Too headstrong. Not an honest horse.

The list of reasons and the laying of blame goes on and on, as if everyone with an opinion witnessed every second of Lighter's training and can expertly deduce the problem of Lighter's loss. Everyone knows exactly why Lighter didn't win the Fountain of Youth, and they argue over it until my face is red from reading. I turn off the phone.

"I don't know how you put up with this," I mutter to my dad as we drive through the security gate at Belmont. Dad gives me a dry smile, eyes on the ice-encrusted gravel drive on our way toward Barn 27.

"Pro tip, July," he says. "Never read the commentary."

I snort. Of course he doesn't read anyone's editorials and opinion pieces. That would be just like him. If you don't know what they're saying about you, there's nothing to get upset about in the first place. Sounds exactly like how my dad has handled most social interaction since I was twelve. After all, if you're too busy working there's no time to do anything like obsess over anonymous thoughts on your job performance. Or, you know, have a life.

"I'll keep that in mind when I get Kali's first test scores back," I say, cringing as I shift in my seat. My ribs ache, all the muscles between them tender to the touch. "I'm sure the comments are going to be colorful."

"You sure you want to work this morning?" Dad asks, eyeing my shimmying.

"Since when have a few bruises kept me off a horse?" I ask in response, and he nods because he knows better than to argue. Besides, he was the one who raised me with the old adage: if you fall, get back up. It's so natural to me now it might as well be like breathing.

I fell. So I'm going to get back up. This morning it's going to be on one of Dad's racehorses, and then this afternoon it's going to be Kali. Spring break started today, which means I have a week to focus just on her. Instead of Practicum and Western Civ readings and lessons, it's only going to me and my horse.

I can't wait.

Dad turns the SUV around the last row of barns, the beams catching on the shedrow. It's lit up from the inside, all orange glow around a soft buzz of activity. Grooms bustle through the shadows, and horses hang their heads over stall openings to blink and yawn at another Monday morning.

Which is when I catch a platinum blond mane wink behind a certain stall grate.

"Dad," I say slowly, stalling halfway out the open door, narrowing my eyes at the shedrow as I study the blond mane and the characteristic copper arch of neck underneath it. Then down to the wild, white-ringed eye. I shift to look back at Dad, who doesn't appear at all concerned by this development. "Why is Lighter in the barn?"

"He came in last night," Pilar says from underneath the dripping eaves. "With me and Gus."

I startle, dumbfounded for only a brief moment. I can barely pick Pilar out from the darkness—her black curls totally obscured by the early morning shadows and her bundled form so tiny it's nearly lost in the cavernous opening of Barn 27. What I can pick out is the flash of her smile before she steps further into the barn lights. Then I leap the rest of the way out of the car, pulling her into a hug.

"You're home!" I say, pushing her back to look her over. She's bronzed from the sun, looking out of place in her winter workout wear.

"What can I say?" she laughs. "I had a longing for a little New York winter."

I raise an eyebrow. "You did not."

"No," she says, wrinkling her nose up at the wetness outside as Gus comes out of Lighter's stall behind her. "I really didn't."

"I'm counting the days to that Dubai flight," Gus announces, reaching out and scrubbing his hand over my knit hat until it's askew on my forehead. "Nobody deserves this weather."

"Lucky you," Pilar grouses in his wake as he laughs and disappears into the tack room.

"Pilar," Dad says by way of greeting on his way past us. Pilar's shoulders straighten, her chin tipping up. I raise an eyebrow, catching the stiffness despite the layers hiding Pilar's usual ease.

"Rob," she nods. "I hope you have something for me to ride today."

"I think I can manage that," Dad says as we enter the office, where Martina is already stationed like she's in a battle command unit, tapping at the computer and drinking her coffee. Her hair is up in a sloppy bun, and her hands are jammed into fingerless, wool mittens. Her sweater is the one she wore yesterday. Truly, she has absorbed the barn. The transformation from law office to racetrack is almost complete.

She looks up at us and takes another sip of coffee as her eyes settle on Pilar.

"Oh good, I was wondering what we were going to do being down a rider," she announces as Dad puts his laptop bag down on the desk, which is quickly becoming Martina's desk. She eyes the bag like it's insulted her, and Dad transfers it to the coffee table, raising his hands in surrender.

"Who's at death's door this week?" Dad asks, because that's running a barn for you. You're never sure who is going to show up, especially with the winter bugs making the rounds.

"Mom is bed-bound," Martina says. "Guess all of that hopping from Florida to New York got the better of her. She was squeaking like a mouse on the phone."

"Fine," Dad says, waving in Pilar's direction. "You up for it, Pilar?"

I look back and forth between them, catching the tightening of Pilar's jaw, like she's steeling herself before she answers, "Of course."

Okay, this is just weird. I glance between the two, hoping I can figure out the source of the tension as though it's written in bold red ink on their backs. But no such luck. Instead Martina raises her eyebrow and points at the whiteboard with all the sets scribbled across its shiny surface.

"Then get out there, both of you," she says, sounding so like Dad. "First set out in ten."

~⁓

Unnamed two-year-olds are big teenagers, full of themselves without knowing their strength, and I don't even have a firm name to yell when they're being bad. It's like riding a blank slate—full of promise and unknowns all at once.

Our set spills onto the training oval in a trickle of hoofbeats, laughter trailing from riders in white puffs. We stop our charges by the outside rail, turning them in and letting them take a moment to breathe. The chestnut colt underneath me huffs big breaths, condensation plumes billowing in the air as he pricks his ears at the training oval. The gray filly under Pilar pricks her ears at the activity on the oval, chewing the bit and probably stewing over the best course to mayhem.

Everything about this morning is routine. Except for the stabbing pain in my ribs and Pilar's strained reaction to Dad. Otherwise totally normal.

I shift in the saddle, wondering if there's a way to sit this horse that doesn't make me want to double over. The colt shifts with me, shouldering against Pilar's filly and getting the side-eye of irritation for his efforts.

"Sorry buddy," I whisper to him, telling myself to just sit. I can do this.

"You look miserable, July," Pilar announces, killing most of my go-get-'em attitude. I sigh into the air.

"Please," I say instead of immediately admitting she's right. "I'm sure this will be like riding a cloud. I've been riding everything Leo can throw at me on top of riding Kali in the afternoons, so this?" I motion to the colt. "This is nothing."

Pilar laughs. "I don't think I'd tempt fate. Two-year-olds have a way of testing it. Poor *Nothing* here might decide to make himself *Something*."

"Fine by me," I smile at her and pick up the reins. "I relish the challenge. Want to stretch their legs?"

"Absolutely," Pilar nods, gathering the reins and heeling the filly into the stream of traffic. I follow along on the chestnut, keeping him level with her as we wrap around the track, warming up until we're going at a good clip down the backstretch and into the turn. Switching leads slips his mind as he starts looking around, gawking like he can't believe he can run this fast.

"This is nothing, buddy," I say into the wind, asking him to switch leads. He flings himself forward, swaps leads, and puts his head down coming toward the quarter pole, where I ask him again to switch leads because I don't trust him further than he's capable of paying attention—which is clearly not much.

Somewhere off the outside rail, Dad is watching us. I take a deep breath, feeling the sharp ache in my ribcage in response, and push it out of my thoughts. It's just a bruise, and I'm just doing what I've been doing for years. I steady the chestnut when he tries a running leap at the next marker, press him down on the rail, and let him loose.

The filly springs forward with us. The track becomes a drone of wind, even though my ears are just as bundled as the rest of me. I crouch over the chestnut's withers, letting him stretch out but not pushing him. This isn't going to be a fast breeze; first breezes never are. We just want to see what we're working with, and so far the chestnut is doing everything perfectly . . . but not as fast as the filly, who keeps pace on our outside before Pilar slowly lets her out and sails by us like it's nothing, passing the finish line a good length ahead and swapping leads like she's supposed to going into the turn.

My little chestnut pricks his ears at the filly's flickering gray tail and forgets, again, about the lead changing phenomenon.

"Lead change, guy," I tell him, getting him to swap as I lift myself off his withers and pat his neck, rewarding him for trying. Sometimes that's all it takes for things to stick; a little kindness and next time he might change leads without being asked. Maybe next time he'll actually give the filly a run for her money.

I give him another firm pat and croon, "Good boy. A for effort, you nameless little unknown."

He swishes his ears back, listening. By the time I pull even with the filly, Pilar is grinning and bouncing up and down to the filly's big trot.

"I'm going to like this one!" she calls to me, slapping the filly's neck.

"Good," I reply. "I hope you're prepared to share her."

She smiles at me slyly. "Don't know, July. What with your poor ribs I doubt you could handle her."

I mock gasp. "Don't force me to convince my dad to send you back to Florida," I threaten, poking her thigh with my crop. She shakes her head, smile falling.

"If that happened I'd quit and start riding for someone else," she says, which makes me give her a double take as her words slam home.

"What?" I ask, all humor leaked from my voice. "You'd quit?"

Pilar shrugs a shoulder. "It's not like I got any rides in Florida," she says. "Paul kept insisting I wasn't ready, which was like arguing with a brick wall. Your dad sided with him. And Lighter . . . well, Lighter went to your Mom in the end, didn't he?"

Ah. Now everything is clicking into place. Pilar's stiffness, Dad's obliviousness. I can feel her frustration seeping off of her because I know what it's like to run up against Dad's blinders. It feels like you're at war with yourself. After all, if the object of your irritation doesn't even recognize you, what can you do?

Stew. And then stew some more. No wonder she came home.

"Maybe Dad thought with your arm . . ." I start and trail off, because I know what a shoddy excuse that is, especially when Pilar gives me a look.

"It's fine," she says. "I get it. I didn't bounce back in time after my arm, not to mention getting my nerves back. I didn't deserve to ride Lighter."

"But you got a good response out of Lighter at Saratoga," I protest, willing her to remember. "And it's not like Mom got him to do much in his last race."

"Even so," Pilar sighs. "I was a glorified exercise rider in Florida, so I came home. I might get some good rides at Aqueduct. I have connections here, despite your dad."

"Does this have anything to do with following Lighter?" I ask, thinking about the colt in his stall. Dad didn't explain the move, but I don't need him to voice what's obvious. Lighter doesn't need to stick around Gulfstream to prove himself; he needs points to get in the gate at Churchill Downs. And if Florida is too hot to accomplish that goal, Dad will put him somewhere a little cooler for the last round of Derby preps. Maybe he'll follow in Star's footsteps to Arkansas.

"Maybe it does have something to do with Lighter," Pilar hedges, bringing me out of myself as we walk the horses off the training oval, heading back to Barn 27. "You read the news, haven't you?"

I make a face. There was once a time when all I ever did was read the news, hoping for some glimpse of Mom. I still have news alerts set up for her name, and I can't quite bring myself to dismantle them yet. They're little fragments of a past that's not far enough in the rearview to safely let go of quite yet, so I keep scanning the news. It's just that now Mom isn't on the other side of the country; she's on our horses. Celia Carter is riding Lamplighter and Feather for Rob Carter of Barn 27 at Belmont Park, and it still feels like a ridiculous fantasy.

"Lighter has dropped out of the top ten list on *The Blood-Horse*," Pilar continues, which I know thanks to the alerts. She shoots me a tentative glance. "And everyone is talking about Feather after that blow out win in the Davona Dale."

I know this, too. The headline from a local Florida paper was *Feather Lands Knockout Punch,* and the photo was of Mom curled over the filly's mud-splattered neck. She was all grins.

"If only she had the points to be considered for the Derby," I say with mock enthusiasm, remembering Mom's interview with the local reporter. *It's too bad,* she said, *that it doesn't count toward the Derby after a win like this.* "It would make a great story," I continue, thinking that sounded familiar, too. Maybe Mom said that in the interview as well.

Because it *would* make a great story.

Pilar says quietly, "It would be a huge leap to assume . . ."

She trails off when I turn a startled look to her, realizing what she's thinking. There's only one way Mom comes off Lighter for the Derby: if she's offered a better ride. So far, there is no better ride on the horizon. No matter how much people talk about Feather she's still Oaks-bound, and no one else has approached Mom for the Derby yet . . . as far I know.

"It's a *giant* leap," I say, shaking my head. "And outside of our control on top of it."

Pilar sighs. "I know. But I can't help hoping. Riding Lighter every morning, and for what? Your father won't put me on him again, just like he won't put me on anything in the afternoons. I'm treading water, July. I need an in, even if it takes a miracle."

Pilar's right—she can't keep waiting on Dad, and she definitely can't hope for something as unlikely as the Derby. But a few races at Aqueduct? She's got those in the bag. We just need to rustle them up.

"We can't focus on getting you on Lighter for the Derby," I say, and she looks down at her hands. "But after? There's a hell of a lot of after, Pilar."

She looks up, taking a deep breath. "Then I need to start riding in races," she says, casting a determined look my way. "Here. I need to start proving myself. I want the ride on Lighter back, no matter if it's next month or Saratoga or next year. I want it back."

I'm silent for a full minute, listening to the scrape and clop of horse hooves on gravel and slush. If anyone deserves a chance, it's Pilar. But that's not how the horse world works. You have to earn your rides. You have to grind yourself down to the bone for them. And still—*still*—you may never get what you want. There are no guarantees.

But I'm still damn sure I want to see Pilar in Lighter's saddle, the two of them blazing down the track together like they did at the start.

"I'll help you," I find myself saying. "Any way I can."

Her eyes slide toward me, dark and unreadable with half her face covered in knit. But then she reaches her hand out toward me, fingers stretched, and I take it.

She squeezes. And I squeeze right back.

Chapter Twelve

Spring break doesn't mean an abandoned barn at Jericho. If anything, it means more free riding time, and by god we're all scrambling to take advantage of it. The indoor arena bustles with horses, their paths crisscrossing over and over. Riders give each other little nods and apologetic smiles as they steer clear, passing left to left.

Kali flinches each time a horse flits by, as though stung. She jumps and shivers, chews the bit like she's trying to gnaw through it. A gray horse that looks a little too much like Holy canters past, and she breaks into a riotous canter, skittering through the corner with her head in the air like a giraffe.

I sit back, ribs aching angrily, and Kali comes back to herself with an indignant huff, as though *how dare* that other horse not know her new, arbitrary boundaries.

"She looks tense," Madeline observes from the bleachers as Kali shakes her head and yanks at my arms like she's back on the track and aching to have her own way. I nod silently, focusing on my horse as she continues to snort and roll her eyes at the indoor arena. Madeline purses her lips. "And so do you. Are you breathing?"

"As much as my ribs allow," I say, watching her nose wrinkle up in reminder of my fall. With my muscles aching across my back, I wish I could forget, too.

"I think you need to back off," she advises. "You're tight, so Kali's tight. I don't know about you, July, but when I fall I spend three days in a warm tub."

"Sounds heavenly," I sigh, letting Kali's reins slip through my fingers, her head nosing down to her knees as her neck stretches down, muscles loosening.

"You probably went straight to the track, huh?" she asks, knowing me so well.

I shrug. "If I'm not broken . . ."

"But you are seriously bruised," she points out.

"Which is not broken," I say. "Riding sore is standard operating procedure, Maddy. I'm fine."

Madeline doesn't look convinced, but she shrugs and says, "In that case, let's loosen her up. Spiral in!"

"Are you standing in for Sophie today?" I ask as she dramatically points to the C-end of the arena.

"Don't talk back, young lady," she demands. "I said spiral in. Pick up a trot, please."

"At least you're polite," I say to Madeline's grin.

Picking up the reins, Kali's body immediately tenses, but she gives me the trot I'm looking for and follows me on the circle. As soon as I have her attention, I nudge her in and her line shifts—a twenty-meter circle becomes an eighteen-meter circle.

"And back out," Madeline calls.

I shift Kali back out.

"And back in!"

Kali's ears twitch as I nudge her back.

"And back out!"

We follow along, Kali's head slowly lowering into my hands and her body loosening. With a dramatic sigh, my mare finally lets herself relax somewhere around the twentieth spiral, her muscles across her back moving smoothly and her jaw nice and soft against my hands. The connection strikes warm and sure, the circuit completed from her mouth to my elbow, through both of our bodies until we're a simple unit moving as one.

And then the damn gray goes gallivanting by again, and Kali's head shoots up, the connection torn in two as she leaps into a running trot. I jump to follow her, catching Madeline stand up out of the corner of her eye.

"Spiral, July!" she calls out. "Keep spiraling!"

I tug Kali into the circle. We circle around, around, smaller, smaller. Twenty, eighteen, fifteen, ten meters. Kali turns the tight circle, her body forced to bend, forced to slow. With a grunt, my mare's panicked run collapses on itself and she falls into a stiff walk.

Then, finally, a halt. I put a hand on her sweat-streaked neck and Kali puts her head down and snorts at the dirt. I look across the busy arena to give the gray the evil eye. Madeline sighs from the bleachers, sitting back down.

"Well, I think we know what's upsetting her," Madeline says, and I nod.

Gray horses. Horses getting too close. Horses crossing her path. Fabulous. I have a horse developing into a head case and she's not even on the track anymore. Isn't it supposed to be the other way around? She's just a horse now, after all.

I swallow the rising lump in my throat and lean over Kali's neck to whisper, "Where's our page, girl?"

From the bleachers, Madeline looks at us critically and says, "Walk-halt transitions. Give her something she can do well to go out on. Build up her confidence before you call it quits."

I lift myself up, settling back into the saddle with a nod.

"I can do that."

Then I pick up the reins and push her into connection.

~~

I'm slipping out of Kali's stall when my phone begins to chime in my bag.

Beck.

"Hey," I say, sliding the stall door shut behind me. Kali is tucked into her hay and I'm more than a little in need of a shower, so I juggle the phone in one hand and pick up my bag in the other, headed out of the barn as city noise speaks tinny and clear behind Beck's voice.

"It's spring break, Juls," he announces. "Where are you?"

"Where do you think?" I laugh, gulping down a breath of chilled air when I hit the parking lot.

"You know, guessing isn't even a challenge anymore," he says. "The more important question is where do you want to go?"

"Is this when you tell me we're shipping Lighter back to Florida?" I ask. "Because we haven't even started working him on the track yet."

He groans. "No. Get your mind out of the track, Juls. I'm talking about coming into the city for the night."

"For the night, huh?" I ask, my stomach doing a little flip. I haven't been back to the city since the last time. The sleepover, during which clothing was optional. I shiver at the thought, my keys falling out of my hand and landing in the slush by my car's tires.

A curse slips out of me and Beck chuckles.

"Is that a good or a bad response?"

"I'll be there," I say, swiping my keys out of the slush and shaking them off. Then I pause, realizing the city noise definitely isn't his brownstone. I'm going to need to take a shower first. "Where am I going?"

He laughs and says, "You've got one guess."

～

The Library is a swath of damp, wool-coated bodies when I get there. It smells like sheep, warm beer, and the salty muck people have tracked in from the street. I wind through the crowd until I catch sight of the booth in the back, where Beck sits like a king in front of a plethora of half-full glasses and an empty pitcher of beer.

I pause in the middle of the crowd, watching for a moment before he can see me, struck for a second at this image of City Beck, the person he is all the time when I'm not around to see it. He looks so easy and happy, grinning at something further off in the bar. One arm rests on the booth's back, draped there carelessly. His hair is tousled and a bit wild. I want to rub my fingers into it, and the sheer need startles me into taking one step forward before I stutter to a stop.

Next to him, Elyse sips at her glass of bourbon. Her long blond hair cascades over the bare skin of her cold-shoulder sweater, makeup on ridiculous point, all of her tucked beside Beck like she likes the shelter and doesn't care about it at the same time. There's a certain knowing and not caring about where she is and how she got there that makes a part of my stomach twist. She looks so sure of herself; satisfied in a way I don't think I ever am.

All around them, their friends are doubled over laughing, locked in an uproarious fit as Sebastian slinks back from the bar and picks up his beer.

"Is that second strike or third?" Elyse asks, her voice cutting across the boys' laughter. Sebastian rolls his eyes at her.

"If you'd just succumb to my natural charm, Lyse, we wouldn't have to keep count anymore," he says, and then winks.

Elyse doesn't miss a beat, looking up at him with eager glee in her eyes. "But then how would we have any fun?"

"She's got a great point," Beck agrees, and Elyse smiles, resting against the booth back. His fingers just graze her shoulder, bare from the cutouts, and all of me wants to scream forward, shove my way out of the crowd and stake my claim.

Which is exactly when Elyse's eyes lock with mine.

She smiles one of those brilliant, white-teeth smiles and smacks Beck's chest with the back of her hand, pointing me out in the crowd like I'm a little lost sheep in a strange flock. Beck shifts, eyes finding me, and unfolds out of the bench seat, coming to me when my feet seem to have rooted themselves to the sticky floor.

"You made it," he says, cupping my jaw in his hands and kissing me hello.

"Finally!" Elyse shouts over the chorus of boy shouts, grinning at us as Beck leads me to the table. She scoots over, patting the bench seat next to her. "Sit with me, Juls. Girls stick together in this crowd."

I'm not sure if that's necessarily the case, since Elyse looks right at home here by herself. The bitter spot in my stomach doesn't slide away when I look at her, feeling like something is off. Some part about her easy smile, her eagerness to pull me into the group, laughing up at Beck like isn't she just wonderful, including me like she is?

But then maybe I'm imagining things. I *like* Elyse. I said so, didn't I? And it's just so predicable to be unnecessarily jealous, because that's exactly what this feeling is—unnecessary.

I slide into the booth. Devon waggles his eyebrows at me and Elyse picks up the empty pitcher, handing it him.

"It's your turn," she says as he groans, getting up and disappearing into the crowd for another round.

"Elyse keeps track of who's paying," Beck explains to me.

"Without her, we'd be lost," Lucas says from his corner of the booth, flat cap pushed up on his forehead.

"Or possibly richer," Jasper points out. "I'm pretty sure she chooses who pays based on spite and vindictiveness."

"It's a complicated system," Elyse says, tipping her nose up. Then she leans over to me and whispers, "Actually, it's not unlike a form of training. One of them is invariably a jerk, and therefore they pay for everyone else's beer. I'm trying to better society one pitcher at a time."

"Does it work?" I ask.

Sebastian falls into the booth across from me, sighing dramatically. "Unfortunately, no," he says as Jasper stifles a laugh. "My averages aren't improving."

"Speak for yourself," Jasper says. "I haven't paid in three weeks."

"Four days," Lucas offers.

Beck looks at the ceiling when I glance over at him, as though silently counting. "One hour and twenty-six minutes," he says finally.

"Some are more resistant than others," Elyse allows.

"And how did you acquire this power?" I ask her, even though I know. Just from looking at her, of course I know. Sebastian said it himself—*if you'd just succumb.*

It was a joke, but underneath the words you can feel the truth sitting there. All of them must feel it. They're simply waiting for her to choose, and until then they're playing a game.

Lucas laughs, pushing his flat cap down over his eyes. "That's like asking how the sausage is made, July."

"Probably best not to ask questions," Beck nods sagely as Devon comes back with the beer, depositing a glass in front of me to Elyse's smirking approval. Beck fills it up until I motion him to stop somewhere near the middle. There's riding tomorrow, as usual.

"How are the ribs?" Beck asks as I wince trying to shove my coat off my shoulders. He pulls it the rest of the way, piling it in his lap as I cup the cold glass in front of me.

"Better," I lie. They're the same, the dull ache sharpening into a stab when I take a deep breath or try to twist in ways my body isn't ready for yet.

"Think you want to take a break from the track tomorrow?" he asks, seeing right through me.

"Nope," I grin up at him. "Lighter's back on the work tab in the morning, so you're not getting a break either."

"Lighter's working?" Elyse asks, leaning forward. "I'd love to see him again. It's been since Saratoga."

"If you can get up in time, you're welcome to brave the elements with us," Beck says before I can warn that Barn 27 is a working stable, not a tourist attraction.

But Elyse is an owner's daughter—she knows exactly what happens at Barn 27. She's probably pulled herself out of bed for the best of her father's horses, slipped through a shedrow at the crack of dawn with a coffee cup in her hand, watching the activity like a silent overseer when she's not asking pointed questions. It's the owner way.

"Wait, what time are we talking about here?" Devon asks suspiciously, breaking through my thoughts.

"Give yourself an hour to get there from the city," I reason with a shrug. "You'd have to be up and ready to go by four."

Every boy at the table falls against the backs of the booth seats, undone by the prospect of waking early.

Beck snorts. "Weaklings," he accuses.

Elyse swallows a sip of her drink, blasé as ever. She puts the drink down on the table decidedly and nods, letting a little smile slip across her face. "I'm in."

Chapter Thirteen

I magine, if you will, showing up for work before sunup in manure-stained boots and dressed like you're planning a day of cross country skiing. Now imagine you've brought a super model with you and she's decked out in cashmere gloves and a wool pea coat, complete with butter-soft leather boots rising over her knees.

Elyse beams at the grooms and riders as we slip down the shed-row, her hair bouncing on her shoulders and her knit cap fashionably jaunty, as though pinned into place to look like it's almost falling off her head. I'm not ready to admit that Elyse's glow this early in the morning irritates me, but I'm quickly verging on it.

I don't know why, exactly.

Which I am pretty sure is a lie. I'm not ready to admit that either. Maybe I just want to see that she's capable of being disheveled, imperfect. *Human.* But no. She glows, and she looks so happy that being annoyed about it feels like not liking a puppy. How can you not like a puppy?

At least Beck is on my level—yesterday's jeans and yesterday's shower. He looks a little bewildered as to how he even got to the track, and makes the coffee maker his direct target when we file into the office.

Martina raises an eyebrow at me as I study the day's assignments on the whiteboard. Elyse and Beck help themselves to coffee, oblivious to Martina's silent judgment. I have to hand it to my sister—she knows when to keep her mouth shut. Or she already knows who Elyse is. Since part of her job is sweet-talking owners, my hunch is she's in the know.

I stay quiet, and Martina keeps eyeing the side of my face as I memorize my morning as dictated by the whiteboard. My name is next to Maggie's. Pilar's is next to Lighter's. I scan the board for Mom's name, but it's absent.

"Mom isn't feeling better?" I ask and Martina shrugs.

"Not as of this morning," she says. "Dad told her to stay home. Pilar has her rides."

Good news for Pilar, I think, downing a huge sip of bitter coffee.

"I'm going to tack up," I announce, mainly for Beck's sake, and walk back into the chill to the tack room, scooping up Maggie's giant saddle and hefting it to her stall. My mare pricks her ears at me, her white-splotched body shifting out of the darkness as she moves closer to the stall door.

She's spotless, thank god. I have no idea how she does it, but Maggie's fastidious nature makes it easy in the mornings. I can literally show up, pick out her hooves, flick off a few errant bits of bedding, slap on her tack, and go. Maggie chews the bit thoughtfully as I jump into her saddle and walk her out of her stall, directing her down the shedrow and up to Lighter.

The white spot in the middle of the colt's forehead reflects the yellow light from the barn. Gus stands next to him, keeping him busy. The colt strikes a hoof against the ground, arching his neck and trying to grab the lead line in his teeth just as Gus swipes it away.

Next to him, Pilar stands quietly, her helmet already buckled and her dark curls pulled back into a braid down her back. Beck and Elyse stand with them, Elyse tentatively offering her palm out to Lighter, who looks at it like she's wasting his time. He bobs his head and snorts, sidestepping away from her.

"He's not the most polite," I say as Elyse wipes her hand on her coat and shimmies her fingers back into her glove.

"I remember," she says, looking up at the colt with a little awe shining in her eyes.

Lighter busily chews his bit, rolling his eyes at Pilar as Beck gives her a leg up. I turn Maggie and she sidles up beside the colt, getting me close enough to put him on the end of my line. Pilar collects the reins and nods affirmatively to my silent question, and we're off.

"Who's the girl?" Pilar asks, hazarding a glance over her shoulder. Beck and Elyse walk behind us, too far back now to hear anything we say. Elyse's step is jaunty, her hands gesticulating mid-conversation as Beck looks at her with his classic charmed bemusement.

"Elyse . . ." I start, fading off when I can't remember her last name. I shrug, shaking my head. "She visited during Saratoga."

Pilar nods slowly. "Right," she says. "The girl with the sunglasses."

I smile at her as we walk through the gap on the training track, Lighter's entire body tightening next to me. I clench the line a little harder, even though I'm going to have to let go soon. It's instinct with Lighter—cause and effect. Out of the corner of my eye, I catch Elyse and Beck joining Dad and Leo at the trainer's stand. Leo does a double take when he sees Elyse, his back straightening as he lifts himself off the railing he's been leaning on to watch the first set.

First impressions are everything, Leo, I think wryly, just before Lighter jerks on my arm, turning his head in toward Maggie and shoving it over her withers. It might as well be a brusque shove to remind me where my mind should be—on him, thank you very much.

Touché, Lighter.

"You ready?" I ask Pilar, who nods.

"Let's let him loose," she says. I release her, the line going slack in my hand.

Lighter jumps into a prancing trot, pale tail rising like a startled deer in mid-leap. I heel Maggie forward to keep pace, shifting her into a rocking canter going the wrong way down the training track's homestretch. Lighter flicks his ears back, cocks them to the side, snorts huge, misty breaths into the morning air, and trots over the tilled dirt in big, effortless strides. Maggie has to stretch to keep up, her ears tipped back cautiously, always on alert. You never know when Lighter might attempt a bolt, drop his shoulder and spin, or just generally be a pain in the ass.

Maggie has her war stories, that's for sure.

Lighter leaps into a stride of canter, but Pilar draws him back to a jog. She tips her face into the bitter breeze, her entire mouth covered in a knit balaclava and her eyes hidden in goggles to avoid tearing. I think she's probably smiling underneath all of her layers, her eyes crinkling up at the challenge of Lighter pushing for more.

He leaps again and shakes his head at Pilar's hold on the reins, gaping his mouth against the pressure to keep him at a jog.

"How's he feeling?" I ask, eyeing him from my position on Maggie's back. The colt looks good—sound as ever, willingly moving forward, like the Lighter of old before he went and threw in a clunker of a race. Sometimes it's hard to see the little problems brewing under the skin of horses. Sometimes you have to feel them to know.

Pilar doesn't look at me. She stares straight between the colt's ears. "Seems full of go," she says as we round the last turn, completing our required lap. Lighter throws in another attempt at something faster, and Pilar draws him back down. He settles in hand, mouths the bit, keeps jogging into the homestretch until Pilar sits back in the saddle, asking him to walk.

Which, shockingly, he does. I slip the line back onto his bridle, leading him toward the gap with a feeling of cautious optimism rising in my chest.

"No one died," I say quietly, and Pilar looks at me and laughs through her balaclava.

"No one died," she agrees. "Did you think someone might?"

"Admittedly?" I shrug. "After the Fountain of Youth I wasn't sure what to expect. I really didn't think he'd be professional this morning."

"He did a lot of growing in Florida," Pilar says, stroking the crest of his neck and combing her fingers through his mane. "We all expected more from the Fountain of Youth, but I think he's just starting to come into himself, you know?"

"And plenty of other horses are, too," I say, thinking of Feather and the three horses who finished ahead of Lighter. Horses do so much maturing in these months that it's usually impossible to find the stand out of the crop.

Then there's the stress. So many races, so many expectations. Even if a horse is fit, the stress can send everything into a spiral. Horses are like sponges. They know more than they let on, and they know what we want from them, especially at this time of year. They just don't know why.

Run in the Kentucky Derby. Win the Kentucky Derby. Win the *Triple Crown.*

Most horses are just here because they like feeling the wind in their face. The really good ones go a step further—they like leaving the safety of the pack, shoving their nose in front. They have the same competitive spirit as the people training them, somehow. It never really makes sense to me, that a prey animal would override all their instincts and sprint to the lead because it simply feels good to get to the finish first.

Lighter is one of those horses, but I still can't explain the Fountain of Youth. Pilar's explanation is the best that fits so far. He's just coming into his own, and sometimes that means new kinks to iron out along the way.

If only we could find them.

~~

"Are you sure you can't go to Dubai?" Elyse asks on our way back to the barn, tilting her head up and batting her eyelashes at Beck, like if only he would say yes, he's going to Dubai, then he'll offer to bring Elyse, too.

Fat chance, I think. Beck laughs, taking Elyse's wheedling far better than I am.

"Tell you what, Lyse," he says. "If you can get me out of three group projects and a fifteen-page paper, then sure. I'll go to Dubai."

She grins. "You're underestimating my serious powers of persuasion."

I tighten my grip on the lead line, Lighter bouncing at my side and shoving into Maggie with each stride. I can't see Pilar's eyes, but I have a feeling she's cutting them over to me. Besides us, Jorge walks alone on a rangy chestnut from another stable, a bright mark of movement in the corner of my eye.

"I'll take you," Jorge calls over to Elyse. "Just say the word."

Elyse's pink cheeks flame deeper into red, and she ducks her chin into her plaid scarf.

"Oh, come on," Jorge laughs, ratcheting up the track talk. "You want to go, don't you?"

"It's not that I don't want to go . . ." Elyse starts, getting cut off by Jorge's dramatic sigh.

"Here I thought you wanted the trip of a lifetime, and now you're changing your mind?" He laughs, pulling his goggles down around his neck and sending a smirk my way. I shake my head at him, which makes him grin wider. "That's fine, girlie. You can't break my heart. I've got plenty of horses who've been there before you."

Elyse stares at him, open-mouthed, and he laughs riotously as he walks the chestnut past Barn 27, turning the corner between barns and disappearing altogether.

"Don't mind him," I advise her, reining in Maggie outside the barn as Lighter and Pilar slip inside to keep cooling out around the row. "He's only playing around. It's just how it is around here."

Elyse nods firmly. "I know," she says. "I just wasn't expecting someone listening in."

Then she really doesn't know Jorge. Or the track, for that matter. We're all loud and in each other's business here. Privacy isn't exactly an expectation when anyone could walk their horse right into your office. I'm surprised she wouldn't know this.

But Elyse is an owner's daughter, I remind myself. I only have to look at her and see Beck's sister, Olivia, all grown up with cool edges and a sharp smile. No matter how often she's been to the track, she's always been given special treatment. I know because I've been on the other end, offering that treatment.

I suppose the surprising thing is Jorge said anything to her at all. Even Leo's kept his mouth shut . . . so far.

"Maybe it's for the best you're missing Dubai," Beck tells her. "It'll give Jorge some time to get over you."

Elyse eyes him, the corner of her mouth quirking.

"Besides," Beck continues. "You've got a horse running at Aqueduct this weekend. Maybe it's not as glamorous, but there's something about the gritty realism of it that's enticing, right?"

She laughs, bumping her shoulder against his.

"I suppose I'll settle," she says, then looks at the barn expectantly. "Is that it for the morning?"

I stay quiet, waiting on Pilar to come back out on Kickabit. We've got races to prepare for this weekend, and Kickabit needs her final breeze. I'm so far from the end of my morning that entertaining the thought isn't worth it.

"Lighter's finished," Beck tells her. "Have somewhere you gotta be?"

"Unfortunately," she says, sighing and pulling out her phone, which is littered with text messages. "Dad wants to do breakfast. I need to get back to the city."

"I can drive you," Beck offers without missing a beat.

Maggie shifts underneath me, reacting to the stiffness zipping up my back, settling in my shoulders and radiating down into my mare like a lightning bolt going to ground. She takes a half-step to the side, tossing her head and sending froth into the air. Some of it splatters across the pristine arm of Elyse's coat. She laughs and pats

Maggie's neck.

"Didn't think I'd get out of here without a little horse slobber," she says, grinning up at me. "Are you staying?"

"Have to," I reply, shrugging, although I wonder what would happen if I simply hopped off of Maggie and walked away. The thought has never occurred to me, not even when I wasn't on the payroll.

I simply exist in this saddle, every inch of me knowing it and the mare underneath it like they're a part of me. Walking away, being done with the day before the day is done with me . . . is that even a thing I'd be capable of?

Beck squeezes my knee as Elyse heads back to his car.

"I'll talk to you later?" he asks, and it actually sounds like a question instead of an assumption. I nod, still feeling a little dazed by the possibilities I'm not taking because the track is at my back and Maggie breathes against my legs, her mouth soft against my gloved fingers.

Beck pats my shin and shoves his hands back into his pockets, walking toward the car. Elyse is already in the passenger seat, waving at me. I wave back, feeling ridiculous as Pilar walks Kickabit out of the shedrow.

"They're leaving already?" she asks, surprised.

"Breakfast needs to be had," I explain, and she snorts.

"You mean, like, with utensils and ordered from a menu?" Pilar smiles wanly. "I think I remember doing that once."

"You mean you don't count the track kitchen?" I ask, turning Maggie and catching Kickabit's bridle, escorting them from the barn. "They have a menu and utensils."

"July," Pilar says seriously, "the last time I ate there I was sick for three days. It was perfect to make weight, but otherwise something I'm not repeating. In any case," she glances at the Mustang as its engine fires up, loud and throaty, "Beck is taking her?"

"It's how she got here," I say, shrugging a shoulder. Pilar narrows her eyes at me. Every little hair on the back of my neck prickles with a sudden onset of instinct I don't care to name.

Jealousy. Suspicion. A certain, primal knowing.

I *hate* it.

"They're friends," I state, and Pilar shrugs.

"Obviously," she says. "So long as that's all they are."

"Beck isn't like that," I say, which is so true I can feel it wrapping around my bones. They feel secure and warm, those words. Like they're the truest words I've ever said.

"But you don't know what she's like," Pilar says, running her fingers through Kickabit's mane absently. "You don't really know people until they chose to show you who they are. That girl . . ." she pauses, glancing over her shoulder at the Mustang as it pulls out of the backside, rumbling through the gate and out into traffic before it's gone in a plume of exhaust. She shakes her head. "You don't know that girl. I can tell."

"Maybe not," I admit, wondering if I'm that transparent. God, I hope I'm not. "But I know Beck."

Pilar nods smartly as we approach the track. "I think it's safe to say we all know Beck. And I know *you*. I don't want you to suffer in silence. You're astonishingly good at that. Talk to me, will you? I'm here."

I smile over at her. "It's appreciated, Pilar. I mean it. But everything is good. Beck is good. Elyse is a friend and she just wanted to see Lighter."

She nods, then stills, looking past me. I turn, finding Dad waving us to stop as he trots down the steps of the trainer's stand, his cell phone at his ear.

"No," he says, voice clipped, in trainer mode. "I'm not letting you do that, Celia."

Pilar stiffens, sending a questioning look my way. I shrug, because I don't know anything more than she does.

"It will be fine," Dad says into the phone. "I've got Pilar here. I'll get her up to speed. You focus on getting better."

We both still so completely we could be statues waiting for the news to drop. Dad shoves his phone in his back pocket and looks up at us before he pins a look on Pilar, who tips her chin up, ready and waiting for the next words to come out of his mouth.

"Are you ready to ride this weekend?" he asks her, and Pilar nods smartly.

"Of course," she says, like she anticipated this.

"Good," he says, and points at Kickabit. "You're on her this Saturday. And Zaatar. Meet me in the office after workouts. We have strategy to discuss."

Before Pilar can say another word, he turns around and heads back to the trainer's stand, leaving us to do the work. I glance back at Pilar, not sure what to expect. It's been months since she's ridden in a race—since Kali left her in the dirt at Saratoga with a broken arm and her bug in question. I half expect to be met with her stoic resolve, like she is before a race with Mom's prayer on her lips, hoping for a safe route home.

But when I meet her eyes I only find bright, ecstatic glee.

Pilar nudges Kickabit closer to Maggie and throws an arm around my shoulders, squealing with happiness. I laugh, even as Maggie snorts and Kickabit tosses her head up, annoyed by the weight shift on her back.

"We did it, Juls!" she whispers excitedly.

"I think we should personally thank Mom's flu," I say, laughing as she settles back into the center of Kickabit's back and pulls her goggles over her eyes.

"Don't think I won't," she laughs, her smile flashing at me as we hit the track, rising in the saddle and waving at me as she dashes off, Kickabit's tail snapping in the stiff breeze behind her.

Chapter Fourteen

Saturday is bitter cold. I swear I can see ice crystals hanging in the air on the way to Aqueduct, like little glints of diamonds hung suspended from nothing. It would be beautiful if not for the way the air burns my lungs.

The Tom Fool Handicap will run later this afternoon, but not with us. So I've neglected to bring anything fancy to wear in the paddock during the allowance and the optional claiming race we've entered our horses in around the big stakes. I figure people can deal with my jeans and my insulated boots. This is a long underwear sort of day.

Hopping out of the truck, I help Gus unload our fillies. Both walk off the trailer and huff giant billows of steam into the air at the sight of Aqueduct shrouded in its icy air and storm-cloud skies.

"It better not snow," Pilar says, glaring up at the sky as she leads Zaatar into the receiving barn. I follow with Kickabit, the filly feeling the cold and yanking on my arm. It pulls at my bruise, and I grimace, covering it up before Dad can see it. Luckily, he's too busy to notice. Race days take priority, then family.

Sometimes I can take advantage of that little nugget of truth.

I put a hand on Kickabit's warm neck, steer her into her stall, and tie her, letting her eye her surroundings as I get the wraps off her legs. It's just as I'm straightening, wraps bundled up in my arms, when my cell phone trills from my back pocket.

We're over in barn 10. Where are you?

Beck's text glows from my gloved hands.

Receiving barn, I type back. Along with a *?* for good measure, because I wasn't aware he was showing up this afternoon. Star is safely ensconced in Palm Meadows, preparing for Dubai with some balmy Florida weather, and Lighter is standing under his heat lamp at Belmont—both horses he could possibly care about warm and happy in their stalls.

Also, who is *we?*

I stand in Kickabit's stall for a befuddled moment, the filly crowding up to me and resting her chin on my head, nuzzling the pompom popping off the crown of my knit hat. My phone doesn't chime again, so I guess that means I have to be proactive about this.

Kickabit tugs at my hat, and I duck out of her reach just as she opens her mouth, big horse teeth aiming for the pompom.

"I don't think so," I warn her, slipping out of her stall as she snorts and shakes her mane out, doing another restless turn over her bedding. She knows what's coming. Her race is four hours away, which means she'll have to be content in her stall without food as a distraction until we take her to the paddock. "Be good," I add, to which she gives me an eyeful, as though appalled at the thought.

Rewrapping my scarf around my neck, I set off across the backside. It doesn't take long to walk two barns; Aqueduct is tiny in comparison to Belmont. It's a simple stretch of eleven scrubby shedrows lined up side by side, with two receiving barns at the end.

Barn ten is next to the test barn, and full of horses munching on afternoon hay. I can tell those who are racing soon—they stand bored and ears cocked backward at the entrance of their stalls, or pace in circles.

Halfway down the row, standing outside the stall of another horse prepped for race day, are Beck and Elyse.

As much as I hate it, my step falters when I remember: *Aqueduct this weekend.*

Elyse has a horse running. I didn't expect Beck to be here, too. They're both hunched in wool coats, too dressed up for Aqueduct in winter. Beck put forth the kind of effort he only musters for Lighter on race days, right down to the leather shoes. Elyse bounces on her toes, which are encased in riding boots that wouldn't survive a barn. The rest of her is in tights and a dress, her gold-blond hair ironed into artfully disheveled curls and pinned away from her face.

There's a clod of manure stuck to the side of my paddock boots, and I'm not sure how well my hat has stood up from Kickabit's mauling. I try not to feel like the track worker I obviously am when I muster up the ability to wave at them.

Elyse smiles and waves back, still bouncing on her toes. Beck pulls me up to him, kissing the side of my forehead. My stomach settles, just a little, as I look in on a stocky bay colt with a startlingly wide white blaze cascading down his face.

"Who's this?" I ask.

"Golden Age," Elyse announces. "He's my dad's. Or, I guess I should say he's the partnership's."

I eye their clothes again. "Let me guess: the Tom Fool?"

She laughs. "We're pretty obvious, huh?"

"Just a little."

"Her dad's a stickler for appearances," Beck says, and I can't help wrinkling my nose.

"Good thing we don't work for him." I wave my hands at myself. "I didn't even bring a change of clothes."

"Well, I'm jealous," Elyse announces, "because this coat seriously isn't cutting it. Who wants to head over to the grandstand a little early?"

"I'm game," Beck says. "I might even win a hand of blackjack this time. You coming, Juls?"

I check my phone and shake my head. "Receiving barn for me."

"Then I'm sure we'll see you in the stands," Elyse says, leaning forward to give an inquisitive Golden Age a kiss on the nose, smearing pink lip gloss across his white blaze. She sighs, and attempts to clean it off. When she's managed to make it a less obvious shimmering blot, she steps back and shakes her head. "Well, maybe it's for the best," she laughs. "A good luck charm."

"You would think that," Beck shakes his head at her and smiles, like this is the kind of thing he's used to seeing all the time from her in the city when they're alone. "Kinda like when you spilled bleach all over me last week and destroyed my favorite shirt."

"That shirt is horrible," Elyse sniffs. "It deserved to be destroyed."

Beck motions at her like he's heard it all before. I raise an eyebrow at all of this, the banter sinking into me in awkward waves. Elyse turns her attention to me, as if for backup.

"You know the one, Juls," she says. "The piñata shirt? It was falling apart. And the message was dumb."

I stare at her like she's speaking a foreign language, and then realize what I'm doing. So I nod. "Surely it deserved to be destroyed."

"Hey," Beck defends. "It's been with me the longest. It had a place of honor in my dresser."

Elyse shakes her head and lets out a long-suffering breath, then squeezes my forearm through my puffy barn coat as she says, "I'll see you in the grandstand. Good luck!"

"Same to you," I say, my throat feeling scratchy all of a sudden. Beck kisses me lightly on the lips, both of us cold and numb. I can hardly feel it.

"I'll come find you," he promises, which might be the closest he's come to reading my mind before I watch them walk down the row, suddenly struck by how similar they are. Owners' kids, all shiny leather and boiled wool coats, laughing about blackjack and who knows what else.

It's hard not to feel a little pang in my chest as I'm left behind for whatever fun they're going to get into before their race, but then I'd been the one to beg off, hadn't I? I'm not at Aqueduct to play the slots and bet the ponies. I'm here to work.

So there's nothing to feel jealous of, really. Nothing concrete to point at and say *this is a problem,* even if the two of them look like a perfectly matched pair.

Golden Age shuffles closer to the stall webbing, stretching his neck out to push my arm with his lip-glossed nose. I shake my head at him and grab his halter, pulling the rag out of my coat pocket I keep around for such problems.

"There," I say after I've scrubbed the pink off his coat. "Good as new."

～

Zaatar runs third in her allowance. Pilar wipes the cold dirt off her face and smiles through it, hands her saddle off to her valet, and pulls at her dirty goggles on her way back to the jockey's room.

I haven't seen Beck and Elyse since I arrived at the paddock. Possibly it's too cold out here for them. Maybe they're busy enjoying the warmth in the owner's booth behind the glassed-in grandstand's façade. The Tom Fool is next, and I don't have time to stick around for it given Kickabit's need to be paddock-bound and Zaatar's need to go back to the receiving barn at the same time.

"Calm down, girl," I tell Zaatar as she jerks her head up, eyeing a seagull swooping over the track to land in the infield. "Seagulls won't kill you."

She huffs animatedly, thrashing her tail around her muddy legs to indicate that she is a *Thoroughbred,* thank you very much, and will freak out at anything because that's her God-given right. I tug on her lead and she lowers her head, the seagull past us now and the threat removed so she can finally let on how tired she is.

By the time I get Zaatar clean, cool, and back in her stall, the Tom Fool goes off without me. Gus watches it on his phone as I come up behind him in the receiving barn, looking over his huge bicep like Kickabit, who stands in a trance with her chin on Gus's shoulder.

The horses sprint full speed around the turn in the six-furlong race, all of them battling for some piece of the front and only a handful making it. I skim through the field, finding Bluegrass's bright yellow silks caught in the middle of the pack, Golden Age leaping out from behind horses into the center of the track and finally starting a run when it's far too late.

A compact chestnut crosses the wire first, a flurry of horses at his heels, and Golden Age in fifth behind a wall of dirt kicking into his face.

"Slow time," Gus comments, pushing his phone into his jeans.

"It hasn't been the same race since it was downgraded."

"They never are," I say, looking up at Kickabit. "Is she ready?"

"Got the all clear," Gus announces, ducking from underneath the filly's chin. Kickabit blinks sleepily and yawns. "She's good to go."

I eye the dozing filly, amazed at the turnaround. Not four hours ago she was pacing her stall. Of course, she perks right up the second she enters the paddock, putting on a show for the sparse audience braving the cold to look into our below-grade saddling area. The paddock is warmer than the track and warmer than at the viewing rail, which are both exposed to the winter wind.

When Pilar shows up, she's bundled as far as she can get without going over weight. Dad tosses her up onto Kickabit and says, "Take her to the front. Don't let go of the lead. Watch for the five horse— she'll come on late."

Pilar nods robotically. "Got it, boss."

And that's it. Gus and I hang out by the rail like two small mammals huddling to keep warm as we wait for the race to run. When I feel hands on my waist, I jump.

"Whoa." Beck lets me go when I whirl around, the chain link fence at my back as Elyse and Beck laugh. "Hey, didn't mean to scare you."

"You sure about that?" I ask. Beck pulls my scarf back around my neck from where it fell during my flailing, and I immediately feel bad. Only Elyse is still hiding her smile behind her hand, and this feels weird.

It feels like Saratoga all over again, when I was the girl with the horses and he was the boy with the well-dressed friends floating through a cloud of owners and their hanger-ons, champagne only a moment's notice away.

I don't like that feeling.

"Sorry," he says quietly into my ear as I turn around, not wanting to look at Elyse. All I can see now is Sunglasses Girl, and I deeply dislike myself for it.

"It's okay," I say under my breath. "I just didn't expect you."

"I said I'd find you, so I did," he says over the noise of the bell clanging and the gates opening up. Horses leap onto the track. "Besides, it's better than listening to Elyse's dad yell at his trainer over the phone."

I wince, my eyes on the horses, finding Kickabit as she thunders past us into the first turn. "Sounds like it's been a fun day at the track."

He shrugs. "Let's just hope Kickabit makes it worth it."

The horses trail into the backstretch, gone from view. I have to watch the giant screen attached to the toteboard to see where Kickabit is in the crowd, which turns out to be easy because Pilar found the lead. The filly bounces along in front of the track like a rubber ball, happily galloping away like there aren't racehorses on her tail.

They curl into the far turn and I lean over the fence, watching as she bursts onto the straightaway first.

They hit the quarter pole—still first.

The eighth pole—first.

Horses strain to catch her, but none are coming close. I start to rock on my toes, excitement zipping through me as our filly keeps going. Pilar keeps at her, crop uselessly flicking over the filly's neck because what use does she need for a crop when no one can touch her?

Kickabit wins it by five!

The announcer isn't as excited as we are. We are a screaming wreck of happiness, dancing around with our hands in the air as Pilar stands in the stirrups and slows Kickabit in the turn. The cold is forgotten for a few delicious minutes as we sit on the high of a win, even one as little and slight as an optional claiming race at icy Aqueduct.

I lean over the fence as Kickabit comes trotting back down the track, Pilar all smiles in her saddle. I yell out to her, "How does it feel to be back?"

She laughs, giving me a thumbs up on her way toward the winner's circle in the paddock. When I turn to follow her, I notice Elyse hanging back, watching thoughtfully.

Then she takes out her phone and begins to tap out a text.

"Hey, you coming?" Beck calls out to her as she hits the send button, the phone making a little *whoosh* noise. Then she pockets it and looks up, all smiles.

"Let's go."

Chapter Fifteen

When I walk the unnamed chestnut off the track the next morning, I have to pull my balaclava down so I can breathe without sweltering.

"What is this?" I ask Pilar, who walks her unnamed gray filly next to me, focused on the filly and obviously not the weather. "Is this . . . spring?"

She barks out a laugh. "It's can't be spring already. Besides, I'm riding Lighter next. I might need the extra padding from all these layers."

"Good luck," I say as we enter the stable yard. "I don't think a few extra layers is enough to cushion anyone from Lighter."

"One can hope," she says, and tilts her head when a shiny BMW slides up to the side of Barn 27. The vanity plates read SUPER T, after the antioxidant tea that funds half the barn, which means it can be only one person.

Khalid Sahadi unfolds out of the front seat of the car, beard and hair so perfectly groomed I am not convinced they are real. He walks toward the barn with more confidence than a person wearing cashmere around horses should, and waves at us when we catch his eye, his whole face lighting up.

"Wish me luck, July!" he calls to me, and I can only nod before he's gone into Dad's office, shutting the door behind him.

"Well that's not suspicious at all," Pilar says as we walk the horses down the aisle, past Lighter's stall, where the blond colt is tethered to the wall and shifting back and forth, eyeing Gus's attempts to get a saddle on his back and crow hopping whenever he gets too close.

I hear a Spanish curse as we pass.

Turning the corner and walking down the other side of the shed-row, we do our cooling down circuit before hopping off and handing the two-year-olds to their grooms. We collect our saddles from the horses' backs and duck toward the next set's stalls. Lighter for Pilar, and one of Khalid's colts for me—a ruddy gray called Sinjab.

The colt greets me with enthusiasm, thrusting his muzzle in my hand for the peppermint I offer him and shoving his face into the bridle. When I'm mounted up, he drags me out of the stall, my feet barely in the stirrups and his energy already at jig-of-sheer-happiness level as we nearly run over Beck on our way into the yard.

"Whoa," he dances out of the way. Sinjab skitters underneath me, shaking his head up and down as I tug him into a trembling halt while we wait on Pilar and Lighter. I peer back into the shedrow, finding Beck leaning against the side of the opening. "Didn't expect to get knocked out by some other horse. I thought that was Lighter's domain."

"Give it time," I tell him. "Lighter's coming out next, so if you really want to check mauling-by-horse off your bucket list he'll be available shortly."

He grins at me, just before he's distracted by the office door opening. Dad and Khalid walk into the open air, nodding like some great deal has been struck and shaking hands. Khalid only seems to notice they have an audience when Lighter screams from inside the barn and Sinjab lifts his head to whinny back.

"See you in Kentucky!" Khalid calls to me on his way to his car, all dazzling white smile before he sinks into the confines of tinted glass. I raise an eyebrow, mirroring Beck almost perfectly.

Before I can pin Dad down with a question, Martina and Maggie lead a jaunting Lighter into the yard, Pilar sitting the rocking and bouncing like a rodeo queen. Maggie flicks her ears back, rock-like and sure next to her charge's wild antics. Martina has a death grip on the lead. "Are we sure we don't want to breeze him?" she asks, throwing a look at Dad over her shoulder.

"Not yet," he says, shaking his head. "Two-minute lick. Get him well warmed up beforehand, Pilar. He's been stiff this morning."

Pilar nods, eager to jump to it. I swing Sinjab around, just in time to catch Dad clap a hand onto Beck's shoulder and steer him toward the training track, walking after us and just out of earshot. Sinjab humps mid-stride, bucking just enough to bounce me forward in the saddle. I stick to him, heel him forward into a rollicking canter through our warm-up before shifting him into a slow gallop.

Martina peels off, heading to the outside rail to wait for us as we churn down the track just off the inside rail. Lighter gallops with his mouth gaping, straining for more room from Pilar, who holds him back with her feet stuck hard in the irons, using her entire body to keep him from going blitzkrieg on Sinjab and blowing into an unscheduled breeze.

My colt doesn't seem to care about his partner's attitude. He puts his head down and goes, galloping into the backstretch and minding his own business. Lighter yanks at the reins next to me, leaping ahead of us in two giant strides before Pilar can get him back into line, grunting with the effort.

"Are you . . ." I start, calling across to her just before Lighter leaps into the air and comes down with a thud, throwing his head down in effort to tear Pilar out of the saddle. Her body flies onto his neck, but she's ready for it, grabbing his mane and sticking. There's only a breath of time before we hit the homestretch and Lighter decides to leap like a stag all the way down to the finish line.

I keep Sinjab well away from him, letting Pilar have her argument with the colt. We pass the gap in the outside rail, where Dad and Beck watch us with baffled expressions. Beck looks a little awed. But at least Pilar stayed on, I think, letting out a breath when Martina grabs the colt and Maggie brings him to a staccato trot.

"Jesus," Martina gasps, straining to keep Lighter at Maggie's side. "What got into him?"

"Think he's just full of himself," Pilar says tiredly.

"If he was this full of himself in Florida he would have won the Fountain of Youth," Martina points out, just as she manages to haul Lighter into a jigging walk. The colt throws his head over Maggie's withers and crowds close, bright mane flying up along his copper neck and getting into his wild eyes. Martina makes a face down at him. I pat Sinjab on the neck on our way off the track just because he didn't pull my arms out of my sockets.

"Good boy," I croon to him as Maggie and Lighter speedwalk back to Barn 27, everything happening on Lighter's busy schedule of pushing everyone around. I let Sinjab go at his own pace, which is decidedly slower now that he's had his two-minute lick around the training track.

A mile in two minutes is a maintenance move, but it's an important one. It's like training for a marathon—running just long enough, just fast enough to keep your stamina. Then, when the strength is there, you pull out the stops and work on the speed.

It's always a delicate balance with a racehorse. Both have to be there—strength and speed. Lighter has both, but sometimes he's lacking the third thing: the head. Who the hell knows where his head is right now. It seems to have flown off somewhere before the starting gate at the Fountain of Youth.

When I ride Sinjab past Dad and Beck, they fall in next to me, both of them still watching Lighter like he's the problem kid who won't stop eating the glue.

"Thoughts?" I ask them. "Opinions?"

"He's gotten strong in Florida," is Dad's comment. "Pilar can handle him for now, but his mind isn't where I want it to be. I'm thinking of changing up his equipment next time out."

"Like," Beck says slowly, "his biological equipment? Or . . ."

Dad and I both look at him.

"Draw reins," Dad says simply as I slowly shake my head, muffling the urge to burst into laughter at the relieved look on Beck's face. "I don't like to use them, but in his case they'll help give Pilar a better handle on the situation until he gets back into an acceptable mindset. We're limited on time if we're going to point him to the Wood."

The Wood.

I still so completely that Sinjab hesitates and comes to a halt, lifting his head and cocking his ears back as if to say *is there some reason we should be stopping?*

Beck and Dad don't notice, so engrossed in training methods

and their plans that Sinjab is a side note. Tapping his sides, the colt bounces back into a happy walk, overtaking them with vigor and thrusting me back into the conversation.

"So you're thinking he's just mentally, what, unsound?" Beck asks, and Dad makes a face to accentuate how little he likes that term—*mentally unsound.*

"I think he needs a change of pace," Dad clarifies. "We'll keep him active and on track. Leo will handle his training while I'm in Dubai with Star, and I trust July will keep things running smoothly until I get back. We'll make a final decision closer to the race."

"What happened to the Florida Derby?" I ask. Beck slides a look over to me, and I shrug my shoulders. I thought Lighter was Florida-worthy. I thought *we all* thought Lighter was Florida-worthy.

"I think it's safe to say we need Lighter closer to home," is all Dad says when we're right on top of Barn 27, where a black Tesla is parked.

"What's with the unexpected visitors?" I ask, just as a man who doesn't look like he could even fit in a car like that opens the door, slamming it behind him and turning once around to survey the land—barn, yard, the horse I'm sitting on. Then his eyes fall onto Dad and a smile breaks over his bearded face.

"Rob Carter!" he booms, hands on his hips. "I've got a proposition for you."

Which is exactly when Elyse gets out of the car.

Chapter Sixteen

"I have questions," I announce after Dad disappears into his office with Elyse and her father, the owner of Bluegrass Thoroughbred Partners. Martina dropped Maggie's reins in my hands and trooped after them, leaving me with my mare and a ton of warring emotions.

Beck rubs the back of his neck and leans against the wall of Maggie's stall as I untack her, pulling the heavy Western saddle off with both hands and draping her bridle over the knob of my shoulder after dunking the bit in her water bucket. Maggie immediately turns to investigate her hay net, poking at it and worrying a few strands into her mouth.

"I . . . may have an explanation," Beck says, which makes me pause before leaving Maggie's stall, throwing him a look suggesting he come clean and quickly. "Elyse's dad wasn't too thrilled with Golden Age's performance in the Tom Fool. I may have . . . sort of . . . talked up your dad a little. After Kickabit won her race by daylight, Elyse might have encouraged him to switch trainers."

I stare at him, head tilted in consideration. He rushes on, "It's not like this is a bad thing, Juls. More horses in the barn, varied group of owners. This will be good if it works out."

"First, it's interesting to me that you think I would think it's bad," I say, turning and letting myself out of the stall. Beck follows me down to the tack room, where I push the door open with my shoulder and dump Maggie's saddle on its post. "A few more horses in the barn is a good thing. A person like . . ." I wave my hand in the general direction of the office.

"Jefferson Lee," Beck supplies.

"Perfect," I comment. "Very Kentucky."

He gives me a look and I smile, shoving aside the image in my head I can't shake—Beck and Elyse, the owners' kids walking side by side. "You're right," I insist. "It's good. Fine. Great, even!"

"Really," Beck says slowly. "Because I'm still not sure where you stand on Elyse. You did just discover she has a name recently, and I got a vibe last time we were together that you might not like her as much as you claimed earlier."

"That's ridiculous and untrue," I say, putting Maggie's bridle on its hook and pulling my helmet off, yanking the bandana after it to scrub my fingers against my scalp. I feel itchy all of a sudden, as though it turns out I'm allergic to truth. "Besides, it's not like Elyse is going to be out here every day. Even if I didn't like her, what would be the issue?"

"There wouldn't be one," Beck says.

"Good," I say, fishing out the tack cleaning kit from the cabinet in the back. I need to keep my hands busy and Maggie's tack is in need of attention. "Then we're in agreement. And I do like Sunglasses Girl. I—"

"Elyse," Beck corrects me, making me duck my head and grit my

185

teeth. "Seriously, Juls," he says, "is this okay with you or not?"

I get what he's asking me underneath it all. It's not about Bluegrass Thoroughbred Partners' horses, and it's not about Elyse showing up on race days or popping into the barn to see Golden Age or any of the rest of their fleet. It's about Beck and Elyse. It's about their friendship. Am I okay with it?

Or not?

Before I can say anything, Leo shoves his head into the doorway.

"Hey," he says, "if the hot blonde is going to be around more often I need more information. Who has details?"

"No one," I say.

"Come on." He leans into the doorway, fixing Beck with a look. "You guys know. You have to tell me. A name is all I'm asking for."

Beck just holds up his hands. "Sorry, dude. I think it's wise to assume I'm under a gag order."

"He'd be right to assume," I say, tossing Leo a sponge from the kit. He snatches it easily out of midair. "And if you want her name, you're going to have to work for it."

The sigh I get in return is deep and dramatic. "You know I have my ways to get back at you when Rob goes to Dubai, right? I can change whole rider line-ups. I can—"

"You live in my house," I remind him casually, wiping the water off of Maggie's bit. "I can change the locks."

And with that Leo gets to work.

In the afternoon, I climb into Kali's saddle. The filly mouths the bit as I sit on her back, gazing down at her orderly red mane and tentative ears that are cocked back toward me before she flicks them forward at the arena surrounding us.

On the ground, Madeline studies a piece of paper. I can just see the black lettering through the opposite side: *USDF Introductory Level*. Then, underneath it: *Walk—Trot—Canter*. We have to be expected to do all three, on top of all the other dressage directives. The paper in Maddy's hands consists of a table. The first column is filled with letters like A and X, which correspond to the points of the arena. The second column explains what will happen at those letters, like *enter working trot rising* and *circle right twenty meters*. The third column is the hardest. It's what you're being judged on, like *balance and bend in turn* and *clear canter rhythm*. It's all the stuff I'm not sure we can do.

Walk, trot, canter? Got it. Memorized it. Kali can do it with her eyes closed so long as mine are open, directing her. It's the dressage part that's questionable.

"Okay," Madeline says. "Let's start by going large. Warm her up. Then we'll get started."

The arena is ours for the time being. If only I could take this quiet moment to clear my head. My ribs ache softly from morning workouts, muscles already stiffening. My brain is still revving from Elyse and her father squirreling away in Dad's office. And my raging insecurity over it is not exactly helpful when focusing on the finer points of trotwork.

I hate this feeling. This undefined, mealy feeling threatening to rise up my throat and choke me, because Beck is right. I'm not particularly okay with Elyse, and I might as well acknowledge that to myself. I'm human, aren't I? I can be stupid about a few things, and Elyse might as well be one of them. I—

"Hello," Madeline waves to me as I trot by her, rising subcon-

sciously to Kali's energetic gait. "Are you listening? Enter working trot rising at A. Halt through medium walk at X. Salute me like you mean it, Juls."

A blush hits my cheeks, even though I've mercifully been keeping my raging thoughts to myself.

"Sorry," I call, turning Kali at A and working down the center line, drawing her back down to a walk and then a halt at X. She should be square on all fours, but she isn't and I can feel it.

Whatever. We'll fix it later. I salute, and Madeline raises an eyebrow.

"At C track right, working trot rising," she says, reading off the chart. "Circle right twenty meters at B."

Easy enough. Kali bends around my leg, comes off the wall easily.

Outside rein, inside leg.

I shove Elyse and Beck out of my thoughts enough to let the mantra take over, and Kali arcs across the arena with her head down, just where I want it, my fingers keeping her just in touch as she holds herself up and carries herself forward.

It feels magical, and for a brief second the glory of the moment takes over. I want to roll around in it and stay in it forever—feeling this good because my horse understands what I want and can actually do it. She can bend and shift and extend, all with a twitch of my fingers and a nudge of my heels.

"At A!" Madeline's voice slams through my thoughts. "Develop working canter in the first quarter of the circle, right lead."

Oh, hell.

I keep my inside leg where it is, flicking my outside leg back and preparing for the shove. Kali's body rises and plunges, her outside shoulder popping out as she over bends on the circle.

Outside rein, outside rein.

The mantra circles in my head, and then I realize Madeline is saying it, too. Kali rocks her way through the circle like a champ, and I let out a needed breath.

We've got this. It's okay.

Then, in the back of my head, I wonder if Elyse's dad is going to bring his whole fleet into Barn 27. I wonder if Golden Age is coming, and all of a sudden I can see myself in the saddling enclosure at Saratoga again. Only this time Elyse and her sunglasses will be standing right next to me as her father's horse parades under the trees.

Then I realize Madeline is shouting instructions.

"Working trot before A!"

I slow Kali, who drops back into a trot with a shake of her head, which she keeps somewhere in the vicinity of my face.

"Change rein at K," Madeline keeps going, pretending to be oblivious to what a dressage judge would be commenting on right now. Probably something along the lines of *horse and rider learned dressage in a field, didn't they?*

"Circle left at E! Develop left lead canter before A! Twenty-meter circle and develop working trot."

I scramble to keep up with Madeline's shouted instructions, heeling Kali into a canter that immediately feels so stilted I have to stop and ask again. *Left lead this time, Kali.* She picks it up and off we go, except Madeline has already moved on.

"Medium walk," she says with a sigh. "F to B. Then free walk to H."

I'm already past F, so I rein Kali back, completely missing trot and plunging straight into an active walk. By B, I let the reins slip through my fingers, and her head goes down to dangle somewhere in front of her knees.

"Between C and M pick up a working trot again," Madeline says. "Then turn in at A. You're done, Juls."

I wrap up the test, Kali trotting happily down the centerline and halting with an exaggerated step to the side, throwing her hindquarters somewhere east of X. But at least she's square. Madeline doesn't look impressed.

"I know," I say, dropping the reins and patting Kali on the neck. She did fine. Better than fine, actually. I'm just a spastic dork who can't get my thoughts in order.

Actually, my thoughts are everywhere else except here. That's the entire problem.

"Good," Madeline says. "Because we have a show in less than a month and you have to actually ride all parts of the test. You do want to do this, right?"

I swallow, immediately struck by Madeline's impressive ability to channel Sophie when she wants to.

"I do," I say. "I've just been . . ." I trail off, thinking back over the day. The *week*. Elyse, Blugrass Thoroughbred Partners, Lighter, Beck . . . it all tumbles into a snarled ball and I can't untangle it.

"You've got stuff going on," Madeline says. "I know. We all do. How are your ribs?"

"It's not the ribs," I say, sighing. "It's the stuff."

Madeline purses her lips, considering me. "Want to run through it again? This time without all the baggage you're dragging around?"

"Absolutely," I say, picking up Kali's reins as Madeline smooths the paper between her hands and begins to read.

"Enter working trot rising . . ."

~~

After I run through the test another three times, committing most of it to memory well enough for Madeline to stand watching me silently from the center of the arena, I lower my aching body into my car and convince every muscle to loosen.

Neck, shoulders, back, abdomen, legs, fingers, toes. My ribs are a lost cause; they throb quietly, reminding me I've overdone it for the day. I'm not sure how I'm going to handle next week, with track, Practicum, Kali, and the rest of school to think about.

Not to even mention Dad will be Dubai-bound this week, leaving Leo in charge and the very real threat of his impending leadership hanging over my head. I stare at the steering wheel, finally letting myself veer off into the cloudy territory of Bluegrass Thoroughbred Partners and Khalid's flashing smile.

See you in Kentucky.

I can draw my own conclusions on that one, but it makes my heart thump a little harder. Feather in the Kentucky Oaks is something I would have laughed at last year, but now? Now it makes sense.

My phone rings, coming through the car's Bluetooth with a sudden trill and yanking me out of my thoughts.

Mom.

I hit the answer button and immediately start talking. "Hey, Mom."

I'm met with a wet cough, and wince for her. "July," she says, her voice hoarse. "I'm so sorry to ask you this, but could you run by the store to get me more Kleenex? I've blown through my supply."

"Sure," I say, turning on the engine. "Anything else? You are eating, right? You have food?"

She laughs, but it degenerates into another cough. "I have a whole list, unfortunately," she admits sheepishly, and I nod to myself as I turn off of Jericho's property, heading back toward the track.

"Good thing I was coming by anyway," I say. "I wanted to tell you that you've got a mount in the Oaks this year, too. Looks like moving back to New York was your best career decision yet."

"The Oaks?" Mom asks, just as I'm done kicking myself for being a brat.

"Yeah," I say, merging onto the highway. "You know. Filly race, lilies, totally overshadowed by the Derby but fun in that we're-all-wearing-pink way. The Oaks."

There's a quiet pause on the other end of the line, and I'm starting to suspect either Mom has passed out or I've said something she wasn't expecting.

"Mom?" I ask, just to be sure it's not the former. "Are you okay?"

"I'm here," Mom says, clearing her clogged throat. "But, July, I don't have a mount in the Oaks. If you're thinking of Feather, she's not even pointing to the Oaks."

"What?" I ask, as Mom keeps talking, her voice raw and inflamed.

"She's going to the Blue Grass Stakes," Mom says. "It's the Derby, July. Feather is pointed to the Derby."

Chapter Seventeen

"Explain," I say as I push open the front door of my mother's house, trooping into the kitchen with a bagful of groceries and dropping a box of Kleenex on the counter. Mom looks up from her chamomile tea and eagerly rips open the box, dabbing at her nose.

"How," I ask, "do we equate doing away with a field of fillies in Florida equals Feather is a logical choice for the Blue Grass Stakes? The *Derby?*"

"Your father didn't want to pit her against Tahr in the Florida Derby," Mom says, blowing her nose and picking up the Kleenex, moving it and her tea into the living room, where it looks like she's lived ensconced in blankets and reality television. "But Khalid wanted to try her against colts, so they compromised."

For a moment, I have to hand it to Tahr. At first, I thought we were avoiding him for Lighter's sake, but it turns out our entire barn is avoiding him. I follow Mom into the living room, staring at her as she settles into her blanket nest.

"I don't understand the rush to push her into that kind of competition," I argue. "She's a solid filly, yes, but against colts?"

"Khalid has it in his head that she can do it," Mom says. "And if your dad agreed to the Blue Grass, it means he thinks Feather has the capability. We both know he'd prefer a more conservative schedule, but this is the reality we're given."

Reality. It's changed significantly since January, when Feather was the little upstart and Lighter was our Derby lock. Since then, the tables might have been flipped over for all reality looks like now.

I sink down onto the sofa next to her. "But then what about Lighter?"

Mom sighs. "Let's not get ahead of ourselves. Feather will have to place second or first to even be considered safely in the gate come May."

"But what if she did?" I ask. "What if she won the Blue Grass? What if Lighter loses the Wood? It would be a pretty stark decision for you, Mom."

She waves a hand in the air. "Hypotheticals," she says, dismissing my what-ifs. "If I spent all my time taking into account what would happen before it happened, I wouldn't ride horses."

"But you'd ride Feather," I insist, wanting an answer. All I can think about is Pilar, about her miracle. I'm so close to seeing Pilar and Lighter blazing down the track together, and the temptation shoves me closer to needing an answer. "Of course you would ride Feather if she winds up having more points."

"She may not," Mom says. "Which is why I'm not committing anywhere yet."

I fall back against the sofa, realizing what she's saying. She's not committing. She hasn't said either way if it's Lighter or Feather, which means she's no longer a lock on Lighter, but then . . .

"Mom, the Blue Grass and the Wood are on the same day," I say. "Are you planning on being in two states at once?"

She opens her mouth and shuts it again, reaching for another Kleenex and worrying it in her fingers. "It would be a good opportunity for Pilar," she finally says. "Since she's been riding at Aqueduct this month and getting races under her belt."

"So it's Feather, then," I say. "That's what you're saying. Ultimately, it's Feather."

Mom shakes her head. "Khalid asked me to ride her in the Blue Grass, and if I'm healthy by then I said I'd do it. The reality is she's—"

"A good story," I supply for her.

"—potentially a very formidable racehorse," Mom corrects me. "You were right in seeing her promise. The fact of the matter is Feather's star is rising. There are ebbs and flows in this business; you know that better than most."

"But if the tide shifts," I say. "If Feather loses and Lighter wins?"

"I'll weigh my options," Mom says, like she's talking to a reporter. I bristle at it.

"Come on," I insist. "You can tell me what you really think."

She sighs. "It's not an easy decision, July. Fillies don't typically win the Kentucky Derby. They hardly ever run—not even the ones who deserve to be there, because we're often too afraid to enter them."

"But Khalid would," I say. "Obviously. She's in the Blue Grass."

"A filly in a field with nineteen colts," Mom muses, wiping at her nose. "It's an intimidating prospect."

And one she would *love*. Deep down, I know she's tempted. I think I even know her answer, because what is Mom without a challenge in front of her? California was a challenge, and she fell into it head first. Martina and I are challenges, and here she is, battling it out in hopes of clawing her way back into our hearts. I see it written all over her.

It's going to be Feather.

Unless I'm wrong. Unless one of the many freak things that can happen do happen, all the stars aligning in the worst ways like they so often do in this sport. Strained tendons, quarter cracks, a misplaced step, a bad break, a stumble . . . a fall.

So many things can happen.

Mom shakes her head. "I'll decide when I need to decide, July."

I nod, my thoughts whirring in circles. The entire landscape surrounding our path to the Derby has changed in the course of twelve hours, and I'm so turned around I can only sit and watch my mother pull another Kleenex out of her box, fold it neatly, and blow her nose into it.

We're all just along for the ride, I think. Especially me. Then I think of the doors opening for Pilar, my heart constricting around the opportunity.

"It's getting late," I say, standing up. Mom looks up at me, surprised.

"Oh, I thought . . ."

"Dad is leaving tomorrow for Dubai," I say. "I have to make sure Leo isn't going to upend the barn first thing out of the gate, which means I have a busy week of putting out fires."

Not to mention school, and Kali, and the show that may be completely impossible to ride in now that all these tables have flipped over, leaving my life in scattered pieces on the floor. I take a big breath, preparing myself to pick it all up.

"Be careful," Mom advises, standing up to walk me out. "You'll end up like me."

I pause as I'm halfway out the doorway, looking back at her stricken face when she realizes what she's said. My instinct is to tell her *no, of course not, I know what I want.* But do I? And would it matter?

Mom knew what she wanted and was pulled in two regardless—between her dreams in California and her family in New York. She had to choose; it couldn't be both. Here I am facing the same problem. Jericho and the track, each eating into my time. Next they'll eat into my sanity, and then into everything else. I thought I could do both, but can I? *Should I?*

I don't know the answer to that yet. But I do know one thing: I don't want to have to regret the same way Mom does. I don't want my life to be a zero sum game, where I can only be one thing over another at the expense of everything else.

Mom pastes on a quick smile, waving her hand like she's trying to disperse the truth in her statement.

"You know what I mean," she says, her voice so hoarse I can barely hear her. "Sick as a dog, surrounded in blankets and tissues."

"Sure," I say slowly, easing back into the house to pull her into a soft hug. "You don't have to work so hard, you know."

Her breath puffs against my hair, her shoulders tight before they loosen and she pushes away. Her face is flushed, maybe because I've said something we both know is a lie. We're horse people. Working hard is all we know to do.

"I'll come by the barn when I'm not contagious," Mom says. "Just try not to kill Leo while your father's gone; he's always been a good kid."

I laugh, wondering how Mom can still see Leo as a kid. But then that's what she's used to—twelve-year-old Leo with his football and his bruises playing in Barn 27's yard. Not our adult foreman who may be plotting my imminent demise over a pretty girl's phone number.

"I'll see you soon," I say. "Rest up. There are plenty of horses that need you in top form when you come back."

She rolls her eyes playfully. "Just like your father."

I groan, and shake my head, letting the screen door slap shut behind me on my way to my car, phone already out of my back pocket and fingers flashing across the keys.

Mom is on Feather for the Blue Grass, I text Beck. Without waiting for a reply, I thumb over to Pilar's number, typing in what she may already know: *Lighter is yours for the taking. Do you want him?*

Three little dots pop up immediately as Pilar writes back. I imagine her fingers furiously flying over the letters until a text appears with a whoosh, short and sweet: *Yes!*

~~

I know I have absolutely no say over who rides Lighter. I've got about as much clout as the daughter of a horse trainer should, which is to say very little to none. The decision is Dad's, but the buck stops with Beck. It was only September when Beck thought it was weird to see Mom on Lighter, because back in the sweaty days of Saratoga it was Lighter and Pilar getting their feet wet together. It was Lighter showing he had a spark in him, and Pilar hoping to ride it all the way to the finish.

But the racing gods are capricious, so here we are; starting all over again with higher stakes. Derby stakes. And I promised Pilar I would try, so that's what I'm going to do, even though Beck hasn't responded to my text, which leaves me flying blind as I pull up to my house . . . and park right behind his Mustang and Jefferson Lee's sleek Tesla.

Well. Okay.

I guess I know now what happened with Bluegrass Thoroughbred Partners, because its owner is currently in my house, which booms with his laughter the second I open the front door.

"To Quark Star!" Jefferson Lee calls from the dining room, champagne glass raised over his head. The name on his lips surprises me, and I stop in the doorway, taking in the scene of my father, Jefferson, Elyse, and Beck all sitting around our table, a bottle of champagne open in the middle. Leo grins at me from the opposite door into the kitchen, raising his glass with the rest of them.

"What did I walk into?" I ask, all of them drinking to toast Star's obvious soon-to-be fame. My dad looks a little pink, like maybe he's been doing this a while. Jefferson looks like he's just getting started, his big body straining the confines of his dress shirt, which he's rolled to his elbows. Elyse smiles serenely up at me.

"Celebrating!" she says cheerfully.

Beck tilts his head at me. "It's a little early for Star, granted. But Barn 27 is going to have a few more horses in its stalls."

"You must be July," Jefferson says, voice rising to the decibels of a jet engine as he holds out his hand to me. "It's always good to meet the family. I hear you'll be riding some of my horses in the mornings."

"It a solid bet," I say, taking his bear claw of a hand and squelching a yelp when he clamps on, shaking hard. I ride through it, grinning, just like I've been taught. Dad allows himself a small smile from his side of the table.

"July's a freshman at Jericho this year," he says, a slip of emotion showing in his voice that sounds like pride. "She helps out at the barn when not riding dressage horses."

"Which makes me wildly jealous," Elyse sighs. "If only I could spend all my time around horses."

Leo pipes up: "You're welcome at the barn any time."

Elyse beams at him, which he clearly loves by the slow smile climbing his face.

"And on that note," Jefferson announces, "I believe it's time to let you prepare for your flight tomorrow." He looks across the table at Dad. "Damn shame you can't see the horses into their new home, but I'll allow that the Dubai World Cup takes some precedence."

"They're in capable hands," Dad assures him, standing up when Jefferson does, Elyse following. Leo straightens up in the doorway, like I knew he would, jumping to see them out with Dad. Only Beck keeps sitting, lackadaisical as always. When the front door shuts, I sit down at the table, eyeing the empty glasses.

"Looks like I missed the party," I say, and Beck shrugs.

"Nothing you had to be here for," he says. "Just Jefferson being Jefferson. He's a little much to handle sometimes, so I expect Barn 27 will get a bit louder after today."

I nod. "Why are you here?"

He eyes me.

"I got your text," he says. "Rob wasn't answering, so I showed up and found the party in full swing."

"What do you think?" I ask, thinking I already know the answer. "Pilar in the saddle for the Wood?"

He shrugs noncommittally, and my heart starts to sink.

"Beck," I say, his eyes lifting to mine, "you said yourself it was weird not having Pilar on him."

"That was three races ago," Beck says. "Everything is different now, Juls."

"Is it?" I lean forward. "Lighter won his first race under Pilar, and then he won his first stakes under Pilar. Since then . . ."

"Since then he came in fourth in a race where he should have finished in the money," Beck says, rubbing his fingers through his hair in frustration. He pushes his glass to the side and leans into the table, fixing me with a look I don't much recognize because this is Serious Beck. The one who comes out only rarely, like when a barn is going bankrupt or a horse is dying.

"*Should have* doesn't mean much in racing," I remind him, and he smiles grimly at me.

"Maybe not," Beck says, "but the plan was Lighter in the Florida Derby. Instead we're here. He was going to have your mom in the saddle, and now he isn't going to have her at all. You want me to put an apprentice on his back . . ."

"An apprentice who is Pilar," I argue. "Who has ridden him. Successfully. Who, by the way, *always* rides him. Pilar knows Lighter better than anyone."

He nods, but I can't be sure it means anything. "He's going into the most important races he'll ever run," he reminds me. "He's also coming off a serious loss. Pilar is just getting back into race riding. You think that's a winning combination?"

"Yes," I say, vehement. "Who are you right now? I thought you'd want Pilar."

"It's not about Pilar," Beck says. "It's about Lighter. It's about him needing someone who knows what they're doing. Someone like Jorge."

I stare at him, falling back in my chair.

"Wow," I say under my breath.

Beck makes a frustrated noise, because this isn't how either of us want this to go. And I know immediately which one of us is right—he is. He's the owner. He gets what he wants, always. And I'm just . . .

I make myself breathe, telling myself I'm more than just a trainer's daughter. I'm sticking up for my friend and I'm pushing for a strategy that will work, even if I'm the only one who sees it.

"Pilar isn't off the table," Dad says from the dining room doorway, surprising me. I look up at him, seeing Leo just behind him. Beck leans back in his chair.

"Seems like she is," I say, throwing a glance at Beck, who looks up at the ceiling diligently.

"We all know there are plenty of factors to consider going into the Wood," Dad says, dragging out a chair and falling into it as though he's exhausted. He must be; between Jefferson, the champagne, and the preparations for Dubai, I'm not sure how he's still standing. "It's a long road yet to the Derby. We're taking Feather to Keeneland, and Celia has elected to follow her. That leaves Lighter. I'm not going to pretend that his training is incredibly encouraging right now, but the Wood is looking less stiff than all other options and I want to give him a chance to bounce back." He pins a look on me. "With or without Pilar. No decisions on jockey assignments until I get back from Dubai."

I have nothing to say, because at least this is a better outcome than Beck's tepid refusal to consider the suggestion.

"Great," I say. "And I assume you've got the detailed training plan for when you're gone all written out and ready to go?"

"Leo has it," Dad says, motioning at Leo. Then Dad stands up, looking at all three of us before his eyes fall back on me. "I trust everything will run smoothly in my absence. Am I right about that?"

We all nod solemnly and Dad takes off his glasses, rubbing his fingers against his eyes.

"Good," he says. "I'm going to get myself ready for tomorrow. Try to practice getting along while I'm doing that. I don't want to be mitigating arguments over international calls the next two weeks. Got it?"

We're bobble heads. Nodding and nodding.

Dad puts on his glasses and retreats upstairs, leaving me with Leo and Beck and a mess of glasses to pick up.

Then Leo decides to speak. "I just want everyone to know that I did get Elyse's number. Granted, it was under the guise of needing to call her about her father's horses, but I think that counts."

Beck pushes his chair away from the table. "And that's my cue."

"Wait," I say, jumping up as he heads to the door, Leo raising his hands because we're both ignoring him.

"Doesn't someone want to reprimand me?" he asks as I dodge around him, following Beck out the door and catching him by the Mustang.

"Hey!" I say, putting my hands on the hood of his car as he opens the door, stopping when my palms slap the metal. "That's it? You're just walking off? What is this, shades of last time?"

"No," he says, shaking his head and resting his body against the open door. "I'm just irritated, and I need a second to not listen to your demands as to what I should be doing with my horse."

"I'm not demanding," I insist, and he stares at me silently. "Fine," I admit. "I might be mildly suggesting."

He shakes his head. "Juls, let's admit for a minute that none of this is going like how we thought it would. Lighter was supposed to be in Florida. Instead we're headed down a road where he may need more help than Pilar can give him. I need you to recognize that, because if we go with someone else I don't want you to be pissed."

"I won't be pissed," I say and he doesn't look like he believes it.

"Sure," he says. "Like you're not pissed about Elyse."

"What does Elyse have to do with anything?" I ask, my heart speeding into a chaotic thumping.

"Come on," he says. "I've known you since we were twelve, Juls. I know when something's bothering you, and that something is definitely Elyse. Jealousy is a weird look on you, which isn't to say I don't like it, exactly, since it's kind of nice to see you get worked up enough to—"

"Oh my god," I groan, cutting him off mid-narcissistic ramble. "I'm not jealous. She's your friend; I get that. It's just disconcerting sometimes, seeing you two together. She knows things about you that I should know, and I don't. And then I think maybe you both like it that way, and then . . ."

Beck comes around the door, slamming it shut with the heel of his hand and scooping me up against him, kissing me soundly on the mouth. I stumble, reaching to grab onto his jacket as I fall into him, a squeak of surprise squelching in my throat. The car is cool against my hip and Beck is incredibly warm, alive and thrumming under my hands as he kisses me.

And I kiss him back, all the little nerves in my fingers firing until I'm a shivering mess when he pulls away, hazel eyes heavy-lidded but bright, shining. I'm breathless, words lost in the hurricane of us.

"It's you, Juls," he says to me softly. "It's always you."

I don't know what to say, so I only nod. His fingers cup around the back of my neck, and his mouth brushes against mine again before we melt into another kiss that makes me want desperately for his bed in the city. For some opportunity we don't have here in the driveway of my house, with Leo pounding at the house's glass front door to startle us apart.

"Have some decorum, for Christ's sake!" he calls at us, cracking the door open to better let his voice carry over the neighborhood. "Some of us don't want to watch your soap opera unfold in the front yard."

"Do you even know what 'decorum' means?" I throw back at him over my shoulder.

"Sure I do," he says. "I've been living with you long enough, haven't I? I know big words now, Juls. All thanks to you."

Beck snorts out a laugh as Leo slams the door shut, stalking into the house.

"I have a long couple of weeks ahead of me," I mutter, resting my forehead against Beck's chest. "Dad gone, new horses, morning workouts, school, Kali—"

"About Kali," Beck says, "what are you going to do about the show?"

I groan. "Please don't remind me."

Beck is silent for a minute, and then says, "Maybe you can do both."

"Both?" I ask, lifting my head.

"Yeah," he says, shrugging. "The race doesn't go off until late afternoon, so what would the chances be that the two conflict? You're riding in one class. How long does that have to take?"

I push aside the fact that Beck is downplaying how long it takes to get to Jericho, groom Kali, obsess over every detail of her braids and the whiteness of my breeches, tack her up, warm her up, show her, untack her, change out of show clothes, and then get to the track.

I have no idea how long that will take or what mayhem will delay me once you take into account that horses are involved.

My ride time and post time for the Wood might be too close together. They might even overlap. I can't do both things at once when they literally happen at the same time.

But I want to believe it's possible. The show and the Wood on the same day can happen, if everything works out perfectly.

"It could work," I say slowly. "If we're lucky, anyway."

Beck gives me a lopsided smile—the one that makes me feel stupidly fluttery. "We're due a little luck, don't you think?"

I laugh, letting myself believe luck is something that can be doled out. That it's something deserved. It can feel like that with horses, where anything can happen. Anything can break or fall apart. And with the work you pour into a horse, when things disintegrate around you in seconds it feels like fate has turned its back. Lately, it seems like we could use a huge helping of luck, even if it is something as simple as a riding time.

"Here's to hoping the racing gods smile in our favor," I say.

"I think you mean the dressage gods," he says, and I rise onto my toes to kiss him.

Chapter Eighteen

"I get it," Pilar says, in her ever-patient way. She shrugs as we stand our horses on the Belmont training track. Lighter pricks his ears at the commotion gallivanting past him, and Sinjab chews his bit thoughtfully next to him.

"You shouldn't have to get it," I say, running my hand through Sinjab's salt and pepper mane. "It's not fair to you."

"What am I going to do?" Pilar asks, looking at me curiously. "Stamp my feet and cry? Race riding is work, and I haven't proven myself yet. That's on me, not anyone else."

"But you have," I say, needing to remind her. "You won the Hopeful Stakes, Pilar."

"And what else?" she asks, raising her eyebrows before she turns her attention back to the track. "I understand the decision. I'm disappointed, but I understand. At least it wasn't a hard no, right?"

I shake my head, because it still stings a little bit. Not being able to talk her onto Lighter wedges into me, just like knowing I didn't have much of a shot at it to begin with. It was never my call.

"Well," I say, digging deep for some optimism. I know it exists in me somewhere, even when I feel like this sport may have trampled it into something a little less shiny and bright. "We have a goal. You on Lighter in the Wood. I think we can handle that, don't you?"

She gives me the side eye and finally smiles. "Then we'd better get these guys moving. I hear they don't breeze themselves."

Sinjab lifts his head and looks around excitedly at the track as we trot in the right direction this time. He knows what's coming, and huffs eagerly when I let him take faster, longer strides. Eventually we're moving along at a good clip, and when we pass our marker for the breeze, I lower myself in the saddle as he leaps forward.

My knees strain to keep me stationary as the force of his plunge grabs at me like someone yanking on the collar of my jacket. The colt is all lunging, cat-like movement around the turn, speeding up on his own at the quarter pole. I readjust the cross in my reins, but I don't have to throw any at him. There's nothing I need to encourage him to do, because he's doing it for me.

The cool spring breeze smacks me in the face, along with the colt's mane as he races down the inside rail for the finish line. I expect Lighter will show up any second now, blazing up on our outside. I expect him like one does a freight train, feeling him and hearing him well before he's suddenly *there*.

Except Sinjab is still alone in the stretch. His body lengthens, legs stretching. Each stride makes little gunshot sounds against the soft training track dirt. I want to look behind me, check for Lighter and Pilar, but the finish line is already flashing by and Sinjab is already switching leads, going full tilt into the next turn if I'll let him.

Halfway through the first turn, I start to ease up on him, swinging a look behind me and finding . . . nothing. Only other people's horses bob along the track, a pair flashing down the inside rail already in our wake.

Then I look ahead of me, easing Sinjab off the rail when I find Lighter standing next to Martina and Maggie by the outside rail. Pilar has one hand on her hip, talking to Martina with confusion etched on her face.

"Hey!" I call as I approach them, Sinjab all huffs and full-of-himself enthusiasm. I pat his neck absent-mindedly, because I know he wants it and it's instinct to do it, even though my stomach is in knots. "Is he okay?"

Martina tightens her hand around the colt's lead.

"He's . . ." she trails off and shrugs. "I don't know what he is, Juls. Physically he looks fine."

"Then what happened?" I ask as we start the long walk off the training oval. Lighter tosses his head, showing off a rim of white around his eyes. Pilar looks down at him with her teeth pinching her lower lip. "Did you even start the work?" I have so many questions. "I didn't see you back there."

"I pointed his nose at Sinjab and asked him to go," Pilar says, like she's recounting important events for a jury and shakes her head. "He wouldn't."

"What do you mean he wouldn't?" I ask, totally confused. Lighter doesn't want to do a lot of things we ask of him: be mannerly, keep his stall in one piece, refrain from sinking his teeth into things he shouldn't, like *people*. But run? Run he'll do.

"He just . . . wouldn't," Pilar says, frustration evident in her voice. "I asked and then I pushed and he said no. Then he *really* said no."

I swing a look at Martina, who shakes her head. "He stopped and reared. Went up on one foot. Thought he'd flip over backward, but Pilar got him back down. We'll check him out when we get to the barn."

My eyes drop to Lighter's feet on instinct, watching the way he walks. He looks fine. No tender steps, no favoring one leg over another. He might as well be a rock with the way he's moving. Of course, it could be something else. His back, maybe. Or his mouth. Maybe it's just his brain.

I look at the blond forelock flipping between his ears and think about all the things cluttered in the colt's head. How are we supposed to know what's going on in there? He can't exactly tell us.

Except he just did, didn't he?

This is another maddening thing about working with horses. They can't tell you what's wrong. They can only show you. Then it's all educated guesses until you hit the right solution to the problem, if you can find it in the first place. No wonder it's so easy to go horse crazy.

"So what was that?" Leo asks from the rail. Beck stands next to him, a sour look on his lips. They're both twin expressions of disgust and worry.

"Wouldn't go," Pilar says. "It was a flat refusal."

Leo looks at us like he can't quite digest Pilar's words. Since when do you have a racehorse—a successful racehorse—refuse to work? It's not like Lighter's a yearling still trying to suss out what we want from him. He's a three-year-old graded stakes winner who knows the job. He knows exactly what we want from him.

And maybe that's the problem.

I stare at his thrashing tail as Martina leads him off the training track. Lighter bobs his head, yanking at the reins as we walk. Leo calls us to stop so he can check out the colt's legs, and Beck appears at Sinjab's shoulder, putting a hand on my knee.

"What do you think?" he asks as Leo straightens, shaking his head in irritation and motioning for us to keep walking. Keep cooling them out.

I know he's found nothing in Lighter's legs except cool, hard tendons.

"Too smart for his own good," I suggest, looking down at Beck as he walks next to my leg. "He knew we were breezing, and normally he loves breezing. That he didn't want to do it means something is off."

"Mentally, you mean," Beck says, eyeing his horse like he's one giant puzzle to be solved.

Which, honestly, he is. We haven't even put the draw reins on him yet, so either his regular equipment is hurting him or he's refusing for reasons only Lighter knows.

"I'm getting the vet out here," Leo says determinedly, acting like the boss we need him to be while Dad's gone. Calling all the shots because Dad can't. "Then I'm getting the chiropractor. How did he feel in Florida, Pilar?"

Pilar shrugs a shoulder. "Fine," she says. "Didn't put a foot wrong at Palm Meadows."

Leo mutters a curse under his breath, and it sticks to me like a little dart, reminding me we're alone for the next two weeks and if we can't get Lighter to work in the next few days, the Wood looks less and less likely.

There are only two preps after the Wood—the Arkansas Derby and the Lexington. The Arkansas Derby would give us the points, and the Lexington wouldn't. Lighter stands at twenty-five points, and he'll need more to even look at the gate at Churchill Downs. At twenty-five, he'll be sitting on the waiting list. He has to finish in the top four in the Wood to entertain shipping him to Kentucky.

Has to.

If we can't get him ready in time for the Wood, it's off to Arkansas. If we still can't get him ready or he tanks his last prep completely then we keep him in his stall at Belmont. It's an unacceptable ending for a colt with such promise, but it's also a pretty predictable one. How many colts have we had that looked promising? How many have made it to the Derby?

One. Two if Lighter makes it. It's not exactly the most optimistic of statistics.

My thoughts veer off to Feather, and I shut them down. I can't think about our filly right now, can't think about which of them will be Mom's Derby horse, much less ours.

Martina hands Lighter off to his temporary groom, who gives the colt a no-nonsense tug toward the barn. With Gus tending to Star in Dubai, Lighter is left with a babysitter. Maybe he's protesting the change. Horses can be persnickety. Although it's not like we can just ask Gus to come home so Lighter can have his way.

Leo is already on the phone with the vet, and Pilar is pulling her saddle from the colt's back with practiced, wooden movements, her shoulders tense. I jump down from Sinjab's back, right into the thick of disappointment. It slicks over me like a heavy blanket, uncomfortable and itchy. And as I watch Lighter walk away from me, hear Leo explaining the problem to the vet as he paces back and forth in the gravel, feel Beck's agitated stillness next to me, I realize there's nothing I can do.

Nothing.

~~

"I don't get it," Madeline says as we finish up Practicum. She leads a rangy chestnut back into his newly cleaned stall, patting him on the hindquarters as she unclips his lead. "He just wouldn't breeze? How does he *not* breeze?"

"Drops his shoulder, bucks, rears," I sigh, finishing up my own stall for a mare called Peanut. I finish spreading the new bedding and lean against the rake, wiping at the sweat on my forehead. How quickly spring goes from crisp, cool promise to balmy and moist. "Basically?" I say. "He just didn't want any part of it."

"That's weird, right?" Madeline asks.

"Pretty much," I say as I unclip Peanut from her crossties and let her wander into her stall, where she immediately starts kicking my hard work all to hell before stretching out her back and relieving herself with a long, satisfied grunt as she eyes me defiantly.

Mares are evil. I'll just say it. Although nothing can eclipse the problem that is Lighter right now.

"What can you do to fix him?" Madeline asks. "*Can* you fix him?"

A scratchy feeling blooms in my chest, starts climbing up my throat.

"I don't know," I admit. "Lighter is a special kind of crazy, and I'm . . ." I look up at the barn's ceiling. Jericho is not the right place to be if I'm going to dedicate time to trying to get Lighter back on track, but if I'm not here there go my grades. There goes Kali and any shot I have at earning her first ribbon.

"Juls?" Madeline asks, waiting for me to finish my thought. I shake my head, letting myself out of Peanut's stall so I can feel less trapped. I close my eyes and take a deep breath, then open them to Madeline's concerned face. "Are you okay?"

"No," I admit, shaking my head. "I don't know what I'm doing."

"What do you mean?" she asks, eyebrows furrowing.

"With Lighter," I admit. "With Kali. I feel like I'm giving both of them half my life and half isn't good enough anymore."

"Hey," Madeline says gently. "Lighter doesn't need you to figure him out. He's got, like, a whole team to help him. And Kali is way better off than you think."

I shake my head, because Kali needs more training than I can give her on my limited schedule, and we both know it. And maybe Leo can figure out Lighter without me, but what if he can't? Then there goes Beck's dream, and Pilar's dream.

I have to be in two places at once, always, and I'm not sure if I can anymore.

"Let's take the horses out for a hack," Madeline says, steering my attention toward something else. Anything else. I can feel my throat closing the longer I think about how caught I am. "It's nice out and everyone needs a reset instead of more training."

"I don't know," I hedge, glancing at the perfectly nice day happening outside the open door. I don't have time to enjoy the weather, not with the show approaching. Not with the Wood so close. I don't have time anymore, period. "Kali actually could use the training."

"It's just one day," Madeline says, turning on the whine in her voice. "Come on, Juls. Let yourself have this for once. Drop the expectations and enjoy something."

She's right. Of course, she's right. But it's still hard to nod along, agreeing that I can do something that's just for me.

"Is that an okay?" Madeline asks, looking at me hesitantly.

"Yes," I manage, my voice cracking. She grins.

"I'm getting Cricket. Meet you outside in ten."

She's gone before I can convince myself arena training this morning is really the better idea, leaving me in a beam of morning sunlight streaming into the barn. It's beckoning and beautiful, and it's been so long since I've ridden Kali outside an arena. A Saratoga sort of long, back when we were both trying to escape reality.

A little escape sounds good right about now.

I put the rake away and grab Kali's equipment out of the boarder tack room, letting myself into her stall. My filly snuffles over me, looking for treats while I get her ready, putting her galloping boots on just in case we decide to go really wild while we're off the dressage grid.

"Look at you," Madeline laughs from Cricket's back as I walk Kali into the bright daylight, the filly blinking at it like she hasn't been outside in eons. "Ready to put her engine to good use?"

"You never know," I say. "Bet you couldn't catch us, though."

Madeline's eyes widen. "Are you kidding? Even a failure of a racehorse would eat poor Cricket for lunch in a race."

Kali lifts her head into the cool spring breeze, nostrils flaring as her lungs expand against the girth I'm tightening. She lets the air out in a whooshing sigh, as though saying *finally*. I pat her shoulder, and then mount up. She immediately starts walking, just like we used to do before, on the track. Moving, moving, always moving. Even before she knew where she was going, it was always about moving.

We hit the trail winding around Jericho's equestrian center. Kali's animated walk outpaces Cricket's, and I keep her checked back to allow the other mare to keep pace as we pass the outdoor dressage ring and the cross country fields beyond. Horses and students scatter over both, preparing for the show on their own and with trainers. It's a perfect day to do it, and with so little time remaining between now and show time I see the urgency.

And here we are, hitting the trail instead.

Madeline sighs, as though this is exactly what she needed when I'm tightening up, wondering if this is the best use of my time. I can sense the seconds ticking away, lost to what? A walk?

"This is perfect," Madeline says, leaning forward to stroke a hand down Cricket's neck. Kali eyes the trail and snorts at a bird swooping low, dancing and shaking her head at the thought of a creature existing in the same space as herself.

"Maybe for you," I allow, reminding Kali that I exist up here with a gentle twitch of my fingers. She lowers her head and mouths the bit, beginning to coil up behind my hold on the reins. "Cricket probably has her test memorized. I'm thinking Kali and I need more arena work so we don't completely embarrass ourselves."

"I think that is what other days are for," Madeline answers primly, eyeing my filly. "Come on, July. Look at her. She's enjoying non-arena life. Maybe you should, too."

I feel a little bristle at the word *should*. I've been running myself ragged based on what I *should* be doing, all on my own. I should be focusing on school. I should be a good daughter, letting Mom in when she might not deserve it quite yet. I should be helping out at the track, regardless of my lack of time.

Time and *should*—my two great enemies.

And really, all I need to do is ride my horse. I need to do it because I want to do it, not because I should. Not because there's a show that needs training for, or a movement Kali can't quite do yet. I should be riding because I want to ride, and that's all.

It's about what I want, not about what everyone else needs.

My chest feels instantly lighter, and I let out a breath that ripples through my whole body. My muscles relax, my fingers loosen on the reins, my knees don't clench the saddle quite so tight. It's feels like a great releasing, and it unfurls across Kali, who picks up a floating trot.

"Hey, wait up!" Madeline calls behind me, Cricket bounding into a trot behind us. But Kali is already going, going, going. Her mane rises off her neck, brushing against my hands when I ask her to canter, perched in the saddle like we would at the track.

She huffs, rounds into my hands, and kicks her hind legs up with excitement. When she gets her hooves underneath her, I let her do what she wants: gallop.

The wind whines in my ears, the sound of hoofbeats thundering in my heart. Kali gallops down the trail with her ears up, and it's hard not to crouch down to look for more speed. To ask her to really stretch and go. It's not her job anymore, I tell myself. She's just doing it because she loves it.

And that's all. That's it, right there.

She's just doing it because she loves it.

Kali leaves Cricket in her dust, hitting the open cross country field and bursting up the first hill. I let her take it, leaning into the rise, until we come to the crest. I tug her back before she can go plummeting down into the thick of things below—event riders approaching questioning fences that look too big and awkward to solve. Kali comes to a shivering walk, and then a halt on the rise, standing overlooking the goings on with her ears pricked and her lungs expanding with each huge, Thoroughbred-sized breath.

It's as if she's saying *I could do that. I could do anything.*

I pat her neck, because I know she's right. She could solve those fences.

She could do anything, simply because she wants to do it.

"Hey!" Madeline calls to me, and I twist in the saddle, watching her canter Cricket up the hill behind us and stop on the rise next to me. She laughs, shaking her head. "Didn't I say you'd eat us for lunch in a race?"

"You did." I nod. "You also told me to enjoy non-arena life, so I am."

She smiles slyly. "Looks like I'm always right. File that away, Juls."

"I'm doing it as I speak," I say, watching a girl turn her horse toward a giant log, both of them arcing over it with a foot to spare. "It's going right next to my solution for Lighter."

"Oh yeah?" Madeline asks. "And what's that?"

"Time and should," I say to myself, turning Kali and pointing her back down the hill.

Lighter can do what we're asking of him. I know it. He just has to want to.

And all we have to do is convince him.

Chapter Nineteen

Lighter is dead asleep in the center of his stall.

"You'd think he worked hard yesterday," I say as Pilar walks by, newly clean buckets in hand. She smirks and shakes her head.

"He has a tough life, July," she says. "We don't know his problems."

Now it's my turn to shake my head. "Speaking of problems, let's get him on his feet. I want to try something this morning."

Pilar eyes me curiously. "Got instructions from the boss?"

She means Dad, not Leo. No one would ever call Leo the "boss" without laughing.

"Nope," I say. "Just have a hunch. Let's wake him up and see if it helps any."

Pilar shrugs and I enter the colt's stall. Lighter remains dead to the world. His ribcage rises and falls, his ears twitching slightly as if he's dreaming about fillies or chaos. I hope he's dreaming about running, but it's probably chaos. Nothing gets Lighter going like a little insanity.

Standing over the colt, I pluck at Lighter's halter a few times, and the colt merely shifts in the bedding. I shove at him, grunting at the effort as Lighter lifts his head from the floor and cracks his eyes open, looking like a grumpy, tired toddler.

"Come on, Lighter." I shove him again as the colt rolls to sitting up, yawning luxuriously now that he knows we want him to do something. I move around him and shove at his other side, encouraging him to get on his feet already.

It takes two firm pushes and Lighter launches to his feet, shaking the bedding from his mane and whipping his head around to show his teeth to me. I leap back before they can sink into my arm.

"Oh, no," I laugh. "I don't think I can weather your teeth like Gus can."

Lighter sighs and stands still, peering at us from underneath his forelock like he can't believe he's being asked to do anything this early.

"I know, buddy," I tell him. "What's the world coming to?"

"So what's the plan?" Pilar asks, and I motion for her to follow me as I lead Lighter out.

We walk into the yard between barns, Lighter dragging his hooves through the gravel in sullen disapproval. Even Pilar seems to be taking her time, like it's too early to ask questions, but also too early for enthusiasm. I stop by the round pen and wave a hand at it.

"We're letting him loose," I declare, and Pilar eyes me like I'm crazy.

"In the round pen," she says, like she's making sure. "By himself."

"Yup," I say. "Look at him, Pilar. He's sleeping in and refusing to run. He's either hurting or he's stressed. Leo had the vet look him over yesterday and nothing's physically wrong with him—"

"So you're going with he's a head case," Leo finishes for me, walking out of the inky morning shadows. I pause, and then shrug.

"It's as good a guess as any."

Leo considers us for a moment, lingering on the colt. Lighter snorts and throws out one leg, bending his neck down to scrub his face against his knee as though he's rubbing the sleep out of his eyes.

"Whatever," Leo finally says with a shrug. "A little free time can't hurt."

"We'll work him last," I say, not bothering to let Leo's authoritative voice bother me. "With Kickabit."

"Did your Dad say . . ." Leo starts, looking worried for a half-beat before he realizes. "He doesn't know, does he."

"What's to know?" I ask. "You talked to him yesterday, and what did he say?"

"He told me to try again tomorrow," Leo says, because we have to get a breeze into him this week. If not today, tomorrow. If not tomorrow, the next day. It has to happen, and if we don't do something different we might as well declare ourselves crazy. You can't keep doing the same thing over and over again, expecting Lighter to suddenly decide today's the day he'll work.

"Lighter liked working with Kickabit in Florida," I say. "She's a speedster. We can use her to give him a fast target. You know how much he hates seeing horses run away from him."

Leo scrubs a hand into his still-short hair, raking his nails against his scalp.

"Fine," he says. "Kickabit was scheduled to go alone anyway, so it's no hardship to push her to the end of the day." Then he looks at me. "That won't happen until you're at Jericho, though. Figure you'd want to see him go."

I take a breath and hold it, considering the ramifications of skipping Practicum. Go groom horses, or see Lighter through to the other side. I can balance them on scales and find them perfectly even, equally important in different ways. I haven't skipped a class yet this semester, but I'm sure I'll get raked over the coals for it. Horses are horses no matter where they are—Jericho or Barn 27—and if someone doesn't show up to clean the school horse stalls that's a black mark on my back.

I'd be the girl who failed to pull her weight.

"I have to go," I say to Leo's raised eyebrows.

"To groom," he clarifies, disbelief evident at my choice. "A few school horses."

"Yup," I say. "To groom a few school horses. And then to ride my horse, the one I need to prepare for a major event in my life that is not the Wood. Think you got this?"

He snorts. "Please," he says, mock-offended. "Since when have I *not* got this?"

I give him a look, since the last time we were solving a Lighter problem it landed him in the hospital with a hole in his head. I don't even have to say anything, because Leo waves me off.

"Yeah, yeah," he grumbles. "Noted. Let's get Lighter in his pen and get you on your way."

The pen clanks as we open it, Lighter pricking his ears at the metallic scrape. I lead him inside, the colt picking up his feet more animatedly, his tail going up in a blond, bedding-studded banner as he snorts at the ground and wheels around to look at us like he can't quite believe what's happening.

"That's right, big guy," Pilar tells him, leaning against the metal fence. "A morning left to your own devices. Go nuts."

"Not too nuts," I say, undoing the lead and slipping out of the pen before Lighter can react, locking the gate behind me as all three of us watch the colt for the incoming explosion.

Which doesn't come. Lighter sniffs the air with huge, blown-out nostrils and then folds himself down on the ground to roll. Once he's up again, he snorts out a breath and wanders over to the fence, checking out the long threads of grass and settling in like this is where he's always been. Nothing is different.

"Well then," I say, stepping back from the fence as a little stab of disappointment hits me in the chest. Is this good? Bad? How can you really know? "Guess that's it."

Leo shrugs and slaps me on the shoulder.

"Let's get the workouts started," he says. "It'll be daylight before we know it, and you have horses to groom."

I smack his arm, and he grins at me.

So I guess we're good to go.

～

"Remember that outside shoulder!" Sophie calls at me from across the arena. "She needs to stand taller on her outside! Get that neck back in the middle!"

I shift. It feels like I've done absolutely nothing, but to Kali, it's everything. Her body curls around my inside boot, and her neck straightens just enough so when I flick my foot back she rolls into a canter without a second thought.

We complete the twenty-meter circle as Sophie calls, "Okay! Now go large!"

Turn off the circle, power down the long wall. Kali flicks her tail happily and rounds into the turn on the short wall, completing another twenty-meter circle as Sophie looks at us from her spot in the middle of the arena and all of my class watching me, finished with their own turns but knowing well enough not to dare talk through the last leg of class.

"Nice," Sophie says, which is such high praise coming from her a blush hits my cheeks almost immediately. "You can transition her down to a trot now, July. Make sure she's still fully engaged. Don't let her drop onto her forehand. Keep her working. Pick your moment."

Our moment comes on the turn, when I sit back and stop the rocking motion that tells Kali to *canter, canter, 1-2-3, 1-2-3*. She slides right into a jaunty, extended trot that makes my heart sing for just a moment before Sophie calls, "Now walk."

And that's it. Kali drops into a peppy, racehorse-inspired power walk I feel should be the envy of all riders everywhere. I loosen the reins, letting her have her freedom as I pat her liberally all over her neck.

"Lots of pats," Sophie nods, approving. "She's done good work today." Then she turns back to the rest of the class as I let Kali cool off, raising her voice, "I hope you're all working on your tests for the show in your free rides. It's tradition that someone from this class earns themselves a ribbon, so I expect to see you all here the next two weekends before the show. Got it?"

We all nod, including me in the far corner, walking Kali on a loose rein, which is when my phone beeps in my vest's pocket. I am so sorely tempted to pull it out, because I know what it is. The timing works out.

But I don't. I keep it there, my whole body shivering with the need to know until I jump off of Kali and stand in the dirt, tearing at the zipper of the pocket as everyone else leads their horses out of the indoor and I have my phone in my hands, my fingers trembling around it as I tap my messages and then the video waiting for me.

Pilar and Lighter in the backstretch, other horses zipping past them. Pilar's dark curls tumble in the wind underneath her helmet and Lighter leaps into the air, plunging with a need that sends my hopes soaring.

Then they're on some other plane of speed, roaring down the inside rail. Lighter is all copper and platinum, a flying streak of precious metal as he rounds the far turn. Pilar shifts subtly in the saddle, readjusting her cross and aiming him at Kickabit's tail as the filly gallops hard to the wire under urging. Lighter switches leads and takes off after her, hardly needing Pilar's encouragement to cut into Kickabit's lead and pull even with the filly at the finish pole, then soaring past her in the first turn. Pilar keeps at him until he's fully past Kickabit before she starts to rise steadily in the saddle a furlong past the wire, slapping his neck heartily as a whole contingent of relieved breaths are released loud enough for the phone to pick up each one.

A text from Beck pops up over the moving image.

Pilar's on him for the Wood, it says. *Why mess with a proven team?*

I squeak, delight scrambling through my exhausted body.

"Good news?" Sophie asks me, as I lean into Kali's shoulder, my knees weak from relief and riding. I've been on five horses so far today, each of them their own challenge. But if I have to be honest, it's mostly the good news that makes me want to sink into happiness here in the dirt. Let myself take a moment to breathe and think we've avoided a catastrophe.

Sophie looks at me like I've got a story to tell. I guess I do.

"Our horse breezed," I say, not knowing if she understands and not stopping to explain. "It's very good news."

"And it wasn't before?" she asks, blinking at me as she glances down at the video still playing out in my hand before it stops, the little play sign appearing in the middle of it.

"Not so much," I say. "We're putting him in the Wood Memorial next month, so if he didn't give us something this week it wasn't too likely he'd run."

"The Wood Memorial." Sophie considers me, then looks at the filly. "Same day as the show, huh?"

"You follow racing?" I ask, surprised. She shrugs.

"Not much," she says. "I pay attention to the Derby. I like to root for the winner of the Wood. Local pride and all."

I smile, imaging Sophie screaming her head off for Lighter. "Hopefully it will be Lighter."

"I'll tell you what, July," she says as I push my phone into my back pocket and draw Kali's reins over her head. "If your horse makes it to the Derby, I'll cheer for him anyway. Winner of the Wood or not."

"I hope that will happen," I say, meaning it.

Everything is so up in the air, undefined and unsettled. There are plans on top of plans, strategies to put in place for any scenario that presents itself, because anything can happen between now and Derby day—like Lighter simply finishing up the track in the Wood, closing his Derby hopes in his face.

Then I'd have to tell Sophie about Feather, our other Derby horse. Our dark horse. I'm sure Dad has just as many plans upon plans for her, too.

"The show can run pretty late," Sophie is saying as we walk Kali into the aisle between indoor arenas and down to the boarder barn.

"Are you planning on being at both?"

Planning, as if I have a choice. I laugh involuntarily, and she tilts her head at me.

"Good point," she says without my having to explain. "Either you can or you can't."

I nod. "Exactly. I can or I can't. Seems to be the motto of my life these days."

"The schedule won't post until the day before the show," Sophie says to me. "I might be able to pull a few strings for you."

I stare at her, mouth dropping just enough for my teeth to click when I snap my jaw shut.

"You can do that?" I ask, stunned as Sophie laughs.

"I can do a great many things," she says, winking at me. "When do you need to be at the track?"

A time pops into my head and is out of my mouth. Sophie nods.

"I'll schedule it so you've got enough wiggle room," she promises.

"Thank you," I gush. "Seriously. I just . . . why?"

She touches my shoulder lightly and I wait for some Sophie wisdom, something I can follow like *straighten her neck* and *I want to see your leg two inches further back.* Something concrete and definitive.

But I don't get that.

"You know your priorities," is all she says, and keeps walking when I stop at Kali's stall, her body smaller and smaller until she disappears around the turn in the aisle and leaves me wondering if I really do.

∿

On Dubai World Cup day, the television in the office at Barn 27 is on permanently. We pop our heads in between workouts to find out what race they're on and ferry back the information to everyone else as we ritually go through horses. Lighter, Kickabit, Sinjab, Zaatar, on and on until the tracks close and I've fallen on the office sofa in the break between the Dubai Golden Shaheen and the Dubai Turf.

"Nope," Martina says from the doorway, rustling me off the sofa and pushing me back in the aisle. "You are helping get the new stalls ready. Then you can have time for Dubai."

"The Bluegrass Thoroughbred horses had to show up today, huh?" I ask, sighing when she points me at an empty stall.

"It's five horses," Martina says. "I just need you to set up this one stall. No complaining, Juls."

"That was an observation," I say, but she's already turning her back, stalking down the aisle to make sure the rest of the stalls are in progress. I turn back to the stall I've been given, nearly jumping out of my skin when Mom says, "Need help?"

Whirling around, I gape at her. "I thought you were still in your blanket nest."

She smiles. "As much as I like the blanket nest, I felt good enough to venture outside today."

"And do hard labor?" I ask, sending a critical look over her. I know she's strong—stronger than me, for sure—but then I wasn't recently felled by the flu.

Mom rolls her eyes and nods her head down the aisle. "You dump, I'll spread. We'll be done in fifteen minutes."

"Which is when the transport is getting here," Martina calls down the aisle, as if she has supernatural hearing. She motions for us to get moving. "Come on, people. We are on a time crunch!"

"She would make an excellent dictator," Mom says, and I stifle a laugh, leading the way to the bedding supply and handing Mom a rake.

We're done just as the semi rolls up, brakes squealing and sweat collecting on my lower back. Martina rushes to meet it, and I hang back with Mom as she puts away the rake and I collect the bags that once contained shavings, making sure all the little staples are accounted for after I ripped them open. The last thing we need is a lame racehorse because of a staple. Especially a racehorse we've only had for a couple of days.

Pilar leads Golden Age down the shedrow aisle, his wide blaze easily identifiable and the yellow wraps around his legs jarringly bright. I wonder, absurdly, if we're going to have to keep that color around or if we can replace it with our more classic white.

Then my brain goes blank, because Beck walks into the shedrow with Elyse on his heels.

My feet root to the ground, heavy and useless until Mom grabs my hand, pulling me out of the way so Pilar can lead Golden Age into his new digs. Elyse skips past Beck and comes to a skidding stop at her colt's stall, watching Pilar give our new charge his full tour—water bucket, hay net, all four corners—before she starts unwinding the gaudy yellow bandages.

"This is so great," Elyse gushes, swinging a glowing look over Mom to focus on me and then settling on Beck. "A new beginning is what he desperately needs."

"He'll like it around here," Beck promises. "Lighter hardly complains."

"That you know about," I find myself saying, Mom's hand tightening around mine. Beck laughs.

"He's back on track for the Wood, isn't he?" he asks. "Seems like his complaints have been taken care of well enough."

"Thanks to July, I hear," Mom pipes up, letting go of me to extend her hand to Elyse. "I'm Celia Carter, July's mother."

"I know that name," Elyse says, taking Mom's hand as her face lights up with recognition. "You ride Lighter."

Pilar shoots us all a look from her position at Golden Age's feet.

"I do," Mom says, then sends a critical eye to our new colt. I wince for Pilar, who turns her focus back to Golden Age's legs. Mom doesn't notice. "Perhaps I'll be riding Golden Age when it comes time."

"That would be so great," Elyse says, plastering on a wide smile that ratchets up the awkwardness somewhere well past what I can tolerate and still function.

"We've got the Dubai races on in the office," I find myself saying. "Want to stick around for the World Cup?"

Elyse hesitates, which tells me she's not used to hanging out with the barn folk. Owners' daughters with the grooms and the tired-eyed assistant trainers aren't exactly commonplace. Still, Elyse keeps that smile on her face.

"Of course," she says, swinging that grin up at Beck, who rocks on his heels like all of this is no never mind to him. "I wouldn't miss Star running for the world."

Oh, please.

"Great!" I say with a little too much chipper inflection. Beck tilts his head at me and Mom maintains her poker face perfectly as I motion down the shedrow. "You know where the office is. I'd grab a seat before it's inundated. Beck, want to help her?"

He looks at me like I've got explaining to do, because mine are not exactly the actions of someone who is totally fine with Elyse popping into Barn 27. I'm going to have to admit it fully now, and then . . . what?

What happens then?

"Come on," Beck says to Elyse, nodding toward the office. "She's right that we need to claim space now. It's going to be a madhouse in a few."

I watch him herd her down the aisle, my heart somewhere in my throat as I try to figure out what the hell I'm doing.

Pilar slips out of Golden Age's stall, shaking her head and clutching the atomic yellow bandages to her chest. Then Mom speaks. "I see plenty has happened in my absence."

"I don't want to get into it," I say, turning toward the office only for Mom to snag my hand, shaking her head.

"Oh, no," she says. "Cool off, July. You're a walking explosion, and that is the newest owner in your father's barn." She sits me down in one of the lawn chairs that have appeared in the shedrow now that the weather has warmed. I immediately try to get up and she shakes her head, putting a hand on my shoulder.

"The race," I start, only for her to immediately contradict me with, "It doesn't start for a while. What are you going to do in there? Stew the time away?'"

"Fine," I say, sighing and leaning back into the chair. "Happy? I'm relaxed and normal. Nothing is wrong. Everything is sunshine and rainbows."

"Sarcasm is not the best defense," Mom advises me, sitting down in the lawn chair next to me and crossing her legs like she knows she'll be here a while. "Tell me what's wrong."

I sit, stony silent and unwilling.

She raises her hands. "I can't help if I don't know."

I shake my head. "There's nothing you can help with. Elyse is here, in the barn, and she's Beck's friend. That's the beginning and the end of it."

Mom nods, looking thoughtful as a few precious seconds of silence pass. "You know," she says, and I wish she wouldn't. I don't need this. "It's okay to be jealous, Juls. It's even okay to feel insecure about something you care about."

"I'm not . . ." I start, but it dies off when she rolls a knowing look at me. My mother, who has hardly known me the past few years, has hit the nail on the head. How is she so good at this? "Fine," I allow. "Maybe I'm both of those things."

Mom nods quietly, because she must have known the second Elyse walked into the shedrow. I must be so transparent to her.

"Beck trusts you, doesn't he?" Mom asks, and I find myself nodding instinctually. It's a bone-deep feeling, like the rush of anticipation I'd felt in the driveway nearly two weeks ago when his mouth met mine, his casual confession.

It's you, Juls.

"And you trust him, don't you?" Mom asks, which jolts me because I do. It's there like a bubble in my chest, past love, past tangled sheets and grinning kisses. It's deeper and true, no matter who he is or who I am.

No matter the distance in between.

"Yes," I say softly, because I feel so dumb. Elyse is just a girl. A friend. A person with thoughts and feelings that don't matter if Beck doesn't act on them. And then there's the fact that I don't know what Elyse feels. Not really.

Mom nods and pats my knee. "Good," she says. "Then I think

you have nothing to worry about."

I look at her, amazed.

"How do you do that?" I ask her, watching her frown at me thoughtfully. "Just cut to the quick of it?" I clarify. "You were gone so long, and . . ."

I don't know what else to say. The words flee, leaving Mom with a gap to fill any way she wants. She fidgets in the void I've created, because neither of us like this conversation. The unknowable why of Mom's disappearance to California haunts me, because no explanation will ever be good enough. *Because of the horses* isn't good enough, since it's just a flat out lie. *It got too hard* is a lie, because how hard could it be to just come home?

But now she's here. Now she's being my mother. Even if I've learned to trust Beck implicitly, I still need to learn to trust *her*. My mother.

"July," Mom says after a second of chewing on the insides of her cheeks. "There isn't a second of my day where I don't consider California a mistake."

I do a double take.

"But it's what you wanted," I say, surprised. "The journeyman jockey experience, through and through, right?"

"It's what I wanted," Mom nods, and shakes her head as though to clear it. "Or thought I wanted. I was alone in California more often than not, and even more when I was on the road. I wanted to come home, back to New York, but by then I felt I'd already ruined things. I was afraid of what I'd missed, afraid of your reactions. July, I was ruled by fear. It consumed me, and I let it."

She looks at me hard. "I was a coward, and I was a coward to jump at the ride on Lighter as an excuse to come home. I should have just come home, but the fear—I never want that to happen again. I refuse to let that happen again, do you understand?"

I swallow, looking at her and feeling like she's finally telling me some semblance of truth. Something that glimmers like the wetness lining her eyes. She swipes at her damp eyelashes and laughs nervously, sucking in a shaking breath.

"I'm a wreck," she says. "I probably shouldn't have left my blanket nest."

"Maybe," I allow, watching her wipe her nose. "But then you wouldn't have saved me from myself."

She swings a look at me, and I swallow.

"Seriously," I say, meaning it. "Thank you."

It takes a few seconds, but she finally nods and pats at her eyes, which are still a little red-rimmed and raw. We sit in silence, listening to the sounds of Barn 27, the horses shifting and calling to each other, the grooms rushing to finish chores as the race gets closer and closer.

"I like being back here," Mom says softly, and I feel something in me break off. Something that was hard and unmoving before, calcified by years of bitter disappointment.

It snaps clean away, and I reach out for her hand.

Chapter Twenty

"It occurs to me," Bri says as she stands outside Kali's stall, "that I have only been to races with you. Never this *dressage* that you kept insisting you did but I never saw any evidence of."

I smile as I work on the last of Kali's braids, my fingers aching and my filly shifting impatiently next to me because there has to be something better to do than stand and have her mane yanked on.

"I know," I say, "I always meant to torture you with a horse show, but somehow it fell to the wayside. Hopefully I'll be able to make it up to you over the next few years."

"Why couldn't you have gone to Dubai?" she asks me. "That one I would have gone to, you know. I wouldn't have even asked questions."

"Maybe there will be a next time," I say to pacify her. "Star finished second and he's only four; he could keep racing next year."

Bri perks up. "Then that's the plan. You, me, Dubai."

I chuckle under my breath as I finish up Kali's braids, taking a step back to admire my work. The little red knots run down the crest of her neck in an orderly line, proving to me that I do know how to style hair, I just don't know how to do it to myself. Kali gives me the evil eye from her tethered spot on the wall, as if she's saying she has no idea what all the fuss is about. She'll only rub them to smithereens the first chance she gets anyway.

"Your ride time is approaching," Madeline sings as she leads Cricket past Kali's stall. Bri flattens herself against the wood, giving the big mare space. I check my watch, the roiling part of my stomach beginning a sharp and painful churn.

Okay, big breaths. It's only been a few years since I've done this, but the important thing is I've *done* this. Sure, it's Kali's first time, but it's not mine. So what if Bri is standing in the aisle wearing her nice race day dress, reminding me I only have a couple of hours to get through the show and get myself to the track? It's possible.

I have to keep clinging to that.

"How do I look?" I ask Bri, spinning around in my show whites.

"I am shocked those pants don't have smudges on them," she says, giving me a thumbs up. "Well done, July."

"Let's see if we can keep up the streak of good luck while I tack her up," I say, opening the stall door and picking up Kali's saddle. She grunts out a sigh as I slide it over her back, shifting when I tighten the girth. Once I have her bridle on, it's not just Bri standing outside my door, but Madeline and Sophie.

"You're on deck soon, July," Sophie reminds me, checking her watch and motioning for me to hurry up. Time is everything in shows, especially when you happen to be riding a newbie trying to use my hip to brush their braids free. "We need to get Kali in the warm-up ring."

"I'm ready," I announce, taking the helmet Madeline thrusts at me on my way out of the stall, Kali looking around at the bustling activity with wide eyes. Sophie falls into step next to me, Madeline and Bri trailing behind.

"I want to work primarily on her canter transitions," Sophie says when we get to the outdoor warm-up ring. She holds Kali's head as I mount up, the filly shimmying underneath me in agitated anticipation. The warm-up ring is a churn of people in white pants and perfectly groomed horses, each one locked in their own little dressage world while trying to keep to their own path at the same time.

It's organized chaos. The track at the height of workouts is more orderly.

Kali pricks her ears at it and huffs, arching her neck against Sophie's hold on the reins.

"Remember straightness," Sophie tells me. "She has a propensity to over bend."

I nod, not saying anything. My attention is on the warm-up ring, and Kali's shivering excitement. A gray floats by us, all extended trot and perfect head carriage. Kali snorts at him, tensing.

Two more horses go by, and then it's my turn. We walk into the arena, sticking to the outside fence as Sophie walks next to it, telling me exactly what she wants from me, from the warm-up, from Kali. It's a list of demands I sort through mentally, all the while keeping an eye on the other horses, feeling Kali's jig underneath me refuse to settle.

"Let's trot," Sophie says in her authoritative way that says trotting is totally possible and will happen instantaneously the second she finishes saying it. I tap Kali—just the slightest movement because otherwise I'm sure she's liable to go bursting into the air—and she shoves off with her head held high.

"Get her attention, Juls," Sophie calls at me across the ring. "I want to see her on your page!"

I throw in a half-halt before the short fence, and another one halfway down the long fence. Kali's body collects underneath me, her head slowly falling down, down, until I have her nearly where I want her.

"Better," Sophie says as we swoop past, her voice lost in the crush of horses until I hear *canter*, but we're already turning onto the opposite long wall, edging out into the arena to pass new horses walking along the fence. Kali lengthens her stride, passing them as though we're racing and she's finally good at it. I croon at her to calm her jets, and she swishes her ears back as though surprised I'm there at all.

We hit the turn and I get just that right amount of bend, the right amount of straightness in her neck, and ask for the canter.

She bursts, striking out perfectly and rounding into my hand as I ask her to circle. I rock in the saddle, giving her little guidelines as we go. *1-2-3, 1-2-3, 1-2-3. Rocking, rocking, rocking.* I catch a glance at Madeline and Bri at the fence, Bri's dress fluttering in the spring breeze and Madeline's smile wide and obvious.

I let myself relax into the perfection of the gait, feeling out Kali's soft mouth to ask for just a little more flourish as we swoop into one last circle because we've got this.

We've *so* got this.

Transitioning down, we trot down the long wall, Kali blazing a path and horses swooping off our line. I turn her into another twenty-meter circle, narrowly avoiding the giant gray warmblood on the inside. The gelding yanks his head down and blows out a breath, then drops his shoulder and bucks, sending his rider onto his neck and sending Kali into a careening, chestnut whirl of hooves and startled snorts.

I sit back in the saddle, pushing her forward as the gray gallivants to the other side of the warm-up ring. Kali leaps ahead, jumping back into a trot that makes me think this is it. This is us on the same page, Kali on the bit and me a pair of soft hands listening to her mouth. Nothing can knock us out, not even a little spook.

Then she bobbles.

It's quick—a trip of hooves, a face plant into the dirt like she was looking at something and forgot about her feet. My body sinks back like it's been trained to do, muscle memory taking over and saving me from flipping onto her neck or over her shoulder. She's up in milliseconds, trot still going, going . . .

Gone.

Kali lurches to the side, the stiffness radiating up her shoulder, into her neck, to her mouth, through the reins, into my hands and straight into my heart, which starts thumping irregularly because this wasn't supposed to happen.

"Whoa," I tug her down to a walk, and Kali complies, chewing at the bit anxiously as I stop her next to the fence and look down her shoulder. Her outside fore looks completely normal, but then that's the way with horses. I nudge her forward, watching, and sure enough the bobble comes radiating up her body, hitting me with a sick, sad slither on my spine.

"Come off of her, Juls," Sophie says quietly, suddenly right next to me as the rest of the warm-up ring slows to a crawl, as if in mourning.

My throat closes as I kick my feet out of the stirrups, landing with a puff of arena dust around my ankles. Kali lowers her head, stretches inquisitively to touch her muzzle to my hip as if asking *why can't we keep going?*

I pat her neck softly, my fingers tingling, and lead her past the onlookers, out of the arena, going slowly the whole way.

Chapter Twenty-One

*H*o*w did it go?*
Where are you?
No, seriously, are you okay?
Post time in two minutes.
Lighter looks damn good.
Also, should I be checking emergency rooms by now?

Then, a few minutes later: *He's in.*

The last time stamp is embarrassingly in the past when I type back *I'm coming. Where are you?*

I know the answer, but I want to give him a chance to respond. *Barn 27.*

I cup my phone in my hands as Bri drives through the gates at Belmont. The sky is streaked with purple, the sun already mostly gone from the sky and the trailer still parked outside of Barn 27, fresh from ferrying Lighter back home from his second-place finish in the Wood.

Second. I breathe a sigh of relief. The sixty-five points that gives us might put Lighter halfway down the list of twenty horses filling the starting gate in the Derby. It's nowhere near Tahr, who's near the top of the list after his runaway win in the Florida Derby last weekend, but it's all we need. Lighter is safe. It's a relief, but I wish I could have seen it.

Which is when I remember Feather.

"What do you think will happen now?" Bri asks after she turns off her car, turning in her seat to watch the replay of the Blue Grass Stakes, of Feather and Mom blazing to the lead in the last few strides of the race, kicking down all the doors between them and the Kentucky Derby.

They're in.

"Guess we'll see," I say, pushing the door open. "We've never had two horses in the Derby. I mean, we usually have none, so this is a little weird."

"Only a little weird?" Beck asks from the shadow of the shedrow. I startle from my path to the office, spinning toward him as he walks toward me, hands in the pockets of his suit. It's one of the suits I love—the vest still done up and the creases still in place. Beck cleans up so incredibly well. In the dimming light, I catch his eyes shift down to my riding clothes, my white breeches smudged and dirty now that it doesn't matter.

"Hey," I say as he stops in front of me, still assessing like he's scanning me for scrapes and broken bones.

"Guess you didn't wind up in the emergency room, huh?" he asks. Bri takes her opportunity to duck out, announcing she's going to get her glass of celebratory champagne in the office after the sound of a cork popping free sounds down the shedrow.

"Congratulations, Beck," she says before she slides away into the dusk, giving him a light-hearted hug and whirling off. I swallow, alone now with Beck and disappointment warring with exhilaration. It's gasp-worthy, feeling these two all-consuming feelings collide in my chest.

He looks at me, waiting for my answer.

"No emergency room," I confirm.

"So . . ." he says, edging closer to me. "Did I get stood up?"

I open my mouth but he shakes his head. "Wait, no, let me savor this feeling for a second. This is the shoe being on the other foot, isn't it? That's what they say?"

"Stop it," I say as he smiles, probably taking great pleasure in my discomfort because he's Beck and this is an opportunity for him to file away so he can say later *remember that one time, when you didn't show up?* I gather myself. "Kali got hurt."

The smile wipes from his face. "Bad?"

I shrug a shoulder, tears threatening to well. "I don't know yet. Gave her some bute and got her comfortable in her stall. The vet's coming out on Monday; we'll know more then. I'm just . . ."

I don't say the rest, my throat closing around the word. *Afraid.* I'm afraid I've ruined her, and we've only just begun.

"Hey," Beck says. "It's going to be okay, Juls. Besides, look at the bright side. Time and money fix most problems. I can't speak much for time, but if you need money . . ." He jerks a thumb down the aisle to where his Derby horse is encased in shadow. Lighter, who's bank-rolled so much the past few months.

"Thanks for the offer," I say, cutting off a sniffle. "But I can handle it."

Beck gives me a look. "Can you?"

I bristle, and Beck slips closer to me, putting both hands on either side of my head. "Hey," he says quietly, "I'm only concerned.

You've taken on a lot between Jericho and the track. And I'd be an idiot if I didn't notice you haven't let yourself take a breath since Lighter came back from Florida."

"Well, he's Lighter," I say, catching sight of the colt shifting in his stall.

"And you're you," Beck says, "always in everything and never knowing when to quit."

I screw up my nose like I've smelled something off. "What should I be quitting, exactly? I'm needed in both places."

"But where do you want to be?" Beck asks, and I stiffen, stubborn as ever.

"Both," I say quietly.

"Maybe you can't have both," he suggests, and rests his forehead against mine. "Where do you need to be?"

I close my eyes, wanting to desperately say *with you.*

I want to be with Beck. But he's in the city all the time, living a life he figured out ages ago. I'm still figuring mine out, and mine is fractured in two. I want both, but then that isn't the issue is it?

Which one needs me more?

"Kali," I say, feeling the truth come out of me with a quiet sigh. "Kali needs me."

And I need Jericho. Barn 27 is only getting larger, spreading out, becoming something that doesn't need my help. Maybe it never did. Maybe I'm just comfortable with what I know—racehorses and turning my face into the wind made by a thundering Thoroughbred. It's addictive, that feeling.

But it's one I don't need. Not anymore. Or, at least, not right now.

"There," Beck says, like he's been waiting for me to say this all along. "That wasn't so hard, right?"

"Oh, wise boyfriend," I say. "What would I do without you?"

He smirks, lifting his forehead from mine. "I honestly have no idea," he says, before he kisses me. "You're like a lost puppy when I'm not around."

"That is not true and you—"

He kisses me again, and when he pulls back he's wearing his more serious face. "I'm sorry about Kali."

"Me too," I say.

"Feels strange asking you to celebrate after everything that went down," he adds, and I nod. It is weird. It feels wrong, because I can only think of leaving Kali in her stall and of what the vet will say on Monday during her soundness exam. Maybe it's nothing. A little strain, some time off.

Or maybe not. Maybe it's *something*. Something there's no bouncing back from.

I strike that from my thoughts. She's young. She's healthy. She's *Kali*.

She'll heal.

"But I want to celebrate," I find myself saying, because I do. I may need Jericho, and Kali may need me, but I didn't work myself to the bone with Lighter only to not celebrate his spot in the Kentucky Derby. This is huge. Bigger than me.

Besides, I might as well go out with a last hurrah.

"Yeah?" Beck asks, raising an eyebrow. I nod.

"Think there's still some champagne left?"

"Oh, champagne we have," he says, holding his hand out to me, ready to lead me to the celebration. I take it, just as Lighter comes to his stall door and lets loose a high-pitched whinny into the approaching night, as though he's telling the world *I'm here. I'm coming for you.*

The lights gleam on his dark eyes, and I can't help but think he has no idea the magnitude of Barn 27's hopes on his shoulders. He's just our crazy colt, doing what he wants to do and dragging us all along in his wake.

Some of the weight lifts off my chest at the sight of him, because if Lighter can pull his life together, so can Kali. So can I.

"Come on, Juls," Beck says softly, and I turn into his warmth, let him lead the way to the open office door spilling light across the shedrow dirt.

And to the celebration within.

About the Author

Aside from her Texas beginning, Mara Dabrishus spent the first two decades of her life in the Arkansas Ozarks. She primarily writes young adult fiction about her first love—horses—although she's also been known to write speculative and paranormal fiction. Her stand-alone novel, *Finding Daylight,* was a semi-finalist for the Dr. Tony Ryan Book Award and her short stories have been recognized by *Writer's Digest* and starred in *Kirkus Reviews,* as well as having won the *Thoroughbred Times* Fiction Contest.

When not writing, she's a librarian at a small college outside of Cleveland, Ohio. She lives with a husband, two ridiculous cats, and a small infant daughter.

Acknowledgments

While I was writing *Derby Horse,* I happened to be immensely pregnant. Writing, editing, and publishing this book has been done through morning sickness, doctor's visits, and the birth and subsequent raising of my daughter. *Derby Horse* has been with me through an incredible life change, and so it's very close to my heart. To all the people who supported me during the past year while I've been writing this book, I say thank you: my editor and absolute best friend friend, Erin Smith; my newest editor and wisest voice, Andrea Robinson; my writing partner in crime, Kathy Noumi; my amazing beta readers, Carolyn Starkey and Linda Shantz; and every single horse book author out there who has been with me in this vibrant and wonderful community—Tudor Robins, Natalie Keller Reinert, Kim Ablon Whitney, Brittney Joy, Mary Pagones, Maggie Dana, and so many more. I owe them everything.

And, of course, to my family. My husband, Mohammad, our new baby girl, and the two cats who rule the house. Thank you for everything you do and are.

Keep In Touch!

Support the Stories
Your opinion is important! If you enjoyed this book, please consider leaving a review on Amazon or Goodreads. Just a few words really help to keep me writing so you can keep reading!

Contact Me:
I love hearing from my readers!

Website: http://www.maradabrishus.com
Facebook: https://www.facebook.com/maradabrishusauthor
Twitter: https://twitter.com/marawrites
E-mail: mara@maradabrishus.com

Printed in Great Britain
by Amazon